A man has his pride. How are you at poker?

Guess you'll have to wait and find out.

The phone remained silent for a couple of minutes. Finally, he typed, *You still there?*

Yeah, I was letting myself into my room. I was thinking I might cook dinner for the three of us. I'll let you bring the dessert. (hint, hint)

That had him grinning. *Message received and understood. I'll be there, pie in hand.*

See you then. Good night.

Still smiling, he headed for his room at the end of the hall and went to bed. Most of the time he came back to an empty house, the same as he had tonight. But for the duration of the brief conversation with Hailey, it had seemed as if he'd actually had someone waiting for him at home.

The feeling wasn't real, but for a second there it sure felt like it.

Dear Reader,

I love Christmas and hanging the ornaments on the tree, especially a set of tatted snowflakes that my aunt made for me nearly forty years ago. They're beautiful works of art that remind me of the good times she and I shared.

Unfortunately, the holidays can be difficult when an important person in your life is no longer there. In *His Holiday Gift*, Hailey Alston recently lost her mother. Rather than face the holidays alone, Hailey decides to visit Jim Morris, the grandfather she's never met, and Finn Cooper, his godson. She hopes to finally learn something about her late father before returning home to pick up the pieces of her life.

But the town of Dunbar has a way of drawing people in and changing their lives forever. As Hailey, Finn and Jim get caught up in the town's celebrations, they slowly begin to focus less on the pain of their losses and start building new memories with each other. Finding the way back to joy is a long journey, but they find that it's a trip worth taking.

Here's wishing you the best of holidays!

Alexis

HIS HOLIDAY GIFT

ALEXIS MORGAN

HEARTWARMING

If you purchased this book without a cover you should be aware that this book is stolen property. It was reported as "unsold and destroyed" to the publisher, and neither the author nor the publisher has received any payment for this "stripped book."

Harlequin®
HEARTWARMING™

Recycling programs for this product may not exist in your area.

ISBN-13: 978-1-335-46017-2

His Holiday Gift

Copyright © 2025 by Patricia L. Pritchard

All rights reserved. No part of this book may be used or reproduced in any manner whatsoever without written permission.

Without limiting the author's and publisher's exclusive rights, any unauthorized use of this publication to train generative artificial intelligence (AI) technologies is expressly prohibited.

This is a work of fiction. Names, characters, places and incidents are either the product of the author's imagination or are used fictitiously. Any resemblance to actual persons, living or dead, businesses, companies, events or locales is entirely coincidental.

For questions and comments about the quality of this book, please contact us at CustomerService@Harlequin.com.

TM and ® are trademarks of Harlequin Enterprises ULC.

 Harlequin Enterprises ULC
22 Adelaide St. West, 41st Floor
Toronto, Ontario M5H 4E3, Canada
www.Harlequin.com

Printed in U.S.A.

USA TODAY bestselling author **Alexis Morgan** has always loved reading and now spends her days creating worlds filled with strong heroes and gutsy heroines. She is the author of over fifty novels, novellas and short stories that span a wide variety of genres: American West historicals; paranormal and fantasy romances; cozy mysteries; and contemporary romances. More information about her books can be found on her website, alexismorgan.com.

Books by Alexis Morgan

Harlequin Heartwarming

Heroes of Dunbar Mountain

The Lawman's Promise
To Trust a Hero
Second Chance Deputy
The Unexpected Family Man
The Firefighter Next Door

Love Inspired Suspense

A Lethal Truth

Love Inspired The Protectors

The Reluctant Guardian

Visit the Author Profile page
at Harlequin.com for more titles.

Acknowledgments

I want to take this opportunity to thank everyone at Harlequin Heartwarming for all of their hard work in making my books shine so brightly.
I appreciate everything you do.

CHAPTER ONE

FINN STOOD UP and stretched from side to side, trying to work the kinks out of his back. Normally he would've knocked off work two hours ago, but he'd stayed late to put the finishing touches on his latest project. He stepped far enough back from the motorcycle to gain some perspective. Other than a couple of smudged fingerprints on the chrome fender, it was perfect. He wiped them off and tossed the rag aside. It was time to call the buyer and let him know he could pick up his custom bike on Saturday afternoon.

There was no time like the present to deliver the good news. He grabbed the work order and dialed the number. After a half dozen rings, the call finally went to voice mail. "Hey, Ben, it's Finn Cooper. I wanted to let you know that you should be able to pick up your new baby on Saturday afternoon. Everything is done except for installing the mirrors. One in the first shipment was cracked, and I had to send it back. The replacement is due to arrive sometime tomorrow. I'll install it as soon as it shows up. If you have any questions, you can reach me tomorrow during working hours."

His long day finally done, Finn turned off the lights in the shop and headed into the small office in the front of the building. He was in the processing of logging out of the computer when the shop phone rang. Normally he would've let the call go to voice mail, but chances were it was Ben calling back, hoping to catch Finn before he left. He answered without bothering to see who was actually calling. "Hey, Ben. How's it going?"

As it turned out, he'd guessed wrong. It was his godfather growling at him from the other end of the line. "I don't know who Ben is, boy, and I don't care. Right now I need you to stop whatever you're doing and come to my house before you go home. See you soon."

"Wait— Hey, don't leave me hanging like this. Is something wrong? Are you feeling okay?"

Considering Jim's health had been a bit up and down lately, Finn needed to figure out if he should call 911 first.

Jim made a disgusted sound. "I'm fine. Just get here."

The call went dead, leaving Finn no choice but to grab his keys and run for the door. He loved the old man and owed him everything. That didn't mean he didn't want to strangle him whenever he pulled a stunt like this. If Jim was really okay, why the rush? It wasn't as if Finn didn't have good reason to worry. The old man was as stubborn as they came and fiercely resisted any attempt to call for the EMTs to haul him to the emergency room even when he was having chest pains. That had happened twice already, and Finn wouldn't be surprised if that was what was going on this time.

The drive from the shop to Jim's home took less than ten minutes. Finn ended up parking on the street since an unfamiliar SUV with a small trailer attached already took up most of the driveway. Despite an increasing sense of urgency, the motorcycle on the trailer momentarily stopped Finn in his tracks. It was one he'd always heard about but never thought he'd see—a classic Vincent Black Lightning. He didn't know enough specifics to determine what year it was made, but that didn't really matter. The British-made bike was beyond rare.

No wonder Jim had been all worked up when he called. The man had often talked about the Vincent Black Lightning his late son Nick had owned, but no one had ever been able to figure out what had happened to it. After all this time, it was unlikely that Nick's bike would have suddenly reappeared, but Finn wouldn't be surprised if Jim had found one listed for sale and bought it in memory of his son. Considering how much they sold for these days, Finn really hoped that wasn't the case. Their custom motorcycle business provided a comfortable living for each of them, but not the kind of money it took to buy that kind of bike.

It was time to head inside and find out what was going on. Picking up speed, Finn charged into the house without bothering to knock. As soon as he stepped into the foyer, he could hear Jim talking in the living room although it wasn't clear if he was on the phone or if there was someone else with him.

Sure enough, Jim was seated in his usual spot in front of the television. This time, though, he wasn't watching his favorite shows. Instead, he was talking a mile a minute to an attractive blonde Finn had never seen before. She looked to be around Finn's own age of thirty, maybe a little younger. Jim had yet to notice Finn's arrival, but his mysterious guest was clearly aware of him standing there. When he didn't immediately speak, she caught Jim's attention and pointed in Finn's direction.

"It's about time." Jim sat up straight in his recliner. "What took you so long?"

Finn bit back the urge to point out that it had been less than twenty minutes since Jim had summoned him to the house. "I had to lock up the shop first, but I'm here now."

Jim jabbed his finger in the direction of his guest with a huge smile on his face. "Good, because I want you to meet somebody. I gotta admit I was suspicious when she first reached out to me several weeks back, and I figured you would be, too. Rather than getting you all riled up for nothing, I decided not to say anything until we had the tests run. The results verified her claim, but I would have recognized her anyway."

By that point, Finn was both confused and increasingly concerned. "I'm not following, Jim. What kind of tests?"

"DNA tests obviously." Jim twisted around in his seat to point at one of the framed photos hanging on the living room wall. It had been taken nearly six decades ago on the day Jim and his late wife, Rhonda, had been married. "Can't you see that Hailey here looks just like my wife did back in the day?"

Looking far more energetic and happy than he had in ages, Jim then proudly performed the introductions. "Finn, I want you to meet Hailey

Alston. She's Nick's daughter, which makes her my granddaughter. Hailey, this is my godson, Finn Cooper."

HAILEY HADN'T KNOWN what kind of reception to expect when she arrived at her grandfather's house in Dunbar, Washington. Over the course of her few interactions with the old man, he'd never once mentioned anything about having a godson. Finn looked to be close to her age and about six feet tall with broad shoulders, dark hair and brown eyes. If she was feeling a bit blindsided by the unexpected introduction, she could only imagine how he felt.

On second thought, she didn't have to imagine it at all. Right now, Finn stood with his hands on his hips as he glared at his godfather, his anger all too obvious. "So out of the blue, some woman calls and claims she's Nick's daughter, and you didn't bother to tell me?"

Jim glared right back at him. "Don't talk about Hailey like she isn't standing right there. I won't allow you to be rude to her. She's a guest in my home, and you will treat her as such."

Hailey watched as Finn struggled for control. Finally, he drew a slow breath before speaking to her directly. "He's right. I apologize, Ms. Alston. I'm guessing it's pretty obvious that your arrival has come as a complete surprise to me. Jim didn't tell me why I needed to come running when he called me. The last two times he did that, he ended up in the emergency room with heart problems. I wasn't expecting him to have company."

His explanation made sense, but she suspected his concern for Jim's health wasn't the only reason for his frustration. "I understand."

She glanced at her grandfather and back toward his godson. "He didn't mention you to me in any of our conversations. I'm sorry if I've arrived at a bad time."

Jim shook his head. "No need to apologize to him, Hailey. You arrived at a fine time."

By that point, Finn's expression had gone totally flat. "You said something about DNA tests?"

"She was the one who suggested the two of us have DNA tests run before we made arrangements to meet in person. After all, there was no sense in getting all involved in each other's lives only to find out we weren't actually related." Jim pointed at an envelope on the mantel over the fireplace. "The results came back two weeks ago. There's no doubt that she's Nick's kid. As soon as I heard that, I invited her to come for a visit."

By that point, Jim was blinking like crazy, his eyes shiny with tears. "We've already missed too much time together. I wasn't about to ask her to delay coming to see me. She drove here all the way from Missouri."

Finn plucked the report off the mantel and took a seat, choosing a chair that faced both her and his godfather. He scanned the report twice before shoving it back in the envelope. "So, you live in Missouri? Is that where you grew up?"

Before Hailey could answer, he tacked on one more question. "How long are you staying?"

"Yes, I grew up a little west of St. Louis." She glanced at Jim before continuing. "I really wanted to meet my grandfather in person, but I can't stay gone forever."

It was no surprise that Finn looked more pleased about her plan to return to Missouri than her grandfather did. Maybe it was time for her to head for the bed-and-breakfast where she would be staying while she was in Dunbar. "Look, I know you two have a lot to talk about, and I should be going. I put in a lot of hours behind the wheel today, and I'm ready to call it a night."

She mustered up a smile for Jim. "It was so nice to finally meet you. I'll call tomorrow and set up a time to stop by again."

Jim frowned big time. "No need for you to pay to stay somewhere else when I have a perfectly good bedroom you can use right upstairs."

"I appreciate the offer, but I can't impose on your hospitality." She picked up her purse and stood. "I'm also not sure what the parking situation is at the bed-and-breakfast. They may not have room for both my SUV and the trailer. I'd rather get that figured out before it gets much later."

Finn spoke up before Jim could protest again. "If you're staying at Rikki Volkov's place, I can tell you pretty much for sure that she won't have room for the trailer. Besides, a bike like that one should be stored somewhere secure. If you'll follow me back to our shop, we can park it inside the building to keep it safe."

His concern over the bike was surprising. "I would appreciate that."

Finn stood up. "Jim, can I do anything for you before we leave?"

The older man pushed himself upright in his recliner. "No, I'm fine."

Then he frowned. "Hailey, in all of the excitement of finally getting to meet you, I never thought to ask if you'd had dinner."

She shook her head. "I haven't, but don't worry about it. I didn't eat lunch until late."

As soon as she said that, she wished she

hadn't. Jim immediately pointed at Finn. "After you lock up the bike and trailer, feed her."

"I don't want to inconvenience Finn, Mr. Morris. I'll be fine."

At that point, her host stood up. "If you don't feel comfortable calling me Grandpa yet, at least call me Jim."

He sounded as if she'd hurt his feelings, which was the last thing she wanted to do. "I'm sorry. I'm still trying to get my head around the idea that I actually have a grandfather. It might take some getting used to, but don't think it isn't important to me."

Jim looked slightly happier. "You two best get going. Finn, like I said, see that she gets fed. Hailey, I'm up early, so anytime is fine for you to stop by tomorrow. No need to call first or anything. Also, I'm not a fancy cook, but I make a mean omelet if you get here early enough for breakfast. Otherwise, we can have soup and sandwiches for lunch."

She offered him a smile. "I'll aim for after breakfast sometime if that's okay. I'm hoping to sleep in a bit. After being on the road for almost a week and crossing two time zones, I need to reset my internal clock."

"Okay, I'll see you then."

The whole time they talked, she was aware of the silent third member of their group. At least

Finn didn't hurry her along, which she appreciated. The only question she had at the moment was if she should give Grandpa Jim a quick hug on her way out of the house. She suspected he'd like it if she did, but it might take some time before she'd feel comfortable with doing so.

"Thanks again for inviting me to visit. I'll see you tomorrow."

Finn rejoined the conversation. "Jim, call me if you need anything. Otherwise I'll be at the shop tomorrow. I'm about ready to start on our next project."

"You finished the last one?"

"Yeah, except for the mirrors. I told the customer he could pick the bike up on Saturday afternoon. His final payment has already cleared our account."

Finn stepped back to allow Hailey to walk past him. Jim followed right behind her, speaking to his godson. "Let me know if you need my help on anything. I plan to spend most of my time with Hailey while she's here, but I can still stop by the shop occasionally if you need me to."

"I'll keep you posted. The customer signed off on the design, and I've already ordered the parts. Most are on their way, but I have to check the status on the others. I also should pay a few bills."

Finn paused to pat Jim on the shoulder. "Like I said, call if you need me for anything. Oh, and do me a favor and write up your grocery list. I want to shop for both of us tomorrow after work. It's either that or starve. The pantry is getting pretty bare at my place."

"I could use a few things if you're going anyway."

By that point, she and Finn were standing on the front porch while Jim stayed just inside the doorway. "Good night, you two."

Finn remained silent until they reached her SUV. "You can follow me to our shop. We should drive pretty slow. There's a good chance the roads are getting icy."

"Thanks for the warning. I don't mind driving in snow, but ice is never any fun."

As she unlocked the driver's door, he offered up another suggestion. "Once we get there, if you're not used to backing a trailer into a garage, I can do it for you. After that, I suggest we grab dinner at the café here in town. The guy who owns it went to culinary school and then worked at some five-star restaurants back East before moving to Dunbar. Titus has never served me a bad meal yet, and I eat there pretty often."

She dredged up a smile. "Having you park the trailer for me is a great idea, and so is getting dinner here in town. I called the bed-and-breakfast when I first got to Jim's to let them know I was in town and that I would check in before nine. I'd rather not be late getting there."

"It shouldn't be a problem. The shop is only a ten-minute drive from here, and the café is about five blocks from there. Rikki's B and B is close by, too."

"That's great. I'll eventually figure out my way around town."

He offered her the first genuine smile she'd seen from him. "Considering Dunbar only has a population of about six hundred people, it's actually pretty hard to get lost."

She smiled at that. "Good to know. See you at the shop."

Finn waited until she started her car and backed out of the driveway before returning to his truck. When they reached the motorcycle shop, Finn made quick work of backing the trailer into an open bay in the garage. To her surprise, he joined her in the SUV rather than driving his truck. "Parking can be rather limited near the café. After we eat, I can guide you to Rikki's place and then walk back to my truck from there."

"I don't want to inconvenience you or interfere with any plans you may have had for tonight."

Finn buckled his seat belt and settled back. "Actually, you're saving me from eating canned stew for dinner. I wasn't kidding about needing to go grocery shopping tomorrow."

She pulled away from the curb. "Which way?"

"Go straight for two blocks and then turn left. The café will be on your right about three blocks down."

He didn't speak again until she'd parked a few doors down from the café. "A word of advice—save room for dessert. Titus makes some of the best pies I've ever had."

"Good to know."

Then he pointed toward another shop down the street. "See that storefront outlined in red and white Christmas lights? If you like good coffee and pastries, be sure to check out Bea's place while you're here. Jim has a fondness for her cake doughnuts. He'll love you forever if you surprise him with some. He mostly drinks decaf coffee these days and likes two sugars with a heavy dose of cream. If you tell Bea who it's for, she'll know how to fix it."

"Thanks for the info. I'll do that."

They got out of the SUV and headed for the café. To her surprise, Finn gently held on to her arm to keep her steady as they crossed the snow-covered sidewalk where he opened the door for her and then followed her inside. He looked around and smiled. "Good, there's no line. It can get pretty crowded at times. It's the only restaurant in town other than a pub and a pizza place that just does pickup or delivery."

A tall man with lots of attitude and tattoos started toward them, grabbing a couple of menus on his way. "Finn, you missed out on the chicken and dumplings again. You know you can't wait this late to eat and hope there'll still be some available."

Finn's disappointment was obvious. "Sorry, but something unexpected came up."

The other man's attention turned in her direction. "Since I haven't seen you around before, I'm guessing you're the something. Titus Kondrat—" he extended his hand to shake hers "—I own this place. You missed out on today's special, too, but there's other good stuff on the menu."

"Nice to meet you. I'm Hailey Alston. Finn already told me the food here is great, and that you also make a mean pie."

"I guess you'll find out. Let's get you seated."

She trailed after him, aware a few of the other patrons staring as she and Finn walked by on their way toward a table against the back wall. He didn't seem to think anything of the attention they drew, so she did her best to ignore it as well. It was a relief when they were finally seated, and everyone went back to enjoying their meals.

Titus set a menu in front of each of them. "I'll give you a few minutes to decide and come back to get your orders."

When he disappeared through the kitchen door, she leaned forward to whisper, "Interesting guy. Not exactly what I pictured when you said he'd been trained at high-end restaurants."

Finn smiled a little at her assessment. "Interesting is an understatement, but the man can really cook."

When he immediately turned his attention back to the menu, she did the same. She guessed there would be time enough for conversation later.

CHAPTER TWO

As he finished the last bite of his pie, Finn mulled over exactly what he wanted to say to the woman sitting across from him. It was hardly Hailey's fault that Jim had chosen to keep her existence secret, but that didn't keep him from being furious about being blindsided with her sudden appearance. It wouldn't be fair to aim his anger in her direction, but he had questions she needed to answer. Might as well get started.

"So, where have you been all these years?"

Hailey had been about to take a drink of water, but she plunked the glass back down on the table hard enough to send a ripple of water splashing over the rim. Clearly, he wasn't the only one whose emotions were running hot right now. She sopped up the spill with her napkin before responding. "Like I told you, I grew up in Missouri."

Okay, so she wasn't going to make things easy for him. Maybe he hadn't sounded as friendly as he'd thought. "I remember that much, but you have to understand why I'm curious about a few things. For example, if you've known about Jim, why haven't you reached out to him before now?"

Once again, she delayed answering, instead staring down at the table while fiddling with her flatware. "That's the thing—I didn't know anything at all about him until very recently."

Hailey slowly lifted her gaze to meet his. "I've never had any family other than my mother. Mom's parents disowned her when she got pregnant over spring break during her senior year of college, so I've never met them. She never talked about them much, but from what I've gathered, they were evidently ultraconservative about such things."

"Boy, that's rough."

"You can't miss what you never had." She shrugged her shoulders in a dismissal that he didn't quite believe as she continued talking. "Despite everything, Mom was determined to keep me and to make it on her own. It was a struggle, but she successfully finished her degree. Being a single mom couldn't have been easy for her, especially when she was so young herself. We managed, though."

Her explanation was puzzling. Yeah, it was a shame that her maternal grandparents had chosen not to be part of Hailey's life, but Finn was sure Jim and his wife would have welcomed both Hailey and her mother with open arms. Too bad they'd never had the chance.

"How does your mom feel about your coming here?"

He immediately regretted the question when Hailey flinched as if his words had caused her physical pain. Before he could apologize, she answered him. "My mother fell ill just about a year ago. She didn't tell me right away, not wanting to worry me until they had all of the test results to confirm the diagnosis. It turned out to be ovarian cancer, and it had already spread to other parts of her body. The prognosis was bad from the start."

The sheen of tears in her eyes made it clear that this particular story didn't have a happy ending. He wasn't about to press her for details. Instead, he said, "I'm sorry. That had to be tough for both of you."

"It was." She blinked a few times to clear away the tears before continuing. "I took an extended leave of absence from my teaching job this fall so she wouldn't have to deal with everything on her own. Since neither my father nor her parents had ever been in the picture, I wanted to be there for her as much as possible."

So why hadn't Nick ever been in the picture?

Had that been his choice or had Hailey's mom just not told him that he was going to be a father? Finn had only been a toddler when Nick died, but everything he'd heard made it sound like he had been a stand-up guy. It was hard to imagine him turning his back on his own child. So far, Hailey's explanation had left him with more questions than answers.

Talking about her mother had already upset Hailey. Considering how tired she looked, he hesitated to continue the discussion. Instead, he gave her a chance to collect herself to see if she'd volunteer more information on her own. After finally taking a long drink of water, she began talking again.

"Mom died about two months ago, naming me as the executor and sole beneficiary in her will. With the attorney's help, I took care of the things that couldn't wait, like paying her final expenses and medical bills, but it took me a while to work up enough energy to start going through her personal items and packing up her condo. It wasn't until then that I found keys to a storage unit I didn't know she had."

When once again she went silent, he figured it was time to call it a night. "Look, maybe we should go. It's been a long day, and we're both tired. We can talk more tomorrow."

Hailey shook her head. "No, I'd rather finish explaining. Besides, there's not a lot else I can tell you, mainly because I don't know much more myself. Mom never told me anything about my father—not his name, not how they met, nothing. I don't know why, and she never explained. I asked a few questions along the way, but her answers were always pretty vague. I could tell it was a painful subject for her, and eventually I decided who he was didn't really matter. Mom and I were okay on our own."

He wasn't sure what to make of her story. "I'm guessing you finally got the answers to those questions when you went to the storage unit."

"Yeah, I did." She leaned back in her chair and stared up at the ceiling as if she couldn't look at him and continue her narrative. "The only things in the unit were a lawn chair, a shoebox containing a letter addressed to me with a bunch of old photographs, and that motorcycle you just locked up in your shop. All I can think is that she used to spend time in the storage area—maybe sitting in that chair, lost in her memories as she looked at the pictures. According to the letter, the bike was all she had left of my father. I guess that's why she held on to it all these years."

That had him sitting forward, shocked to the core. "Seriously? That's Nick's actual bike?"

When she nodded, Finn shook his head in

amazement. "I've heard about that motorcycle my whole life. Jim and Nick rebuilt it together and took it out cruising whenever Nick came home on leave. When he got stationed stateside toward the end of his enlistment, he took the bike back East with him. That was the last Jim ever saw of it, and no one could figure out what happened to it after Nick died. I guess that's because your mom kept it hidden all these years."

Hailey sighed and then pulled an envelope out of her purse and held it out to him. "This contains the letter and some of the pictures she left for me."

When he hesitated, she slid it across the table to him. "If you don't want to read it for yourself, I'll tell you all I know. You can believe me or not. According to Mom's letter, she was on spring break when she met Nick. He'd recently left the army and wanted to see a bit of the country before returning to Dunbar to join the family business. Instead of flying directly back home, he decided to drive his motorcycle and take his time. He and Mom crossed paths at a resort on Lake of the Ozarks back in Missouri. It sounds like they fell hard and fast for each other, because he proposed to her within days."

"Wow, that was quick." Finn shook his head in wonder at the idea Nick upending his entire life in such a short time.

Hailey seemed to agree. "Yeah, it's hard to imagine my very practical mother doing anything wild like that. Anyway, the main problem was that his home was here in Dunbar, and she didn't want to change schools when she was so close to graduation. Nick offered to stay with her in Missouri until she finished her classes. Then, once she graduated, they would decide what to do. Rather than tell his parents the big news over the phone, he left the bike with Mom since he expected to come right back to her as soon as he talked to his folks."

She'd finally reached the part of the story that Finn already knew. Nick had wanted to surprise his folks, so he'd asked Finn's parents to pick him up at the airport. Thanks to a drunk driver, the trio never made it back to Dunbar. Life had changed drastically for a lot of people that night, Finn included.

Meanwhile, Hailey was still talking. "Mom kept waiting to hear from Nick. She didn't know if he'd changed his mind about marrying her or if something else had happened. Finally, she called the only number she had for him—the motorcycle shop. Whoever answered the phone told her that Nick wasn't available. When she pressed them for answers, the person finally told her about the accident."

"She didn't bother to tell them who she was or why she was calling?"

Hailey shook her head. "Obviously not. By that point, she'd already told her parents that she was expecting and knew she was on her own. I think she may have been afraid that Nick's parents would reject her claim or, worse yet, try to take legal custody of me or something. Maybe she was wrong about that, but I can understand why she was afraid to reach out to total strangers considering how her own family reacted."

Yeah, he could understand why she'd think that way.

"Thanks for explaining the situation." Finn had more questions, but they'd have to wait. Hailey looked as if she was running on fumes, so he thought they'd better wind things up for the evening. But before leaving, he figured he should check out the contents of the envelope for himself. After quickly scanning the letter, he set it aside and flipped through the faded pictures. Hailey definitely looked like a mix of her parents. She might have her mom's facial features, but she definitely had Nick's smile, blond hair and bright blue eyes.

His curiosity satisfied, Finn shoved everything back into the envelope. He handed it back to Hailey and picked up the bill that Titus had dropped off when he delivered their desserts. "You've had a long day, and I'm betting you're ready for it to be over. I'll settle up with Titus, and then we can head over to the bed-and-breakfast."

"Sounds like a plan."

FIFTEEN MINUTES LATER, they were parked at the B and B. Finn jumped out of the SUV and waited for Hailey to open the hatch so he could carry her luggage.

"I can handle it."

He waved her off. "I'm sure you can, but it would take you a couple of trips. Since I'm here, let me help."

"Okay. I really appreciate it."

Hefting the two biggest bags, he let her lead the way up the steps to the porch. The front door opened before Hailey could ring the doorbell, and Max Volkov stepped into sight. He offered her a friendly smile. "Hi. You must be Ms. Alston. I'm Max Volkov, co-owner of this fine establishment. My wife had a meeting tonight and sends her apologies for not being here to greet you herself."

Hailey smiled back at him. "No problem. She warned me she would be gone when I called to let her know I was in town. I'm sure I'll meet her in the morning."

"That's true. In case she didn't mention it, breakfast is between seven and ten."

He stepped back out of the way. "Sorry, I didn't mean to keep you standing out in the cold. Please come on in. I'll help you with your bags."

That was when he finally noticed that Hailey wasn't alone. "Finn! I'm sorry I didn't see you there. I didn't realize you knew Ms. Alston."

Figuring Hailey's reasons for being in Dunbar were hers to share, not his, Finn offered a version of the truth. "She brought a classic bike to the shop."

If Hailey wondered why Finn had made it sound as if she was there on business, she didn't say anything. After handing off her luggage to Max, Finn pulled out one of his business cards and handed to her. "This has the numbers for the shop and my cell in case you need anything."

"Are you sure you don't want me to drive you back to your truck? It's pretty cold out here."

He waved away her concern. "No, it's only a few blocks, and the exercise will help work off the huge dinner I just ate."

Then he headed off down the street, ready to get home and call it a night. Tomorrow would be soon enough to figure out what, if anything, he should do about the newest member of their small family.

HAILEY DIDN'T JUST like her room at the bed-and-breakfast, she loved it. Decorated in soft shades of blue, it was spacious, with a comfortable bed and a private bathroom. Since it had been too late last night to check out the view from her window, she had done so as soon as she got up. The mountains were on full display, the snowcapped peaks tinted a soft gold by the morning sun. She loved the Ozark Mountains back in Missouri, but they were radically different from the rugged Cascades that loomed over Dunbar.

She didn't yet know how long she would remain in town, but it would be nice to explore some of the area before heading back home. Looking back, it might have been smarter to wait until spring to reach out to her grandfather, considering how unpredictable the weather was in late December.

After enjoying a delicious hot breakfast downstairs, she had returned to her room to shower and get dressed for the day. She checked the time. Grandpa Jim was probably impatiently waiting for her to come over. Oddly enough, she was more nervous about seeing him this time than she had been yesterday evening, possibly because she'd been nearly numb with exhaustion by the time she'd reached his front door. Now, though, she was rested and worried.

On the surface, Jim had seemed thrilled to meet her. What if he no longer felt that way?

After all, she was a reminder of all that he'd lost. She also wouldn't blame him if he was angry that her mother had chosen to keep them apart for almost thirty years. If so, Hailey didn't want to hear about it even though she had her own issues with her mother's decision to withhold the identity of Hailey's father from her. Too bad there wasn't a time machine or magic spell that would let her go back into the past long enough to ask her mom why she'd maintained her silence on the subject until after she was gone.

Hailey sighed. Ever since learning of her mother's illness, she felt as if she'd been cut adrift from the life she'd known. Making the decision to reach out to her grandfather was the first definitive action she'd taken. Her instincts were telling her that there was no reason to think that Jim would be anything but pleased to see her again. Finn's feelings might be a little more mixed, mostly because he still needed more time to come to terms with her unexpected arrival.

On the way to Jim's, maybe she would pick up some coffee and treats for Jim at the bakery in town. While she was at it, she would also buy something for Finn as a thank-you for everything he'd done last night.

Feeling better about her plans for the day, she

trotted down the steps to the small lobby at the front of the bed-and-breakfast where Rikki was hard at work. As Max had promised, Hailey had met his wife earlier at breakfast. She'd also met their young son Carter, a real cutie.

When Hailey stopped in front of the counter, Rikki saved her file and then looked up with a smile. "Hello again."

Hailey smiled back. "Hi. I'm on my way to visit Jim Morris. We haven't made any firm plans for the day, so I don't know how late I'll be getting back."

"That's not a problem. I normally leave the front door unlocked until about nine o'clock in the evening. If you think you might be later than that, I can give you a key to use while you're here."

Hailey thought about it and then held out her hand. "If you don't mind, maybe I should take one."

Rikki immediately unlocked a small drawer and pulled out a key. "Here you go."

"Thanks, I appreciate it."

Rikki gave her a curious look. "I think I've only met Mr. Morris once, but he seemed like a nice man. Have you known him long?"

How to answer that? In a town as small as Dunbar, there was a good chance almost anyone she met would know either Grandpa Jim or

Finn or, more likely, both of them. All things considered, she should've expected the question to come up and formulated an answer of some sort. It wasn't as if she wanted to lie about the situation, but she wasn't excited about the idea of pouring out her muddled family history to everyone she met.

She settled on sharing a small part of the truth. "I recently inherited a classic motorcycle and brought it to Dunbar to have Jim and his godson check it over for me."

That clearly surprised the other woman, probably because she knew how far Hailey had driven to deliver the bike. "From what I've heard, they do good work."

"That's what I've heard." She checked her watch. "Oops, I'm going to be late. Have a great day."

To avoid any further questions, she practically bolted out the door. Outside, it looked as if it had snowed a little more overnight. The huge cedars and Douglas firs were dusted with snow, making the neighborhood look like a Christmas card come to life. She paused long enough to look up and down the street. Virtually every home featured strands of twinkling lights on bushes, trees and the houses themselves. There was also a scattering of giant inflatable Santas, snowmen and reindeer in front yards and up on the roofs.

She actually preferred how Rikki and her husband had decorated their Victorian house in a much more traditional style. They'd outlined the roof with Christmas lights, looped fresh cedar garlands along the porch railings and hung a huge wreath in each of the front windows. As Hailey breathed in the rich scent of the cedar boughs, she felt the slightest stirring of holiday spirit, something that had been in short supply since her mother's passing. Both Halloween and Thanksgiving had barely registered on Hailey's radar.

In fact, one reason she'd decided to make the trip to meet her grandfather was because it provided her with an excuse to avoid the hustle and bustle of her friends cheerfully preparing for Christmas. Although several people had invited her to their holiday celebrations, she'd politely turned down the invitations. This would be her first Christmas without her mother, and she didn't have the energy to fake having a good time when all she really wanted to do was cry.

But enough about that. It was time to get moving. Jim was expecting her this morning, and she didn't want to keep him waiting too long.

CHAPTER THREE

FINN ARRIVED AT the shop at his usual time only to find a decidedly unhappy Titus Kondrat already waiting for him. His friend stood next to his monster of a bike—a 1990 Harley-Davidson Fat Boy. Titus normally maintained the bike himself, but once in a while he rented one of the stalls in the shop in order to use some of Finn's more specialized tools.

"Morning, Titus. What's up? Is your bike needing some attention?"

"Yeah, but the kind I can't give her myself. She needs your expertise this time."

He stepped to the side, giving Finn his first clear view of the Harley. He winced at the amount of damage the bike had taken. While Finn hated seeing the classic bike so banged up, he was more concerned about its owner. There were no obvious injuries on Titus's face or arms, but he could still have cracked ribs or other problems.

"Are you okay? Were you in an accident?"

Titus looked thoroughly disgusted. "I'm fine. I wasn't riding her when it happened. Someone ran into her while I was in the grocery store last night. They didn't bother to leave a note, and no witnesses spoke up."

He studied his bike for a few seconds, his expression grim. "Look, I know you're always booked solid with your custom design work, but I was hoping maybe you might have time in your schedule to work on her. If not, can you recommend someone else in the area?"

Finn waved away his concern. "I make time for my friends, so let's get her inside. I'll put together a detailed estimate of what it will cost to restore your lady to her prior glory, less the friends-and-family discount, of course."

Titus frowned and shook his head. "Look, you don't have to do that. It's enough that you're willing to squeeze her into your already busy schedule."

"Don't worry about it. I'd do the same for any of my friends." Finn circled the bike again. "It shouldn't take me long if you want to wait."

His friend checked the time. "I wish I could stay, but I've got to get back to prep for the lunch crowd."

Finn let himself into the building and then raised the door on one of the repair bays. After

Titus wheeled the bike inside, Finn asked, "Do you need a lift back to the café?"

"No, that's okay. Moira should be swinging by anytime now to give me a ride."

As they waited for Titus's wife to arrive, Finn circled the bike, taking notes. "I'll hop online this morning and track down a replacement fender for the front end. I'll also go over the engine and other mechanical systems to make sure they're okay. Once I've got everything nailed down, I'll come see you with a repair plan."

Titus was looking decidedly happier. "Thanks, Finn. I really appreciate this. Let me know if an extra pair of hands would help."

"I'll do that."

A motion outside the window caught Finn's attention. He'd expected to see Moira pulling up in front of the shop, but instead it was Hailey. What was she doing there? She hadn't mentioned stopping by today when he left her at Rikki's last night. When Titus turned to see what had caught his attention, Finn did his best to look unconcerned.

Unfortunately, nothing much got past Titus. "You didn't exactly explain who she was last night at the café."

"No, I didn't."

"And you don't want to talk about it now."

No reason to deny it. "Let's just say things are complicated."

Rather than go into more detail about Hailey's unexpected relationship to Jim, Finn pointed toward the next bay over. "I'm actually surprised you didn't notice what's sitting on that trailer. It belongs to her."

As soon as Titus realized what he was looking at, he let out a low whistle and headed straight toward the bike. "Man, I've heard about these beauties, but I've never actually seen one."

He pointed at the Missouri license plate on the trailer. "Did she bring it all the way here just so you could work on it?"

Not exactly, but it was a good cover story. "I need to give it a thorough going-over. From what I understand it's been close to thirty years since it was last ridden."

Titus lightly ran his fingers over the leather seat and the back fender of the Vincent Black Lightning. "This thing must have been well protected wherever it was stored all that time. Most barn finds have some kind of damage from critters or the weather."

"Apparently it was kept in a storage rental unit. Maybe the place was climate-controlled or something. That would explain the bike's near pristine condition."

By that point, Hailey had entered the shop

carrying a cup of coffee and a bag marked with the logo from Bea's bakery shop. Her smile looked a bit tentative as she approached them. "Sorry, I don't want to interrupt anything, and I won't be staying but a minute."

Finn forced himself to smile. "I was just telling Titus here about your motorcycle."

Titus gave the bike another admiring look. "It's a real beauty. I've been crazy about motorcycles since I was a kid, but I never expected to see a Vincent Black Lightning in person. You definitely made the right decision to bring it to Finn. No one is better at working on classic bikes and doing custom work than he is."

"I'm glad to hear it, because I don't know much about motorcycles. In fact, I've never even ridden on one." She stared past them at the bike. "This one belonged to my father, which makes it special to me."

The beep of a car horn interrupted their conversation. Titus stepped back from the trailer. "That's my ride, so I'd better get going. Hailey, it was nice seeing you again. Finn, stop by the café for lunch or dinner, and we'll talk about the repairs."

Then he was gone, leaving Finn alone with Hailey. "Was there something you needed?"

He hadn't meant to sound brusque but figured he hadn't exactly come across as welcoming when she grimaced and thrust the bag toward him. "I followed your suggestion about picking up some cake doughnuts and decaf for Jim at the bakery. While I was there, I got you a fritter and coffee as a thank-you for everything you did last night."

Now he felt like a complete jerk. He peeked into the bag and caught a whiff of the heavenly scent of fried pastry, apples and cinnamon. "Good choice. I love Bea's fritters. Thank you."

Hailey held out the coffee. "She said you take your coffee with cream, no sugar. I hope that's right."

"That's perfect."

Evidently, he wasn't the only one who had run out of things to say. Finally, he nodded toward Titus's bike. "That's another classic bike, but nowhere near as rare as yours. Titus really babies it, and he's pretty upset that someone ran into her last night and didn't even leave a note."

Hailey sighed. "I can't believe people do things like that. It's so inconsiderate. Are you going to be able to fix it?"

"Yeah, the damage appears to be mostly cosmetic, so it shouldn't take long to have her back to her usual gorgeous self."

Hailey arched an eyebrow and gave him a curious look. "She? So tell me, how do you tell if a bike is male or female?"

He laughed. "You'd have to ask Titus that. He's the one who thinks his bike is a girl. I don't think I'd have the guts to question his opinion on the subject."

That had her smiling, too. "I'm not sure I would either."

She took a step back from the Harley. "Well, I should get going or Jim's coffee will be cold before I get to his house."

He followed her toward the front door. "Remind him I'll be stopping by to get his grocery list later this afternoon."

"I will. Maybe I'll see you then."

Not sure how he felt about that possibility, he limited his response to a quick nod. When she drove out of sight, he went back inside feeling a little unsettled. Having not one, but two unexpected visitors before he'd even had time to turn on the shop lights had thrown him off his game. Picking up his tablet, he headed out to finish inspecting Titus's Harley. After that, he'd start working on the new custom order. If he had time left over, he'd take the Vincent off the trailer and see what kind of shape it was in.

At least he had enough on his plate to keep him busy and his mind off Hailey's arrival in Dunbar. He certainly understood her need to satisfy her curiosity about her father and his family, but he was concerned about the long-term effects of her sudden appearance in Jim's life. The old man's health had been pretty fragile lately, and the doctor had warned them that any undue stress on his heart could cause more problems. Then there was the business that Jim and Finn co-owned. Her father had been Jim's only heir. As Nick's daughter, would she now lay claim to his half of the business? Rather than worry about it now, he'd enjoy his fritter and then get back to work.

"COME ON IN, GIRL. I've been waiting all morning for you to show up."

At least one person was genuinely happy to see her. "I got off to a pretty slow start today, but I was also late for another reason."

Hailey held up the cardboard tray that held two coffees and the bag of goodies she'd brought. "Finn mentioned last night that you were fond of cake doughnuts, so I picked some up at Bea's bakery in town. I also bought Finn a fritter and coffee. I dropped them off at the motorcycle shop on the way here."

Jim studied the bag with a big smile on his face. "I'm surprised Finn told you that. He's always on me to eat more healthy food."

"Sounds like good advice."

"I'll tell you what I told him. I've lasted this long eating what I like, not what someone else says is good for me. It's too late to change my ways now." He held out his hand for the bag. "Besides, Finn isn't above bringing me a few treats once in a while."

She surrendered the bag and handed him his cup of decaf. "Speaking of food, he asked me to remind you that he'll stop by later to pick up your grocery list."

"Already have it written out for him. I could do my own shopping if we had a big grocery store right here in town, but the nearest one is twenty miles away. You saw firsthand how the roads can get a bit dicey this time of year. It worries Finn if I venture too far from home whenever the conditions aren't perfect." He shook his head in disgust. "Heck, I was driving in winter weather long before that boy was even born. Not sure when he got the idea that he could decide what I was allowed to do for myself."

Jim might find that frustrating, but it sounded like a reasonable policy to her. While he seemed to be mentally sharp, she doubted he had the same reflexes that a much younger version of himself used to have. Rather than express that opinion, she changed the subject. "I suspect we'll need to warm up our drinks a little in the microwave."

"Come on into the kitchen. While you zap

the coffee, I'll get out plates and napkins for the doughnuts. Then you can tell me your first impressions of Dunbar."

When everything was ready, they headed back into the living room. As soon as Jim was ensconced in his recliner, Hailey took a seat on the sofa. She set her coffee on a coaster on the end table and picked up her doughnut. "I haven't been in a shop like Bea's in years. It was hard not to buy one of everything."

"That woman has a gift for two things—making doughnuts and gossiping. Bea considers it her duty to keep folks up to date on everything going on here in town." He pointed an arthritic finger in Hailey's direction. "Just so you know, chances are your name will be bandied about as soon as she catches wind of your arrival and what brought you here."

Hailey didn't much like the sound of that. Maybe that was life in a small town, but she valued her privacy. "Would it be better if I avoided her place in the future?"

Jim looked amused by that idea. "Probably not. I've known that woman for decades, and no one has ever found a way to stop her lips from flapping. Having said that, though, she's not usually mean-spirited. Bea keeps the hurtful stuff to herself."

An inveterate gossip who evidently had

a conscience seemed like a contradiction in terms, but Hailey would have to take Jim's word for it. He finished his first doughnut and moved on to his second. "I know you haven't been here long, but have you seen anything else about our fair town that you liked?"

"I haven't had a chance to look around very much, but the people I've met have been friendly." Figuring he'd want a few details, she started naming names. "Besides you and Finn, I've met Titus, the guy who owns the café in town. Twice, actually. We had a great dinner at his place yesterday evening, and he was at Finn's motorcycle shop this morning when I got there."

"Actually, it's only half his."

Was he talking about Titus's café or Finn's shop? Her confusion must have shown, because he went on to explain. "Back in the day, Finn's grandfather Bill and I started the motorcycle business together. When Bill died, his half passed to Finn's father and from him on down to Finn."

Jim frowned a bit before adding, "My half should've gone to your dad, so I guess that means now it would come to you. Guess I'll have to have a talk with Finn about that."

Hailey wasn't sure that was a good idea. "We can talk about that later."

She didn't want to hurt Jim's feelings, but what would she do with a half interest in a bike shop two thousand miles from where she lived? It wasn't as if she'd come to Dunbar looking for an inheritance. All she wanted was to learn something about her father, hoping the knowledge would help fill the hole his absence had left in her life all these years. When Jim looked as if he wanted to argue the point, she launched back into her list of people she'd met.

"I really like the bed-and-breakfast where I'm staying. My room is great, and the view from the window is amazing. I'm not used to seeing gorgeous mountains everywhere I look. Both Rikki and Max Volkov have been very welcoming, and their son Carter is adorable."

Jim looked pleased by her assessment of her lodgings. "I don't know the Volkovs very well, but then I don't get out as much as I used to. You might be surprised to hear that Max caused quite an uproar when he first came to town a while back. He made a bunch of wild threats and demands that had a lot of people stirred up."

She'd only spoken to Max once, but that behavior sounded out of character for him. "But he seems like such a nice guy."

"Oh, I'm sure he is, but nice goes right out the window when there's money involved. You see, our local museum has a huge chunk of gold on display as the centerpiece of its collection. At some point it was dubbed the Trillium Nugget since it's shaped like the flower of a trillium plant. Anyway, turns out the nugget was originally found by Max's great-grandpa Lev. Max got it in his head that the town had stolen it from Lev or some such silliness, and he demanded it be turned back over to his family."

Wow, she could imagine how well that had gone over with the locals. "What happened then?"

"The police chief and the museum director finally figured out Lev gave it to the town for saving his life. After that, Max dropped his claim with the museum's promise to give Lev credit for the nugget's discovery and to tell his story. They did a real nice job on the new display, so everyone's happy. I hear tell that Max is writing a book all about what happened. I'm looking forward to reading it."

"I'll tell him that when I see him again."

Jim popped the last of his doughnut into his mouth and washed it down with coffee. "You should visit the museum while you're here. It won't compare to one in a big city, but it's part of your family history."

"I'll do that."

What else could she talk about? Inspiration hit when she glanced at the view offered by the big picture window that faced the street outside. Like the people who lived near the bed-and-breakfast, Jim's neighbors took decorating for the holidays pretty seriously.

"There's another thing I really like about Dunbar. I've had a hard time getting excited about the holidays this year, since my mother passed away. However, seeing all the amazing Christmas decorations here in town reminds me of how much Mom enjoyed breaking ours out every year. It's nice."

When she turned back to Jim, she realized she might have brought up a touchy subject. He definitely didn't look happy. Christmas Eve was only two weeks away, and she should've noticed there wasn't a single decoration or Christmas card in sight at Jim's place. "Sorry, I didn't think to ask if you celebrate Christmas."

He struggled to muster up even a hint of a smile. "With it just being me living here, I haven't bothered dragging out the boxes of decorations in years. It was my wife who always did all of that. Rhonda had a knack for turning our house into a real showplace at Christmas. The kid and I might have grumbled a bit about having to haul all that stuff in from the garage every year, but neither of us could ever tell that woman no."

Jim stopped talking for several seconds, making her suspect his thoughts had drifted back into the past and happier times. Then he drew a deep breath and released it slowly. "This is the first time in years I have something worth celebrating. Maybe it's time to get out the decorations again."

She hadn't been hinting that he needed to get with the program. "You don't have to do that, Jim."

He sat up straighter in his chair. "Yeah, I do. Your grandmother wouldn't like knowing how I've let things slide. Heck, I'm the only one in the neighborhood who hasn't even put up a wreath. That's not right."

"I'm sure it's fine, Jim. Not everyone celebrates the same way."

He wasn't having it. Pushing himself up to his feet, he motioned for her to follow him. "I'll put Finn to work on bringing in the heavier stuff when he gets here, but you and I can manage the smaller boxes. He won't mind if we start without him."

Jim obviously knew his godson far better than Hailey did, but she suspected he might be wrong about that. Regardless, she had no choice but to follow her grandfather out to the garage. It looked like they'd be spending the afternoon unpacking Christmas decorations.

CHAPTER FOUR

IT HAD BEEN another long day and was about to get longer. Finn pulled up in front of Jim's house and turned off the engine. Rather than immediately heading inside, he lingered in his truck for a few seconds as he rubbed his temples and thought about putting off going to the grocery store for another day. He'd eaten an enormous late lunch with Titus while going over the plan for repairing the Harley. Even a bowl of cold cereal would do for dinner. The trouble was that he'd promised to restock Jim's kitchen for him, and he tried to keep his promises to his godfather whenever possible.

Hailey's SUV was still parked in Jim's driveway. He was sure Jim was enjoying getting to know his granddaughter, and Finn could understand why. The pair had a lot of catching up to do. He only wished he knew what Hailey's end game was. Was this a one-and-done visit, or did she have long-term plans in mind to spend more time in Dunbar now that she'd met her grandfather? She certainly hadn't been very specific about how long she intended to hang around this time. All Finn knew for sure was that the longer she stayed, the harder it would be on Jim when she left.

Yeah, the two of them could always stay in touch by phone or video chats, but that wouldn't be the same as having her close by. All of which had Finn wondering if Jim had already broached the subject of her relocating to Dunbar permanently. It would be surprising if he hadn't, and Finn hoped she would at least consider the possibility for Jim's sake.

He'd delayed long enough. Hiding in his truck was cowardly and wouldn't change a thing. Before heading inside, he got a bottle of ibuprofen out of the glovebox and washed down two tablets with a quick swig of cold coffee. It was time to get moving.

As he approached the front porch, he stopped just shy of the first step and stared at the door. It had been ages since Jim had bothered to display a wreath. Looking back, both he and Jim had lost all interest in decorating the place after Jim's wife died. No surprise there. Rhonda had always been the strong one and the driving force in their small family. From the beginning, she'd been the one who convinced Jim they should set aside their own grief and provide Finn with a safe home where he could recover from the loss of his parents. He'd lived with them until his late teens and owed the couple more than he could ever repay.

Rather than linger outside lost in events of the past, he trudged up the steps and let himself inside. Just as he suspected, the living room was filled with dusty plastic crates. Thanks to the Christmas music blasting on the radio, neither Jim nor Hailey had heard him come in. He watched as Hailey unwrapped one of the shepherds from the nativity scene and gently set it on the side table in the corner. She stepped back to study the pieces and then moved a few around until she was satisfied.

"How does that look?"

She'd directed the question to Jim, but Finn answered first. "The blue wise man goes on the left. The red one goes on the right. Not sure why, but that's where Rhonda always put them."

Jim had been bent over, rummaging around in another crate. At the sound of Finn's voice, he jerked upright. In the process, he came close to dropping the blown glass angel he'd been unwrapping. After carefully setting it on the mantel, he snarled, "Dang it, when did you get here?"

"Just now."

"Well, don't sneak up on a man like that. I almost broke one of Rhonda's angels."

"Sorry, Jim. I didn't mean to startle you." Finn paused to look around the room. "Looks like you two have been busy."

Jim went back to rooting around in the crate he'd been unpacking. "Christmas is almost here, and I thought it was time we do a little decorating. We'll need you to bring in the crates from the top shelf out in the garage. Hailey isn't tall enough to reach them, and I don't do ladders anymore."

"Can that wait until tomorrow evening? I still need to do the grocery shopping."

Hailey had finished rearranging the nativity scene. "That would be fine with me. We still have a couple more crates that we haven't gotten to yet, and I'd like to get back to the bed-and-breakfast before it gets really late."

When Jim didn't immediately agree, Finn upped the ante. "I'll come straight here tomorrow after I close up the shop. I'll also bring dinner, so no one has to cook. How does that sound?"

Jim gave him a narrow-eyed look. "Pizza, or something good from the café?"

Finn had been thinking pizza, but he was willing to compromise. "Whichever one sounds better to you."

"I'll let Hailey decide." Jim walked over to the coffee table and picked up a piece of paper. "Here's my grocery list. Run on along, now. She and I have work to do."

Finn scanned the list. "I'll be back in a couple of hours. Text me if you have any last-minute additions."

Jim just waved his hand as if shooing Finn on his way. "Make sure you buy that chunky peanut butter I like. Last time you got the smooth stuff, and I don't like it as well."

That again? "Like I told you at the time, they were out of the chunky."

"Yeah, yeah. See you when you get back."

Finn lingered in the entryway for a minute, watching as Jim picked up an ornament and held it out to Hailey. It was another angel, but this one was carved from some exotic wood. "My wife bought this one on our trip to Germany. She collected angels wherever we went, but this was a particular favorite."

Hailey gently cupped the small figurine in her hands. "It's beautiful. I can see why she loved it so much."

Jim's smile took years off his face. It had been a long time since he'd looked that happy about anything. Finn was glad to see him enjoying himself, but it was hard not to be a little jealous. Rather than dwell on it, he let himself out and left them sorting through the decorations. The groceries wouldn't buy themselves.

As Hailey handed the angel back to Jim, she happened to glance in Finn's direction, meaning to say goodbye. She bit back the words when she saw the bleak expression on his face. He was obviously unhappy, but she wasn't sure why. Did seeing all of the decorations bring back bad memories of some kind? Or happy ones that somehow caused him great pain?

She quickly turned away, not wanting Finn to catch her watching him. Instead, she went back to unwrapping the remaining pieces of the nativity set. All that was left were the animals. She arranged them around the periphery of the scene, wondering the whole time if she was putting them in the right places. Jim hadn't said anything about where things went, but she could always ask Finn tomorrow night.

After putting the lid back on the crate, she added it to the stack of empties in the far corner. "Looks like we're done for tonight, and I should be going."

Jim grumbled a bit. "No reason to hurry."

"It's getting late, and I'm ready for some downtime." She put on her coat and picked up her purse. "When Finn drops off your groceries, tell him I'm fine with whatever he wants to bring for dinner tomorrow night. I haven't had pizza in ages, but I'm guessing we'd also get dessert if he orders from the café. I rarely eat a lot of sweets, but I don't think I have the strength of character to turn down a slice of one of Titus's pies."

That had Jim grinning. "I'd never admit it to him, but I had some serious doubts about that guy when I first met him. I'm not sure what I thought a real chef looked like, but Titus definitely didn't fit the image. But like a lot of folks here in town, all it took was one serving of his chicken and dumplings to convince me that man knows his way around a kitchen."

By that point, they'd reached the door. On impulse, Hailey kissed Jim on the cheek and then gave him a quick hug. After spending most of the day together, it felt natural to her. He acted a bit surprised by the gesture, but then he hugged her back. His eyes looked suspiciously shiny, but he was smiling big-time as he let go. "Drive safe, missy."

"I will." She shook her finger at him. "And don't think I'll show up with doughnuts every day. It's not good for either of us, and I won't be able to fit in my jeans by the time I head back home to Missouri."

Just that fast, his smile dimmed. "I'll see you tomorrow."

"Yes, you will."

He started to say something but stopped. She suspected he was about to ask how many more tomorrows they would have together. It was a relief that he hadn't. She didn't have an answer for him, because she hadn't yet decided how long she would be able to stay. Not because she had to be back home on a specific date, but because she feared the longer she stayed, the harder it would be to leave at all.

EARLY SATURDAY EVENING, Finn put his debit card back in his wallet and picked up the insulated picnic basket that Titus had set on the counter. "I'll bring this back tomorrow."

"No rush. Not many people go on picnics this time of year."

Considering how hard it was snowing outside, the man wasn't wrong. "Well, I'd better be going."

Titus followed him toward the door. "I couldn't help but notice you ordered dinner for three."

Finn really didn't want to have this conversation right now. "Since when do you keep track of how many people I buy dinner for? Don't tell me that you and Bea are having a competition to see who can find out the juiciest gossip first."

Looking chagrined, Titus took a step back

and held up his hands in surrender. "Sorry, you're right. It's none of my business. Forget I even asked."

Deciding maybe he'd overreacted, Finn glanced around the café to see if anyone was close enough to hear what he was about to say. "Sorry, Titus. I didn't mean to snarl at you, and I know you don't go spreading rumors."

He drew a slow breath and then said, "The truth is that Hailey isn't a customer. She's Jim's long-lost granddaughter."

Titus's eyes went wide with surprise. "Wait a sec. I've always thought you were the closest thing to family he had."

"Yeah, so did I. As it turns out, though, Jim's son Nick had a daughter that no one knew about. In fact, that Vincent Black Lightning she brought with her was actually his bike. The rest of the story should be Hailey's to tell."

Still keeping his voice low, Titus asked, "How is Jim taking the news?"

"He's thrilled. To be honest, I haven't seen him this excited about anything since Rhonda died."

"But I'm sensing you're not as happy as he is."

There was no use in denying it. "To be honest, I haven't figured out how I feel about the situation. Don't get me wrong. Hailey seems nice enough, and I can understand why Jim is happy about her being here. I'm more upset that he's known about her existence for a few weeks now and didn't bother to tell me until she showed up on his doorstep the other night."

"I don't get it. Why would he keep her existence a secret?"

That was a puzzle, all right. "I'm not sure, and I haven't had much of a chance to talk to him about it. I will, though, if I can ever get him alone."

Titus clapped Finn on the shoulder, his expression sympathetic. "I'm sure you'll get things figured out. Now, you'd better go before the food gets cold."

Finn nodded and headed out into the darkness. It was only five o'clock, but the sun set by four this time of year. He made his way across the street to where he'd parked his truck, doing his best not to fall on the slushy pavement. Although the sidewalks had been shoveled and salted, the street hadn't been plowed since earlier that morning.

A few other hardy souls were out on the road, but at least everyone was using common sense and driving carefully. He almost wished that there was a traffic backup, anything that would buy him a little more time to tamp down the confusing tangle of emotions stirred up by the short conversation he'd had with Titus about Hailey. It wouldn't go over well with Grandpa Jim if Finn did anything that would make Hailey feel less than welcome. The old man was happy to have her in his life no matter how Finn felt about it.

Better to go with the flow until he saw how things played out. If she hung around town for a short time and then went back home, life might go back to normal. Things could get more complicated if she decided to pull up roots and move to Dunbar to be close to her grandfather. Until that happened, Finn would continue running the business by himself to give Jim all the time possible with Hailey. Anything to keep the peace.

By that point, he'd reached Jim's house. After grabbing the basket out of the back seat, he headed toward the house. He stomped his feet on the welcome mat to knock off the snow and ice before opening the door. Inside, he left his work boots under the bench and hung his coat on a peg before padding into the living room in his stocking feet.

At the moment, Hailey and Jim were nowhere to be seen, but it wasn't hard to see how the pair had spent their day. The pile of empty storage crates had taken over the back corner of the room, and almost every horizontal surface was covered in Christmas decorations. He would bet that it had been Hailey who'd set up the Victorian Christmas town on the long narrow table to the right of the fireplace.

Finn set the basket down and went over to check it out. As a kid, he'd always been fascinated by the amazing details in the pieces that made up the collection. One of his fondest Christmas memories was going shopping with Rhonda every year to choose a new house or set of figurines to add to the village. His personal favorite was the small pond with skaters who glided effortlessly around in circles. Just seeing them improved his mood considerably.

"Did I get it right?"

He'd been aware of Hailey's approach, but he'd kept his focus on the village. "You did fine. Rhonda and I changed it up a little every year. She said it made the town seem more real. The only rule was that we put any new additions in the front."

He finally turned to face her. "As far as I know, she never ordered anything from a catalog or online. She told me that when Nick was a kid, she'd take him with her to pick out new pieces for the village. She continued the tradition with me. The two of us would drive up to Leavenworth, a town near here that has the whole alpine village vibe going on. We'd have lunch and then visit a bunch of stores that carried what we were looking for. I swear there were hundreds of possibilities to choose from."

He pointed at a small pack of dogs sporting red ribbons around their necks. "I picked out those myself."

"I like them. I thought about scattering them throughout the town, but I decided to keep the pack together." Hailey reached down to stroke the head of a St. Bernard with her forefinger. "It's nice you have such wonderful memories of her. My grandmother must have been pretty special."

"She was." He picked up another favorite figurine. It was a woman with white hair and a sweet smile. "I chose this one because it looked so much like Rhonda."

"I wish I'd known her."

There wasn't much to say to that, at least nothing that might not come across as criticism of Hailey's late mother. He set the piece back down on the table. "We should probably eat before the food gets cold. Where's Jim?"

"Taking a nap." She glanced at the clock. "He's been asleep for almost two hours. He said to wake him when you got here."

That was worrisome. "He normally doesn't nap that long during the day. Was he feeling all right?"

"As far as I could tell. He seemed fine to me."

They both knew she hadn't been around Jim enough to know what was normal for him. Finn pointed toward the basket. "How about I go check on him while you start unpacking our dinners? We usually eat at the kitchen table instead of the dining room."

By that point, Hailey looked pretty concerned. "Should I have called you?"

He gave it some thought. "No, it's fine. I would've let him nap myself. I'm probably overreacting."

The problem was solved when Jim appeared in the doorway and asked, "Is dinner ready?"

They both spun around to face him. It was a relief to see him looking like his usual self. "I was about to come wake you up while Hailey unpacked the food."

She held up the basket to show him. "It won't take but a minute. I set the table a little while ago since I knew Finn would be arriving about now."

Jim followed her into the kitchen as Finn trailed along in his wake. After Jim took his regular seat at the table, he asked, "What did you get us?"

"I ordered the fried chicken with all the usual fixings. I hope that's okay."

Hailey smiled. "Sounds good to me."

It didn't take long to serve up the food. Finn

watched as Jim tucked into his dinner with his usual appetite. The knot of tension in his own chest eased up, and it was time he turned attention to his own meal.

But before he did, he had one more thing to say. "Neither of you specified what kind of pie you wanted for dessert. I got my usual banana cream and four of Titus's mini pies. Hopefully you'll find those to your satisfaction, because there's no way I'm sharing mine."

Jim snorted. "I'd say that was rude, but I can't blame you. Titus doesn't make a bad pie, but the banana cream is one of his best."

Finn grinned at him. "Good thing I made sure that two of the minis are banana cream. The others are Dutch apple and peach."

Hailey had been following the conversation, looking amused by their banter. She pointed her fork first at Finn and then at Jim. "I call dibs on the peach. No arguments, gentlemen."

Jim laughed and held his hands up in surrender. "Fair enough."

Having secured her choice of desserts, Hailey smiled at Jim. "I finished unpacking the Victorian village while you were sleeping, and it's simply gorgeous. Finn told me that it was your wife's collection and that she added to it every year."

"Yeah, she did. I used to tease her that eventually it would take over the whole house. She loved taking Finn here shopping with her, especially since I didn't have the patience for cruising through different shops to find the one perfect addition to the set." Jim smiled, his thoughts focused on those happier days. "I wish now I'd gone with her anyway, but it's good that Finn has those memories of spending special time with her."

"She knew you loved her, Jim, and the two of you had your own special times together." Finn glanced at Hailey. "You wouldn't believe how often I caught them dancing in the living room or canoodling on the couch."

Jim's face flushed a bit at that last part, while Hailey laughed and said, "Seriously? They were canoodling?"

Finn grinned. "That's what Rhonda called it, giggling like a teenager the whole time."

Jim cleared his throat and gave Finn a hard look. "This is hardly proper conversation for the dinner table."

Rather than embarrass his godfather any further, Finn obligingly changed the subject, directing his next question to Hailey. "Did you and your mother have any special Christmas traditions?"

At first, he didn't think she was going to answer, but finally she set down her fork and dabbed her mouth with her napkin. "Actually, we did. We both loved snow globes, and we each picked out a new one every year, often from wherever we vacationed."

She sighed before adding, "I guess this is the first year that I won't be adding to the collection."

Abruptly, she picked up her plate and headed toward the kitchen counter. "I'll wrap up the rest of this chicken and stick it in the fridge, Jim. Maybe you can have it for lunch tomorrow."

Jim looked at Finn as if asking for advice on what to say or do next, like he'd have any better idea. It wasn't as if either of them knew her all that well. By that point, Hailey was already walking out of the kitchen back into the living room. Jim jerked his head in that direction, ordering him to follow her.

Rather than argue, Finn left the table, wishing like heck he had some idea what to do when he caught up with her.

CHAPTER FIVE

HAILEY FOUND HERSELF drawn back to the Victorian village. She watched as the ice skaters whirled around the small pond in aimless circles, a perfect metaphor for how she felt at the moment. She'd come to the realization that she hadn't put enough forethought into planning this trip. It might have been smarter to wait until after the holidays or even until spring before driving all this way.

Not that she regretted finally meeting her grandfather. Jim had been nothing but welcoming since she'd showed up on his doorstep. Finn was more cautious, but she figured that was understandable considering he'd been totally unaware of her existence before they'd actually come face-to-face.

The real problem was that her own emotions were still too raw from the loss of her mother. Her grief over her mom's passing was hard enough to deal with, but finding out that her mom had known all along that Hailey had other family seemed like a huge betrayal. At the same time, she felt guilty for being so happy to find out that she wasn't totally alone in the world. The potent mix of contradictory emotions kept knocking her off-balance.

"I'd ask if you're okay, but it's pretty clear that you aren't."

Finn inched closer without crowding her too much. "Grief is a funny thing. You can think you've got it under control, but then it will hit you full force again when you least expect it."

He waited until she glanced at him before continuing. "I can't say that I really know what it's like to lose a parent. I was only three when Nick and my folks died in that car accident. If it weren't for photographs, I wouldn't even remember what they looked like. Even so, there's always been a hole where they used to be. Rhonda was the one who stepped up and took charge of me that awful night. Jim, too, but she's the one I remember holding me for what must have been hours at a time. She kept both Jim and me steady, not just back then but right up until the day she died."

Finn picked up the same figurine he had earlier, the one he'd said reminded him of Rhonda. "She was definitely the glue that kept us going. We've both been a bit lost without her. Now that you and Jim have gotten out the decorations, I feel bad that I didn't insist on doing it sooner. She would've wanted that."

He returned the figurine to its appointed place. "I'm sure your mom would understand why you didn't feel like getting out the snow globes this year, especially since you were making the trip out here for the holidays. That said, I'm betting she would want them to remind you of the good times you shared, not just what you've lost."

By that point, tears were streaming down Hailey's cheeks. She started to turn away, but Finn stopped her. Instead, he enfolded her in his arms, holding her carefully as if he was afraid she'd break. It was the first time since her mother's death that she found true comfort.

Before she could say anything, an alarm went off from somewhere close by. Finn lurched back a few steps as he dug his cell phone out of his pocket. After swiping across the screen to shut off the signal, he muttered, "Sorry if that startled you. I'm a volunteer firefighter, and that's our all-hands-on-deck signal. I have to go."

Jim came charging out of the kitchen. "Do you know what's happened?"

Finn sat down on the bench in the entry to pull on his boots. "Not yet. I'll text you when I get a chance."

As he put on his coat and gloves, he turned to her. "Are you going to be all right?"

She wiped the last of the tears off her face with the sleeve of her sweater. "I'm fine. Like you said, the emotions hit hard sometimes. Be careful out there."

He nodded. "I always am."

Then he was gone. She and Jim stood by the front window and watched until Finn's truck disappeared into the night. "I didn't know he was a firefighter."

"We don't talk about it much. Finn knows I don't approve of him taking such foolish risks, but there was no stopping him when he decided to volunteer. The problem is that our town can't afford to staff a professional fire department of its own. I'll even admit the volunteers do a fine job at great personal risk. The hard part is never knowing what kind of situation he's heading into. It might be a medical emergency, a car accident, or a cat that's stuck up in a tree."

At least that last one didn't sound all that serious. Well, maybe it was to the cat's owners. Still it seemed unlikely they would've issued an all-hands-on-deck call for something like that. She couldn't help but wonder how many nights Jim had stood at the window, all alone and worried about his godson. What could she do to distract him?

"He promised he'd text when he could. Until then, what do you say we play cards or something?"

Jim's expression immediately brightened as he gave her a considering look. "Your father was a positive fiend when it came to playing cribbage. He was only about twelve when he started beating me on a regular basis. Any chance you inherited his passion for the game?"

"So that's where I got it from. Mom eventually refused to play with me." She smiled as she looped her arm through his. "I tell you what. Let's play on the kitchen table. While you get out the cards and the cribbage board, I'll make us some tea to drink with our pie."

He patted her hand. "Sounds perfect."

TWO HOURS PASSED before they finally heard back from Finn. The message was short and to the point. The fire is out. No one hurt. Details later. Will head home soon.

Jim set his cards down, his shoulders slumped in relief or maybe exhaustion. Hailey figured it was likely a mix of both.

"Let's call this game a draw." She added her cards back to the pile, pulled the pegs out of the cribbage board and stored them in the compartment on the back. "It's past time for me to head back to the bed-and-breakfast."

That Jim didn't try to convince her to stay longer made it clear he was ready to call it a night, too. "Thanks for the pleasant distraction."

He also didn't fuss when she added their cups and plates to the dishwasher and turned it on. "You're welcome."

"Text me when you get to the B and B."

"Okay, but don't worry if it takes me longer than expected. I have to clean the snow off my car first, and I'll be driving slowly."

She led the way to where she'd left her coat and boots by the front door. When she was all wrapped up and ready to leave, she gave him a hug. "I'll want a rematch soon."

"It's a deal." He squeezed her back, chuckling a little. "Your coat is so puffy it's like hugging a marshmallow."

"This time of year it's better to go for warmth rather than fashion."

"Smart girl. I'll see you tomorrow."

"Are you sure you're not getting tired of my company?"

There was something both sweet and sad in his answering smile. "Honey, being with you is like getting back a little of so much that I've lost. You have your father's eyes and smile, both of which he got from my wife. So, no, I'm not ever going to be tired of your company."

She kissed his cheek. "Right back at you."

Finn mustered up enough energy to drag himself out of his truck and inside the house. Unlike some of the other volunteers, he had no one waiting for him at home. That was why he usually stuck around the firehouse to wrap up any last-minute details so the others could get back to their families. It had taken longer than usual this time, and it felt good to be almost done for the day.

Once inside, he dropped his keys on the counter and considered what to do next. Jim was probably in bed by now. Just in case he was wrong about that, he sent one more text to let Jim know that he'd made it back home. On a whim, he also sent one to Hailey, just to check in on her. *I'm guessing you're back at the B and B by now. Thanks for hanging out with Jim while I was out on a call. I know he worries.*

He wasn't sure she'd answer, but he was concerned about her. Hailey did a pretty good job of pretending everything was okay. But the more time he spent around her, the easier it was to know that she struggled at times. He suspected Jim had noticed as well.

He should turn in for the night, but he really needed to eat a little something before taking a shower and crawling into bed. Fighting the fire had definitely taken a toll on him. The grease fire had started in the kitchen and caused quite a bit of damage to that end of the house. The upside was that no one had gotten hurt. They'd also been able to contain the fire and prevent it from spreading to the neighboring houses. The downside was that place wouldn't be livable for a long time. The kitchen was pretty much toast, and everything else reeked of smoke and ash. They'd also have to dry the whole place out before repairs could begin. At least the Parsons had family close by where they could stay until repairs were completed.

To refuel his lagging energy levels, Finn made himself some bacon and scrambled eggs. His toast had just popped up when his phone pinged. It was Jim saying he was glad all was well and that he was headed for bed. Finn replied with a thumbs-up emoji to indicate the message was received. Telling himself he wasn't disappointed that it had been Jim and not Hailey texting him, he buttered his toast and sat down at the kitchen table.

Two bites into his meal, the phone pinged again. Sorry I was slow to answer. I was still driving when I got your message. Glad you're okay. Jim and I played cribbage. Boy, he's intense.

Finn chuckled. Jim was no doubt thrilled to have found another victim to play cards with.

Finn could give him a run for his money, but the old man had some serious card skills. He takes the game pretty seriously. Who came out on top?

Me. I took three games out of five.

Remind me not to play you anytime soon.

Keep buying me pie from Titus's café, and I'll take it easy on you.

Not happening. A man has his pride. How are you at poker?

Guess you'll have to wait and find out.

The phone remained silent for a couple of minutes. Finally, he typed, You still there?

Yeah, I was letting myself into my room. Whew! I'm ready for this day to be done. I'm going to turn in soon.

Finn was, too. I'm heading that way myself. I'll probably see you at some point tomorrow. I need to go into the shop for a while, but I usually stop by to check on Jim after that.

I was thinking I might cook dinner for the three of us. I'll let you bring the dessert. (hint, hint)

That had him grinning. Message received and understood. I'll be there, pie in hand.

See you then. Good night.

Still smiling, he headed for his room at the end of the hall and went to bed. Most of the time he came back to an empty house, the same as he had tonight. But for the duration of the brief conversation with Hailey, it had seemed as if he'd actually had someone waiting for him at home.

The feeling wasn't real, but for a second there it sure felt like it. Not sure what to make of that, he rolled over to his side and went to sleep.

CHAPTER SIX

"You can't go home. Not this soon."

Hailey flinched at the fierce determination in Jim's voice. "I'm sorry, but I did warn you that I was only coming for a short visit. My employer has been pretty patient about my extended leave of absence, but she can't hold my job forever. They've already had to have a substitute covering my classes for me longer than expected."

Her grandfather ran his fingers through his hair in frustration and then shoved his hands into his pockets. "Surely she won't expect you to come back this close to Christmas. At least stay through New Year's. Tell her to expect you back the second week of January. That would allow you to spend the holidays with us with plenty of time left over to drive back to Missouri."

The idea was tempting. If she left Dunbar, all she had waiting for her was a long drive back to an empty apartment. "Are you sure you and

Finn won't mind me intruding on your plans for Christmas?"

Jim snorted. "What plans? The last couple of years, we've ordered a turkey dinner from a restaurant in a nearby town. He bought me a sweater. I bought him some new tools. That was about as exciting as it got. With you here, we'll make more of an effort."

He gave her a sly look. "Any chance you know how to bake a turkey along with all the usual fixings?"

She could guess where this discussion was headed. "Even a small turkey would've been too much for just Mom and me, so we always kept things simple. We usually baked a turkey breast with boxed dressing, canned cranberry sauce and store-bought pies."

Jim didn't bother to hide his disappointment. "Well, we can still order from the restaurant."

She couldn't resist his sad, puppy-dog eyes. "I'll call my employer. If she agrees to let me wait to come back mid-January, I'll stay through Christmas. As far as cooking a big dinner goes, I can follow recipes. If you two pitch in to help, I'm betting we can manage to put a decent holiday meal on the table."

Looking much happier, Jim rubbed his hands together with great satisfaction. "I can't wait to tell Finn. He'll be thrilled."

She wasn't quite so sure about that, but Jim knew his godson better than she did. "Do you still have your wife's cookbooks? I'll need to start making a list of what we'll need for our Christmas dinner."

He charged off into the kitchen, leaving Hailey to follow along behind. "Her books are all on that shelf. Most of them are pretty old, but good recipes never go out of date."

After scanning the row of books, she pulled out two of them and headed for the kitchen table to study the table of contents. Jim picked up a wooden box and set it beside the cookbooks. "This has all of your grandmother's recipe cards in it."

Hailey opened the box and flipped through a few of the cards. "I bet we'll find some great dinner ideas in these. I should start taking notes. Do you have a pad of paper and a pencil I can borrow?"

"Coming right up."

He slid a spiral notebook across the table to her and sat down across from her. "So should we start with a menu?"

"Sounds logical."

Before writing down anything, she stopped to ask, "Shouldn't we ask for Finn's input before we commit to a definite plan?"

"Might not be a bad idea. I'll text him to see when he'll get here."

Before Jim could start typing, the front door opened. Jim was instantly up and moving. "Finn, perfect timing. Looks like Hailey will be staying through Christmas. She's gonna cook us a big holiday dinner."

She followed him into the living room. "Whoa, there. I'm not going to spend the whole day in the kitchen by myself. You two have to contribute to the effort. That's the deal."

Finn finished hanging up his coat before joining the discussion. "If there was a deal struck, I wasn't here to be part of it. Leave me out of the discussion."

The twinkle in his eyes belied his refusal. Even so, Jim wasn't having it. "I was trying to protect your interests, Finn. Besides, she's the one who wanted to wait until you got here to set the menu."

Hailey pointed toward the kitchen. "We've been checking through cookbooks for ideas. If we don't find anything that sounds right, we can always look online. Once we have everything nailed down, we can start a shopping list."

Finn headed toward the kitchen. "Can I at least get a cup of coffee first?"

"Sure thing. I just made a fresh pot a little while ago."

Jim added further incentive. "She also made another trip to Bea's shop. She made me leave one of the bacon maple bars for you."

Finn picked up speed. "I love those."

Once he had his coffee and his treat from Bea's, he joined them at the table. "So meatwise, I assume we're sticking with tradition and having turkey."

"That's the plan." She wrote that down, and then asked, "Do you like dark meat or white meat?"

Finn looked confused by the question. "I'm sorry, but don't turkeys normally come equipped with both?"

Okay, that was funny. "They do, but a small turkey would've been too much for my mom and me, so we always just cooked a breast. However, I am willing to give cooking a whole bird a try. It can't be that hard."

"Jim and I will help any way we can. When the time comes, I'll do the shopping, although it would probably be better if I take you with me."

She didn't even hesitate. "I'd be glad to help."

"Do you know what else I really miss?" Jim paused to give Hailey a hopeful look. "Watching Rhonda go into a baking frenzy. Any chance we could make a bunch of cookies before Christmas?"

Hailey didn't have the heart to say no. "I'll start a new list."

On her way to Jim's house Sunday morning, Hailey had stopped at the store to buy everything she would need to make dinner and bake some sugar cookies for the three of them. The last batch of cookies had come out of the oven just in time to put the meatloaf in. To keep things simple, Hailey had added a baking sheet filled with carrots, parsnips and fingerling potatoes to roast. It should all be done in another few minutes.

Finn joined her in the kitchen and sniffed the air. "That smells delicious."

"It's my mom's recipe. She always said the secret to a great meatloaf was using a combination of meats, not just ground beef."

He crowded closer and lowered his voice. "I've been meaning to thank you for getting Jim involved in all the holiday stuff. I haven't seen him this excited about anything for a long time."

His appreciation meant a lot. "It's been good for me, too. This can be a tough time of year for a lot of people, me included. I wasn't exactly expecting to actually do much celebrating this time around."

She wiped her hands on a dish towel before turning to face him. "I do have one problem that maybe you can help me with. I'd like to buy Jim something for Christmas, but I don't know what he'd like. He said you usually buy him a sweater, but I wouldn't even know what size to get. I'd also like to get a small gift for the Volkovs' little boy. I'm thinking I can order a few things online and have them delivered to the bed-and-breakfast."

Jim spoke from the doorway. "You don't have to buy me anything, but I think it's nice you want to buy something for the boy. But instead of shopping online, I have a better idea. Finn can take you to the mall."

She hadn't meant to put Finn on the spot, and it was hard not to notice that the man hadn't made the offer himself. Trying to give him an out, she said, "That's okay. I know you have to work."

Finn shrugged. "Actually, the shop is officially closed on Mondays. I usually work some anyway, but I don't have to. We can make a day of it and go to one of the shopping centers closer into Seattle. Maybe even do a little sightseeing if we have time. How does that sound?"

"I'd like that if you're sure it's no bother."

Jim answered for him. "He'll be glad to take you."

Hailey wasn't so sure about that, but the stubborn set to Jim's jaw made it clear that he wouldn't budge. As far as he was concerned, his godson would take her shopping whether he wanted to or not. "Monday will be fine."

Before Finn could comment, Jim issued another order. "After dinner, the two of you need to go to the tree farm and cut us a Christmas tree."

Finn didn't look thrilled by that idea either. "Why can't we use that little artificial tree out in the garage? You know, the one we bought after Rhonda passed away."

Jim crossed his arms over his chest and glared at Finn. "Because I want a real one this year."

Hailey might not have known Jim for long, but she bet he wouldn't back down easily. She didn't particularly want to intervene between him and Finn, but the last thing she wanted was for Finn to be forced into spending more time with her against his will.

"Look, it's already dark outside. Maybe we should wait to do that when we could go while it's still light out."

Jim still wasn't having it. Pointing out the kitchen window, he said, "In case you haven't noticed, it gets dark by late afternoon this time of year. The family that runs the tree farm know that most people can't get there in the middle of the day. That's why they string up lights so people can see to pick out trees. The sooner we get one, the sooner we can decorate it."

Finn pinched the bridge of his nose and sighed. "Should I go warm up the truck now or can we eat dinner first?"

Jim looked surprised by the question. "Well, sure. No use in letting the food get cold."

Finn gave his godfather one last dark look and left the room.

THE SILENCE DURING dinner wasn't particularly comfortable. It probably wasn't fair to Hailey, especially since she wasn't the one Finn was upset with. While he didn't usually mind running errands for Jim, Finn would appreciate being asked rather than being ordered to do something. At the very least, Jim could've asked if Finn had other plans for the evening.

Not that he did, but it was the principle of the thing.

He also wasn't doing justice to the meal that Hailey had cooked for the three of them. In an attempt to rectify that, he took another helping of the roasted vegetables. "I've never been a fan of parsnips, but evidently I didn't know how to cook them."

Hailey looked pleased by the compliment. "Fixing dinner for one is never fun, so I try to keep it as simple as possible. Over the years, I've learned lazy ways to cook vegetables."

That made him laugh. "Maybe you should write a cookbook called *Lazy Recipes for Vegetable Lovers*."

She grinned back at him. "I just might."

Jim gave her a sly look. "Wouldn't the laziest way be to simply eat them raw?"

Hailey tapped her chin with her forefinger and pretended to be intrigued by that idea. "That's genius. I could do a whole chapter on that alone. I should get a pen and paper to write this stuff down."

Finn was relieved that the small bit of silliness successfully broke through the tension that had been casting a pall over the meal and allowed them all to relax. He finished the last of his meatloaf and pushed his plate back from the edge of the table. "If we're going to do the tree thing tonight, we should probably get a move on."

Hailey gathered up her own dishes and carried them over to the counter. "I'll put the leftovers in the fridge, and then we can go. I'll do the dishes when we get back."

Jim joined her at the sink. "Nope, I'm on cleanup duty. Right after we got married, Rhonda and I agreed that one of us would cook and the other one would clean up. Tell her, Finn."

"Yep, that was the rule."

Hailey still looked hesitant. "If you're sure."

Jim pointed toward the door. "I'm sure. Now you should get going. It's only going to get colder out there the longer you delay."

That pronouncement spurred the two of them to get bundled up and hustle out to Finn's truck. By the time they were underway, Hailey was looking pretty excited. "So how far away is the tree farm? How does all of this work? I've never cut a fresh tree before."

"Really?"

"Yeah. Back when I was little, Mom and I used to go to a Christmas tree lot in a local shopping center parking lot. Then when I was around ten or so, Mom realized that her allergies acted up every Christmas. It finally occurred to her that she was reacting to the tree. Maybe some kind of mold or something. Anyway, after we bought an artificial tree, she didn't get sick."

"Jim and Rhonda always cut their own tree, so that's all I've ever known. Well, except for that poor excuse for a tree that we put out for a couple of years after Rhonda passed."

He paused to glance at her. "But to answer your question, the place we're going is about fifteen miles from town. The Halkos have owned the tree farm for at least three generations that I know of, and they make a big deal of the whole process. There's a place for customers to park that's within easy walking distance of the fields where the trees are. But if you don't mind waiting for a little while, they have a horse-drawn wagon that picks people up and drops them off at the barn to check in. If it has snowed a lot, they switch out the wagon for a sleigh. They also serve fresh-baked cookies and hot cider, which is especially welcome on a cold night."

"Boy, this sounds like fun! I know this isn't how you planned to spend the evening, but I'm sure Jim appreciates you doing this for him."

Finn wasn't convinced of that. Right now Jim was far more focused on Hailey than his godson, but he figured that was understandable. A short time later, they turned off the two-lane highway onto a narrow road that wound along the side of the mountain to the small valley where the tree farm was located. "We're almost there, so start thinking about what kind of tree you'd like to get."

That elicited another look of surprise. "How many kinds are there?"

"If I remember correctly, they raise at least five varieties. The most popular are Douglas firs and noble firs. They'll also have Fraser firs, grand firs, and I think maybe some kind of pine. It all depends on whether you like trees with long needles or short. They also vary in color a bit. Rhonda always liked the Frasers best. They have a sort of silvery white color on the back of the needles."

"Hmm. This is more complicated than I expected. It might take me some time to decide."

She didn't sound too upset by that prospect. Good thing they were both dressed for the weather. "The entrance is up there where you can see the lights."

Ten minutes later they stood waiting in the back of the parking lot with several other customers. The sound of sleigh bells signaled the imminent arrival of their ride up to the barn. Finn couldn't help but notice that Hailey's excitement rivaled that of the kids who were there with their parents. For once the shadows that haunted her eyes were missing, and the warmth of her bright smile seemed to take the chill off the night air. Her enthusiasm was contagious, and he found himself unexpectedly looking forward to wandering around in the moonlight, sipping hot cider as they searched for the perfect tree.

Actually there were two wagons headed their way. The first one was pulled by a pair of draft horses. A second was hitched to a tractor and carried the trees that belonged to the customers returning to their cars. The horses slowed to a stop right in front of where Hailey and Finn waited. Several people stepped down off the wagon and headed off to claim their trees. The driver and a teenager hopped down off the tractor to help everyone secure their trees on the roofs of their vehicles. Meanwhile, the new arrivals climbed aboard the horse-drawn wagon, which then set off for the barn in the distance.

As soon as he and Hailey were settled on the front bench, she picked up where they'd left off in their discussion. "So do you want to get a Fraser since that's what Rhonda liked?"

"I'd suggest that we look around and pick out the kind of tree you think looks the best. We'll aim for one around seven feet tall, so roughly a foot taller than I am. Jim's house has nine-foot ceilings, so the tree will still fit even with the star on top. The stand also adds a couple of inches to its height."

When the wagon rolled a stop, Finn dismounted first and then held out his hand to assist Hailey to the ground before leading her into the barn. She hesitated just inside the doorway to look around, a big smile on her face. "Wow, they've really gone all out on decorating in here."

He'd almost forgotten how the Halkos transformed their ordinary barn into a winter wonderland. Besides the free cider he'd mentioned to Hailey, they sold all kinds of Christmas decorations and also had a photographer on duty to take pictures of kids with Santa. "If you'd like to look around for a few minutes, we can."

To his surprise, she looped her arm through his. "This is going to be fun."

They strolled up and down the aisles but didn't stop to buy anything. In the last aisle, Hailey coasted to a stop to study the snow globes display. She looked a bit wistful as she picked one up that held a pair of cardinals inside. "Mom would've loved this one."

After setting it back on the shelf, she moved on. "I may have to come back here to do a little shopping."

Finn thought that was probably true for him as well. Meanwhile, it was time to move on to their main reason for being there. "Let's go get a saw, a map, and pick up some cider to help ward off the cold."

She gave the globes one last look and then followed him back across the barn.

AFTER LEAVING THE BARN, they studied the rows of possibilities, stopping to check out any trees that might fit the bill. Half an hour later, they'd narrowed the choices down to three trees, each perfect in its own way. They'd already revisited the noble fir before circling back to their second option. Hailey sipped her cider and studied the Douglas fir from all angles. "So, what do you think?"

"I think it would be fine."

Somehow, she wasn't convinced he actually meant that. Her suspicions proved correct when Finn suddenly led her back toward the last tree that had made the short list. "Let's look at the Fraser again."

It was fuller and taller than the Douglas fir. As she studied it, Hailey was all too aware of Finn standing a few feet away, quietly waiting for her to make up her mind. She had to admit that his patience had surprised her. For a man who hadn't wanted to go tree shopping tonight, he didn't seem to mind the amount of time it was taking them to find the perfect one. She drank the last of her cider and then nodded, her mind made up.

"Let's get this one."

He stepped closer. "Are you sure? You seemed to really like the noble fir a lot."

"I did, but this one is definitely the best. It will be beautiful."

Finn held out his cider. "Hold this for me while I cut it down."

From the efficient way he wielded the saw, it was obvious that this wasn't his first tree-cutting rodeo. In a matter of minutes, he gave her a playful wink and called out, "Timber!" as the tree tumbled to the ground.

After taking back his drink, he picked up the tree by its trunk. "If you'll get the top end, we'll head back to the barn. After we settle the bill, we'll hitch a ride back to the truck on the wagon."

Hailey let him take the lead as they started back down the aisle. She couldn't help but enjoy watching the impressive flex of his muscles as he bore the lion's share of the tree's weight. She liked the way he moved, all power and confidence. Because of her mother's illness, it had been a long time since she'd spent time in the company of an attractive man, and she missed it. As if feeling her scrutiny, Finn suddenly glanced back at her. "Am I walking too fast?"

She realized she'd gradually slowed down as they walked. "Not at all."

"Let me know if that changes." As he picked up speed again, he called back over his shoulder, "If it's okay with you, I'd like to get a refill on the cider before we leave."

At least it was too dark for him to realize she was blushing that he'd caught her staring. She managed a small smile. "Sounds good to me, too."

Twenty minutes later, they were back in Finn's truck and pulling out of the parking lot.

"That was definitely a lot more fun than picking out a tree in a parking lot. Thanks for taking me. I really hope Jim likes it."

"He'll love it because you chose it."

There was an odd note in Finn's voice, like maybe he wasn't happy that her opinion might outweigh his. "But we picked it out together. It wasn't a solo effort."

"It's still your opinion that will matter for him."

Why would Finn think his opinion no longer mattered to his godfather? She wasn't about to ask as it was clear that his mood had undergone an abrupt change. The man was as unpredictable as they came. She settled back in her seat, glad they didn't have far to go. Maybe he was simply tired and ready to go home. It was either that or he'd simply had enough of her company for one night.

Well, she had news for him—that road ran both ways. Too bad they were scheduled to spend tomorrow together as well. With that happy thought, she leaned back in her seat and stared out into the darkness.

CHAPTER SEVEN

Monday morning, Hailey climbed into the front seat of Finn's truck, but she didn't act as if she planned to stay there for long even though they were supposed to go shopping together. "Finn, it's your day off. You shouldn't have to spend it shepherding me around."

Yeah, he did. They both knew it was mandatory just like last night had been. Admittedly, the trip to the tree farm had ended up being more fun he'd expected. But even if it had been a total disaster, Jim would never let Finn get by with leaving Hailey on her own today. Rather than belabor the point, he said, "Buckle up."

Hailey studied him for several seconds before complying. "Okay, but we don't have to make a whole day of it. Let's just go to the closest place where I can grab a Star Wars LEGO set for Carter and a new shirt for Jim. Then we can call it a day."

Then she folded her hands in her lap and settled back in the seat, her mouth set in a straight line. That had him chuckling. Looking puzzled, she frowned at him. "Did I say something funny?"

"No, but I'm pretty sure you would have that same expression on your face heading into the dentist's office for a root canal."

Her cheeks flushed pink. "Very funny."

It was. Sort of, anyway. The truth was he wasn't hating the idea of spending the day with her. "Seriously, I need to pick up a few gifts myself, and I've been putting it off. I hate shopping at the best of times, and the crowds this time of year only make it worse. It will be nice to have some company for once."

"Really?"

"Yeah, really."

"Okay, then." She smiled for the first time since he'd arrived. "I'm not fond of traipsing through the mall by myself either."

Now that all of that was settled, he backed out of the driveway. It didn't take long to leave Dunbar behind, following the state highway that would lead them south toward the interstate. Hailey stirred restlessly as if the silence bothered her. Finally, she said, "So, have you always liked working on motorcycles?"

"It keeps food on the table."

She sounded a bit puzzled when she responded, "That isn't exactly a resounding yes."

He kept his eyes on the road, not wanting to meet her gaze, not sure what his own would reveal. "I like the creativity of it, especially listening to what the customer says and translating what is often a pretty vague description into reality. There's a lot of satisfaction when I get it right."

"I can understand that. Do you also do a lot of repair work like you're doing for Titus?"

"Not as much as I used to, mainly because I've always preferred doing custom work. Our company has a solid reputation for quality design work, and we're usually booked six months out. That said, I make room in my schedule for friends and established customers whenever possible. Besides, it won't take long to restore Titus's bike once the parts arrive. If necessary, he and I can knock out the repairs after regular business hours."

"I bet Titus is relieved that you're doing the work for him."

"Yeah, he's really attached to that bike. From what he's told me, the Harley was in pretty poor condition when he bought it. He put a lot of time and elbow grease into restoring it."

She gave him a teasing smile. "His bike is a 'her' as I recall."

"So she is." He laughed. "Whatever you do, don't tell Titus I got it wrong. The man is a bit touchy on the subject."

"Don't worry, I won't tell him."

Evidently, she hadn't yet run out of curiosity about the family business. "Jim said he and your grandfather started the business back in the day."

Finn waited until he passed a slow-moving truck before responding. "Yep, that's true. In the beginning, they both held down other full-time jobs and worked on bikes weekends and evenings until the business began earning enough to support both families. The second generation joined in when they got old enough. My dad started working at the shop when he was still in high school and went full-time when he graduated. Unfortunately, his father died of a heart attack just after Dad turned twenty. According to the terms of the agreement between Jim and my grandfather, my father automatically became Jim's new partner. Nick also helped out at the shop after school and on weekends. The expectation was that he would join the business as soon as he finished high school."

Hailey kept her focus on the scenery on her side of the truck. The only sign she was a bit nervous was the way she was tugging at the pendant on her necklace, sliding it back and forth on the chain. She gave him a quick glance. "I have to wonder how he felt about that."

"I can't say for sure, but he enlisted the week he turned eighteen and reported for duty the Monday after he graduated. I do know Jim wasn't happy when Nick re-upped after his first enlistment was over."

Hailey shifted to look at him more directly. "So I guess Jim and Rhonda wouldn't have been happy to learn Nick wasn't going to move back to Dunbar until after my mother finished college, if then."

"Maybe not, but again there's no way to know. Either way, you shouldn't feel guilty about it. None of what happened was your fault. Anyone's really, except for the drunk driver who caused the accident. If he'd taken a cab home instead of getting behind the wheel of his car, we would have all lived very different lives."

After a brief silence, Hailey spoke again. "If I haven't said so before, I'm sorry you lost your parents like that."

"Me, too, but it is what it is. I was lucky to have Jim and Rhonda. Without them, I would've probably ended up in foster care. Both of my parents were only children, so they'd asked Jim and Rhonda to be my guardians if something ever happened."

"You were lucky. They weren't related to you

by blood, but they were family by choice. I actually had family, but they never wanted me."

She'd told him that before, but it was no less shocking this time. He surprised both of them when he reached across the console to give her hand a soft squeeze. "That's on them, Hailey. They're the ones who have missed out all these years."

She smiled and squeezed his hand in return. "Finn Cooper, that's one of the nicest things anyone has ever said to me. Thank you."

He felt the impact of her smile as if it had been a physical touch. "You're welcome."

Feeling a bit unsettled by the surprisingly intense reaction, he redirected their conversation to a safer topic. "So what sounds good for lunch?"

"I'm always up for a good sandwich or pizza, and it's my treat this time. You have a better idea of what's available where we're going."

"Why don't we hit the mall first and then decide?"

"Good idea."

BY THE TIME they made it back to Dunbar, Hailey was ready to kick back and relax for a while. They'd managed to finish their own shopping fairly quickly, but on their way out Finn had spotted a booth where the local fire department was collecting toys for kids. He'd headed right back into the mall to spend a small fortune on toys and games. Deciding he had the right idea, she'd joined in the fun and added to their purchases. After dropping off several shopping bags full of goodies with the firefighters, they headed back to Dunbar.

Instead of taking the most direct way back to town, Finn had opted to take what he called "the scenic route." That entailed taking the bridge across Lake Washington toward Seattle before turning north. She loved seeing the iconic Space Needle and a smattering of boats out on the water, not to mention the occasional glimpse of the Olympic Mountains to the west and the Cascades to the east.

She suspected Finn was amused by her excitement over the scenery, but who wouldn't be dazzled by such beauty? For sure she wanted to do some serious sightseeing the next time she came back to the area.

But right now, she hauled her shopping bags up to her room, intent on taking a long nap. It was only late afternoon, but she was tired. After stashing her purchases in the dresser, she kicked off her shoes and stretched out on the bed. It felt so good to get horizontal and relax for a while, but sleep proved elusive. With nothing else to occupy her thoughts, she kept reliving every moment since she'd left home to make the long trek to Dunbar.

The trip had definitely been a series of emotional ups and downs. She'd spent most of the drive from Missouri to Washington fretting over what it would be like to finally meet her grandfather. Would he actually be happy to see her? What kind of relationship could she expect to establish with him at this late date? The questions had circled through her head on a constant loop of worry.

So far, her interactions with Jim had proved to be everything she could have hoped for, but Finn was a little more problematic. His mood seemed to run hot and cold when he was around her. Maybe that was normal for him, but she had no way to know for sure. They'd had a good time at the tree farm and also while out shopping. They'd had no problem finding things to talk about over lunch, keeping to relatively safe topics like sports.

Their conversation gradually coasted to a stop on the way back to Dunbar. For the most part, it hadn't felt uncomfortable. She'd been content to admire the scenery, and she knew that Finn needed to put in a few hours at the shop after he dropped her off at the bed-and-breakfast. That might have accounted for his silence if he was thinking about everything he had to do when he got there. Her own thoughts were focused on how much she wished she could tell her mom about meeting Jim and Finn.

She'd like to think her mother would understand why Hailey wanted to find answers to the questions she'd always had about her father and why he hadn't been part of their lives. But she might never understand why her mother hadn't simply explained the situation herself when Hailey was old enough to understand instead of leaving her a letter.

So many questions with no answers. If that wasn't frustrating enough, as much as she wanted a nap, sleep wasn't going to happen. Finally, she admitted defeat and sat up on the side of the bed. What should she do now? It was too early to leave for Jim's house, and she'd finished the only book she'd brought with her. Rather than sitting there and twiddling her thumbs, she decided to check out the books Rikki had available for guests to borrow.

Slipping her feet back into her shoes, Hailey went downstairs to the living room area. She was surprised to have the place to herself. Come to think of it, though, Rikki hadn't mentioned having any other guests when they'd spoken earlier that morning, so maybe she was the only one currently staying at the bed-and-breakfast.

That was too bad, because she could have

used a bit of company right then. She browsed the bookcases that flanked the fireplace. The books were sorted a little haphazardly. Fiction was on one side, divided by genre but beyond that in no particular order. The nonfiction was on the other side and covered a pretty mixed bag of topics. After reading the back blurbs on several books, she finally settled on a romantic suspense written by one of her favorite authors.

She considered taking the book back to her room, but the warmth of the fire tempted her to stay where she was. One chair was perfectly located to afford her a view of the fireplace as well as the street outside. Thanks to the twinkling lights and other decorations, it was if she were looking out at a real-life Currier and Ives print.

She hadn't expected to enjoy anything about the holidays this year, but right now the soft glow of the Christmas lights warmed a spot in her heart that had been cold since her mother's passing. She whispered, "Mom, you would've loved this place. I also think you and Grandpa Jim would've really hit it off."

The sound of approaching footsteps had her wiping away any possible evidence of tears. After drawing a calming breath, she turned toward the door as her hostess entered. Holding up the book she'd chosen, she said, "I thought

I'd sit here and read for a while. The fire is cozy, and the view out the window is spectacular."

Rikki looked pleased by Hailey's comments. "I'm glad you're enjoying yourself here. I heard you coming down the stairs and thought maybe you'd like a late-afternoon snack. I brought you a cup of tea and some cookies. They're fresh from the oven."

As Rikki set a small tray within easy reach on the table next to her chair, Hailey thanked her. "This is very kind of you."

Then Hailey noticed there were two cups on the tray. "Aren't you going to join me?"

Rikki picked up the second cup. "Well, there's a stack of paperwork waiting for me on my desk. I've been ignoring it all day, telling myself that stockpiling cookies and muffins was a far better use of my time. Unfortunately, I've run out of room in the freezer, which means I've also run out of excuses."

She offered Hailey a smile that was definitely on the hopeful side. "Unless you could use some company?"

Recognizing a hint when she heard one, Hailey motioned to the chair next to hers. "I can honestly say that I would love some."

Rikki happily sat down and helped herself to a couple of the cookies. Once she'd made herself comfortable, she asked, "So are you enjoying your time here in Dunbar? I've heard you've been spending a lot of time with Finn Cooper and his godfather."

Then she wrinkled her nose. "I probably should've warned you that the gossip telegraph is alive and well in Dunbar. It was the same when Carter and I moved here. Strangers definitely stand out in a town this small."

That was putting it mildly. "I've noticed I get a lot of looks, especially when I'm at the cafe or the bakery."

"Yeah, I experienced the same thing, but everyone went out of their way to make me and Carter feel welcome." She grinned a little. "Of course Max had a much rougher time of it, but that was because of why he came here in the first place."

Should she admit that she'd already heard that story? Probably.

"Jim told me a little about the Trillium Nugget and Max's great-grandfather. He's looking forward to reading Max's book when it comes out. I meant to tell Max that the next time I saw him."

"That's nice of Mr. Morris. I'll let Max know. He's worried that he'll be the only one interested in the story, but I think he's wrong about that. A lot of people in town enjoy learning about local history, and it sounds like Grandpa Lev lived a pretty adventurous life."

"Jim said I should check out the display about Lev at the museum here in town. He also said there was some information about my family there, too."

She hadn't meant to let that last bit slip out, but it was too late now.

"Really?" Rikki set her tea down. "I didn't realize you had family here. I thought your decision to come all the way to Dunbar had something to do with the motorcycle you brought to Finn's shop. From what Max heard, it's an incredibly rare model."

How much did she want to reveal? Hailey gave it some thought before continuing. "The bike is only part of the story. The real reason I came is that I recently learned that Jim Morris is my paternal grandfather. I've never met him before this."

Rikki didn't say anything for several seconds. Then she kept it simple without pushing for details. "I bet he's glad you came."

Even so, Hailey could almost see the torrent of questions swirling through Rikki's brain. It was hard not to laugh. Not knowing how familiar Rikki was with Jim's situation, she gave her a brief summary of past events, ending with, "It obviously all happened before I was born."

"It's all so tragic."

"Yeah, it is. Anyway, Jim and Rhonda never knew anything about my mother or her relationship with their son." She stopped to sip her tea before continuing, sharing only the highlights of what had come next. She ended by saying, "When I finally got up the courage to reach out to Jim, he invited me to come for a visit, and here I am."

"I bet he was thrilled. I'm happy for you both."

"Thanks. It's been a lot to deal with for not just Jim and me, but for Finn as well."

"How so?"

"I think it's kind of like it was for my mom and me. My whole life it was just the two of us and suddenly I have a grandfather. After Finn's parents died, Rhonda and Jim became his only family. Now he has to share Jim with me. I'm not sure he's happy about that."

Okay, that didn't come out quite right. "Don't get me wrong. He's actually been great. Unfortunately, Jim didn't give him any warning about me until the day I got here, so my arrival came as a shock to Finn. I wouldn't be surprised if he's wondering about my motives. To be honest, I would if I were him. He's understandably protective of Jim, and he wants to make sure that I'm legit."

"And how does he expect you to prove that? DNA tests or something?"

Hailey reached for a cookie to buy herself a little more time. "Actually, we had those done before I ever agreed to make the trip. I'm Jim's granddaughter, all right, so we wanted to meet each other. I was only going to stay a couple of days, but Jim asked me to stay through Christmas. After that, I need to get back home while I still have a job. I'm sure Jim and I will stay in touch, though."

"It's a shame you live so far away, but at least you'll have the holidays together."

"That's true." Then she checked the time. "Speaking of the holidays, I promised Jim I'd come over for dinner again tonight. Afterward, we're going to decorate the Christmas tree."

When she started to get up, Rikki stopped her. "Your story differs from mine in some ways, but there are some similarities. It was just you and your mother. The same with Jim and Finn. Until we moved here, it was just me and Carter. I won't bore you with the details, but I know from experience how hard it is to let other people in. Max had his own issues and actually left town after he learned the truth about his great-grandfather's story. I couldn't admit it at the time, but I didn't want him to go. Neither did Carter."

She stared past Hailey toward the flames dancing in the fireplace. "Thank goodness Max returned to town. He might have used the excuse of researching his book, but he really came back for us. I'm thankful every day that he did. Our life is so much better with him in it."

Was she hinting that Hailey should stay permanently? She pointed out the obvious. "My home is in Missouri."

It was definitely time to get going, but Rikki had more to say. "I know that's where you live, Hailey, but ask yourself a few hard questions. Are you going back because you have people there who really matter to you? If the answer is no, then maybe consider if you might not be better off living where you have family."

Rikki stood. "And now I'll get my nose out of your business. I hope the three of you have fun decorating the tree. That's always one of my favorite things to do this time of year. We'll be putting up a tree in here in the next day or so for our guests to enjoy. We'll also have one in our apartment upstairs that is just for the three of us. We'll decorate it with ornaments that Carter and I have collected over the years mixed in with some handed down from Max's family. We plan to add in our own over the years, so eventually the tree will reflect all of our best memories."

Hailey liked that idea. Too bad she couldn't go back home just long enough to pack up some of her mom's snow globes and a few of the decorations they always put on display. There was no way she could have foreseen wanting to have a few of the ornaments she and her mom had collected to add to the tree tonight. As she drove toward Jim's house, a small voice whispered, "There's always next year."

At least, she hoped so.

CHAPTER EIGHT

FINN STOPPED TO draw a deep breath as soon as he stepped into Jim's house. Boy, something smelled good even if it was an odd mix of scents. If he had to guess, he would say there was a whiff of cinnamon and apples as well as a hint of his godfather's special spice blend. After kicking off his boots, he hung up his coat and headed for the kitchen to see what was going on. Sure enough, Jim stood at the stove stirring a huge pot of chili. As soon as he spotted Finn, he grabbed a spoon and offered him a taste. "You got here just in time. Tell me what you think."

After blowing on it, Finn took a taste. "The spices are right on the money, but I'd throw in a little more salt. Do I need to grate the cheese or anything?"

Jim sneered, his usual reaction when someone added toppings to his special dish. "Good chili doesn't need cheese."

"Yep, you've made that perfectly clear in the past. I, however, love cheddar on chili."

Jim pointed at the fridge. "Since I know I'm fighting a losing battle, check the fridge. You'll find cheese, sour cream, avocado and minced onion all ready to go."

"Perfect." Finn sniffed the air again. "But why am I smelling apples and cinnamon?"

"Evidently Hailey and her mother always made mulled cider when they put up decorations. She bought the ingredients and put it on to simmer in my slow cooker."

Finn lifted the lid on the cooker to check it out. "That's a nice tradition."

"I thought so."

Finn served up two mugs of the cider. He set one on the counter where Jim could reach it before sitting down at the kitchen table. "So where is she?"

After adding more salt to the pot, Jim put the lid back on and then joined Finn at the table. "Last I saw of her, she was in the garage going through all of the boxes with the decorations for the tree. I told her that Rhonda changed the theme every year, and she wanted to check out the various choices."

Okay, this could be bad. "Did you tell her how much the two of us really hated the year we had to look at a tree full of pink flamingos?"

Jim snickered. "Nope, I thought I'd wait and see how she reacts. Besides, the year of the parrots was almost as bad."

"True enough. Hopefully Hailey will go with something more traditional like polar bears, snowmen, or Rhonda's huge collection of Santas."

The door from the garage opened, and Hailey stepped inside. She was carrying a plastic bin piled high with ornaments. After setting it down on the table, she picked up the one on top and dangled it from her fingertip. "Seriously, gentlemen? Flamingos?"

Finn cracked up as he raised his hands in surrender. "Don't blame us. That was all Rhonda. One year she asked us whether we wanted snowmen or Santas. The two of us made a huge mistake by saying it didn't matter."

Jim chuckled even as he shuddered. "Boy, we sure never made that mistake again, but you should've seen it. When we came home the next day, the whole tree was awash in pink—the garland, the lights, everything. Even the skirt was hot pink with sequins. I never could figure out how she managed to pull it all together that fast."

Hailey joined in on their laughter as she sat down across from Finn. "That's hilarious. I'm even sorrier I never got to meet her."

Finn suspected Rhonda and Hailey would have really hit it off. Jim's own smile looked a bit sad. "You two would have kept me and Finn hopping, that's for sure."

Then he pointed toward the bin. "So other than the flamingos, did any of the other collections catch your eye?"

"I brought in one from each set to see what you prefer." She laid the ornaments out one by one on the table. "They're all great. If you want to stick with one type of ornaments, I'd go with the Santas. But if it were up to me, I'd pick some from each set and mix them up."

Finn exchanged looks with Jim, who shrugged. "Whatever makes you happy is fine with me."

"Okay, flamingos it is."

Jim had been taking a sip of his cider and nearly choked. When he could breathe again, he wheezed, "Don't joke about that. Rhonda left that tree up until the needles fell off just to make sure we'd learned our lesson."

It was hard not to laugh as Hailey carefully set the flamingo aside. Next, she held up a parrot for several seconds before setting it down next to the flamingo. "I won't even ask what you two did to warrant a macaw Christmas."

One by one, Hailey considered each of the other options, dividing them into two groups—

the rejects and the possibilities. When she was done, she pointed to the first choice. "Show of hands, please. Who wants the snowmen?"

When no one raised their hand, she moved on. "Polar bears?"

That left one last choice. "Santas?"

Finn raised his hand, but Jim still hesitated. "Come on, Jim. We have to choose one."

Jim met his gaze head on. "I know we've always done things the way Rhonda wanted, but Hailey should have some say in the matter. If she wants to do a mix of the ornaments, we should do that."

Finn dropped his hand back down onto the table with a heavy thud. "Fine. Do whatever you want. I'll go put the tree in its stand."

He ignored both Jim's angry protest and Hailey's startled response as he escaped to the garage, slamming the door shut on his way out. By the time he reached the tree, which they'd left standing in a bucket of water since they brought it home, his temper had faded from furious to a bare simmer. The truth was he didn't know where the flash of anger had come from. Hailey certainly hadn't done anything wrong, and it was Jim's Christmas tree. He could decorate it any way he wanted to.

Resigning himself to having to apologize to each of them, he got the tree stand down off the shelf in the corner and set it next to the bucket. It would be easier to maneuver the tree into position with a second pair of hands, but he wasn't about to ask for help until he had a few minutes to regain control. Unfortunately, he wasn't going to get that time. The door had just opened and someone was headed his way. Without even looking, he knew it was Hailey.

"Can I help?"

He closed his eyes and reached for the last bit of control he had. "I would appreciate it."

She crept closer. "Tell me what I can do."

"Steady the stand so I can transfer the tree into it out of the bucket. Then I'll support the tree while you tighten the screws."

"Got it."

When she was in position, he shoved his hands through the thick branches to grab the tree by its trunk. "On the count of three."

He counted down and then manhandled the heavy tree up and over into the stand. Luck was with him, because he managed to do it without knocking over the bucket and soaking them both. Hailey made quick work of tightening the supports. When she was done, they both stepped back. Finn checked the tree from several angles. "Does it look straight to you?"

Hailey frowned. "I think it's leaning a little to the left."

He went down on one knee to make the necessary adjustments and checked again. "Is that better?"

"It's perfect." She offered him a tenuous smile. "It's also every bit as beautiful as when we picked it."

"Yeah, we did good."

When he stood up, he made himself face her directly. "Look, I'm sorry about how I acted in the kitchen. It's no big deal how we decorate the tree."

"But it clearly is, Finn. From what I gather, this is the first time you and Jim have really gone all out on decorating for Christmas since Rhonda died. I, of all people, should've known that you would want to honor her memory in every way possible." She edged closer to him as she added, "After all, the main reason I drove all the way out here was because I wasn't ready to face the holidays without my mother there to share them with me."

He hadn't expected her to be so understanding, but maybe he should have. "I still shouldn't have taken it out on you. I'd feel better if you either did some yelling or maybe took a swing at me."

She smiled just a little and immediately punched him on the arm, not that she put much oomph behind it. "There. Feel better now?"

He rubbed his arm that didn't actually hurt at all. "Maybe a little."

"Always glad to help a friend." Then she shot him an impudent grin. "Especially since I suspect Jim is only waiting until he gets you alone to do some yelling."

"No doubt."

Might as well get the lecture over with. "If I take the base of the tree, can you handle the other end again?"

"Sure."

Jim was hovering just inside the door as they wrestled the tree inside. As they passed by him, Hailey asked, "Where do you want it?"

He led the way into the living room and pointed toward the front window. "We always put the tree there so that passersby can see it from out front."

Once they'd wrestled the tree in place, Finn checked one more time to make sure it was still straight. While he did that, Hailey returned to the kitchen to fill a pitcher with water for the tree stand. As soon as she left the room, Jim gave Finn a hard look. "You were rude."

"I was, and I'm sorry about that. I've already apologized to her."

"Not sure what upset you so much, but you shouldn't have taken it out on her. Me, either, for that matter."

"Like I said, I apologized to her."

To his surprise, Jim patted him on the shoulder. "Good. Look, I know there's a lot going on right now. I guess I should've expected there to be some fireworks at some point. Having someone new in the family is bound to have all of us a little off-balance."

Having both Hailey and Jim being so understanding only made it harder for Finn to find his equilibrium. It was time to change the subject. "Should we eat first and then decorate or the other way around?"

"Let's eat first. The chili is ready."

"Sounds good. I'll go set the table."

Finn took that as the peace offering it was. "I'd appreciate that, but I do have one question for you."

"Which is?"

"How are you going to react if Hailey likes cheese on her chili?"

Jim laughed. "I'll smile and then pass her the sour cream and avocado."

"That's what I thought."

HAILEY HANDED FINN the tree topper. It was a silver star, the one exception to the otherwise all-Santa theme of the tree. He settled it in place and then climbed down off the small ladder that Jim had dug out of the hall closet. The three of them stepped back from the tree to admire their handiwork. She smiled at both men. "It's beautiful. I'd also forgotten how nice it was to have the scent of a fresh tree inside the house."

Pulling out her phone, she said, "I want pictures. Would you guys stand on either side of the tree for me?"

When they positioned themselves, she said, "Say ho, ho, ho!"

After she snapped several shots, Finn held out his hand. "Give me your phone, and I'll take some of you and Jim together."

Rather than standing with the tree between them, she stood next to her grandfather as he put his arm around her shoulders while Finn took more pictures. When he started to hand back her phone, Jim stopped him. "Can you take one of all three of us together?"

"Sure."

There was a minor scuffle as she tried to put Jim in the middle, and he insisted that was where she should be. Surrendering to the inevitable, she took her assigned spot. It felt strange to have two men she'd only met days ago put their arms around her, but it also felt surprisingly right.

"I'll forward each of you the best pictures."

Jim headed for his chair and sat down. "I'd appreciate that, but is there any way we could get them printed? I'd like to add them to my album."

Finn took one end of the sofa. "I think the drugstore in town still has a machine that can do that. We just have to upload the files and tell it how many copies we want. If not, I'll get the prints done next time I go up to Leavenworth."

Jim huffed a small laugh. "I'm glad you two understand what all of that means."

They all lapsed into silence for a few minutes, the only sound the crackle of the logs burning in the fireplace. After a bit, Jim spoke. "I've been meaning to tell you something I saw in the paper this week. They're having that annual Christmas carol sing-along this coming Wednesday night at the community church. You two should go."

Rather than responding right away, Hailey waited to see how Finn reacted to Jim once again ordering him to spend another evening shepherding her around town. Instead of answering Jim himself, Finn raised his eyebrow, silently asking her what she wanted to do.

Since he didn't immediately object, she figured he was at least open to the idea. "I would enjoy that as long as Finn doesn't have something else he needs to be doing. But if we do go, won't you come with us?"

"I'll think about it."

Although she didn't call him on it, Hailey suspected that meant he had no intentions of joining them. Jim had only left his home once that she knew of in the short time she'd been in Dunbar, and that had been in the middle of the day. Maybe he was reluctant to be out and about when there were still patches of snow and ice on streets and sidewalks in town. Falling was a definite risk, especially for senior citizens. She also hadn't forgotten what Finn had said about Jim having health problems that had resulted in him ending up in the emergency room.

At that moment, Jim yawned. That spurred her into finishing off the last of her cider. "Before I head back to Rikki's place, I'll put the mugs in the dishwasher and set it to run."

That Jim didn't immediately protest was a bit of a surprise. When she got closer to him, she thought he looked a bit pale. "Hey, are you feeling okay?"

Finn lurched up off the couch and gently pushed her aside to kneel in front of Jim. "What's wrong? Is it your heart?"

The older man waved him off. "No, I'm just really tired. That's all."

"Are you sure?"

Jim's practically growled, "Yes, Finn, I'm sure."

Finn must have decided to take him at his word, because he stood up and took a step back.

"I know that you hate that I worry, but promise you'll call me if that changes...right after you call 911."

"Fine, I will." Jim sighed and pushed himself up to his feet. "You two can let yourselves out. I'm going to bed."

Hailey watched him stalk off down the hall. When he disappeared into his bedroom, she whispered, "Do you think one of us should stay?"

"I've offered before, but that only makes him madder." Finn ran his fingers through his hair in frustration. "All we can do is trust that he'll call if anything changes. To tell the truth, I started sleeping better once I got him one of those medical alert things to keep by his bed."

"That was smart of you."

There didn't seem to be anything else they could do for Jim, so she made good on her promise to finish loading the dishwasher. By the time she got back to the living room, Finn had turned off the Christmas lights but left a night-light in the hall on in case Jim had to get up during the night. He was waiting for her by the front door with his coat and boots on. "If you'll give me your keys, I'll start your car for you, so it can warm up before you come outside."

She tossed him her keys. "Thanks. I'll come

back over in the morning and spend the day with Jim. I'll let you know how he's doing."

"Thanks, I would appreciate it."

"Will you be here for dinner tomorrow night?"

"No, I'm supposed to work on Titus's bike with him. Besides, Jim could probably use a break from my company. He hates it if I hover too much." His dark eyes looked haunted. "Since he's not been coming to the shop as much lately, I've been putting in extra hours. Eventually I may have to hire some part-time help, something else Jim won't like."

He smiled finally. "But that's a fight for another day. Drive safe."

Then he was gone.

She watched from the window as Finn drove away into the night. He might be a bit prickly at times, but he was a good man at heart, the kind she would have enjoyed dating. For sure, she would really miss him when it came time for her to leave. Too bad there wasn't more she could do to help him, but they both knew she wasn't going to be around for much longer. At least she could help keep an eye on Jim for now so Finn could concentrate on other things.

CHAPTER NINE

"Don't worry, baby, you're still beautiful to me."

Finn couldn't help but laugh. "Titus, does your wife know how emotionally involved you are with your bike?"

The other man patted the motorcycle on the handlebars as if offering it comfort. "Yes, she does. Luckily, Moira isn't the jealous type. Well, at least as long as her competition has two wheels and an engine."

"Good to know." Finn leaned back in his chair. "I do have a question I've been meaning to ask you for a while now."

Titus parked himself on the chair next to Finn's. "Ask away."

"Why do you think that bike is feminine when it's a Harley-Davidson Fat *Boy*?"

Looking mildly insulted, Titus gave Finn a superior look. "I calls 'em as I sees 'em."

"That makes a lot of sense."

Not really, but then no one said love of a vehicle had to make any sense at all. He checked the time. "The pizza should be here soon. Once we eat, we can start working on your lady."

"I appreciate you're willing to stay late to work on her tonight. It's not that I mind driving my truck, especially in this kind of weather." His expression darkened. "But sometimes... well, let's just say I need to outdistance a few bad memories."

As he spoke, he rubbed his knee. Not for the first time Finn wondered what exactly had happened in Titus's past that put those shadows in his eyes. He wasn't going to ask, though. If Titus ever wanted to talk, he'd listen. For now, he changed the subject. "No problem. I'm glad the parts came in so fast."

"Me, too."

They were saved from further discussion when the doorbell by the front entrance chimed. "Sounds like dinner has arrived."

Titus jumped up and headed for the door. While he did that, Finn cleared off one of the small roll-around tables he used in the shop and then set out paper plates and stack of paper towels to use as napkins. Then he pulled two soft drinks out of the small fridge in the corner. By the time he was done, Titus was back with a huge pizza box with the logo of the local carryout place in town.

Titus set it on the nearby workbench and flipped up the lid. "I hope you like a mix of pepperoni, sausage and bacon. I also asked for black olives, mushrooms and bell pepper."

"Sounds perfect."

Titus picked two slices and put them on his plate. "I've been looking forward to this ever since you called me this morning. I have to admit that I occasionally get tired of my own cooking."

Finn joined him by their makeshift table. "What's Moira having for dinner if you're eating here with me?"

"She's on patrol duty tonight, so I packed her a meal before she left for work."

"That's a nice husbandly thing to do."

Titus arched an eyebrow at the comment and looked mildly insulted. Finn immediately apologized. "Sorry, I didn't mean that the way it sounded. I'm actually jealous. One reason I eat at your place so often is that I hate cooking for myself. It would be a real treat to having someone to pack me a lunch to take to work."

"Yeah, I get that."

They ate in peace for several minutes. Considering how quickly Titus wolfed down not just the first two slices but a third as well, the man had been seriously hungry. After washing down the last bite with his drink, he wiped his hands clean with a paper towel and packed up the last of the pizza and stuck it in the fridge.

When Titus sat back down, he faced his bike but watched Finn out of the corner of his eye. No doubt the inquisition was about to begin. Finn savored the last few bites of pizza and waited to see when Titus would finally muster up the courage to ask whatever was on his mind. It didn't take long.

"So—" Titus shifted to face him more directly "—how are you and Hailey getting along?"

The question wasn't exactly a surprise. "We're doing okay."

His friend snorted. "More than okay, at least from what I've heard."

Finn closed his eyes and groaned. "Why? What have you heard?"

"Nothing bad, but some people have noticed the two of you have been spending a lot of time together. Mind you, I'm not sure where Bea gets her information or how accurate it is. But according to her latest news broadcast at the bakery shop, the two of you had fun out at the Halkos' tree farm the other night. You were also spotted driving out of town together heading toward the interstate the next day. The initial story that went around was that she came to Dunbar to have you check out that motorcycle over there. I haven't told them any different but you can understand why people are wondering why you're socializing with her instead of working on her bike. You know, since that's your job."

Sometimes Finn really hated living in a small town. "I plan to check out her bike after we finish with yours since there's no big rush on it. Besides, other things have taken precedence ever since Jim convinced her to stay until after Christmas. We haven't put much effort into celebrating the past couple of years, but now he's pulling out all the stops for his first Christmas with his granddaughter. That meant cutting a fresh tree at the Halkos' farm. Hailey also needed to do some Christmas shopping. She was going to do it online, but Jim strongly suggested I take her to a mall."

Titus frowned. "Sounds more like Jim was issuing orders than making suggestions."

There was no reason to deny it. "Pretty much, but it was no big deal. We needed a tree anyway, and I had some shopping to do myself."

Titus didn't say a word, but his expression spoke volumes. Finn raised his hands in surrender. "Okay, fine. We did have fun at the tree farm and shopping together. It was nice to get away from town for a few hours. Besides, she's good company."

His friend shot him a sly look. "Not to mention really attractive."

Titus wasn't wrong, but rather than veer off into dangerous territory, Finn redirected the conversation. "There's a definite upside to having Hailey here even for a short time. Considering the scares we've had with Jim's health lately, I like knowing that someone else is with him while I'm at work. The night she arrived, he really scared me. Without telling me what was up, he called and said I need to get to his house ASAP. I drove like crazy to get to his house to make sure he was okay. As it turned out, he was only excited about Hailey being there and wanted me to meet her. I counted myself lucky Moira didn't catch me ripping through town like that."

"She would've understood if you explained what was going on."

Finn wasn't sure about that. People had a tendency to drive a lot more conservatively since Moira moved back to Dunbar and joined the police department.

"Anyway, my point is I can get more done around here when I'm not having to check on him constantly."

He paused to look at their surroundings.

Lately, those cinderblock walls had felt more like a cage than a place of business. "The business was designed to be at least a two-person operation, but Jim can't work the long hours he used to. I do all the paperwork, order all of the parts, and keep track of the shipments. I also handle most of the design work. We're going to need to make some changes around here soon if the business is going to survive."

Titus frowned. "What kind of changes?"

"The kind that Jim will likely fight tooth and nail." Finn huffed a small laugh that had nothing to do with humor. "For starters, I want someone to work in the office a few hours a week. Jim won't like having an outsider involved in the business in any capacity, but I can't keep up with it all by myself. Maybe I could if I cut back on the number of jobs we take on. The problem with that is we need to maintain a certain level of income in order to support both of us."

To his surprise, Titus said, "I get that. Other than Moira, no one else knows what I'm about to tell you, so mum's the word. I almost changed the café's hours to cover only breakfast and lunch so I could be home more. If I did that, though, I'd have to also cut back on the number of employees I have working for me, and they need the jobs. It's not like employment opportunities are thick on the ground in a town this size. Besides, there are a lot of folks who eat at my place several nights a week."

He grinned at Finn. "You among them."

Having the only café in town closed in the evenings was an appalling thought. Finn wasn't a bad cook, but he really didn't like the idea of having to fix dinner for himself seven nights a week. He could always drive the twenty miles to the nearest town that offered more options, but that would get old fast. "You're right. Me starving would be a distinct possibility. A man can live on canned soup and frozen entrées only so long without it affecting his overall health."

Titus grimaced at that thought. "Good thing I rejected the idea pretty quickly. I wouldn't be able to sleep at night for worrying about you starving."

It was time to move on to the other issue Finn needed to solve soon. If he was going to whine about stuff, he might as well get it all out of his system. "The other problem is that Jim rattles around in that big old house all by himself far too much of the time. Maintaining it is also more than he can handle by himself these days, and I don't have the time to take care of both his place and mine."

He raised his arms over his head and leaned from side to side several times to stretch out a few kinks. "I know without asking that he won't consider moving to one of those senior care places where someone could check on him and make sure he's taking his meds and stuff like that. Personally, I think he'd enjoy being around more people every day once he got settled into a new routine. However, I'm quite sure he won't give up his independence without a huge fight. That leaves only one other option—me moving back in with him and renting out my house for the foreseeable future. To be honest, I'm not sure how he would react to that idea."

Too restless to sit still any longer, he decided it was time to get to work. "Enough about my problems for one night. Let's get started on your bike and see how far we get."

"Sounds good. Considering we both have to work tomorrow, I don't want to keep you here to all hours."

They both rolled their stools over to the Harley. Titus took one side while Finn settled in on the other side and began unbolting the damaged parts. Three hours passed as they worked mostly in silence, speaking only when one or the other needed an extra hand or to borrow a tool. By the time they were ready to knock off the night, they'd made an impressive amount of progress on the bike. At least they'd reached the stage where they were starting to bolt on a few of the replacement parts that Finn had ordered for the bike.

He finally called a halt to the proceedings. "I think that's enough for one night. I can handle the rest of the repairs on my own. It shouldn't be another day or so before I finish the paint and bolting on the last few pieces. Barring any surprises, you'll likely have her back by the end of the week."

His friend looked decidedly pleased by the good news. "Moira will be happy to hear that. She's getting a bit tired of me sulking about my other girl being out of commission. Granted, the weather hasn't been particularly conducive to riding a motorcycle, so it's not like I'm missing the chance to take her out for a spin. It's knowing I couldn't even if I wanted to that's the problem."

Finn could sympathize with that feeling. "I can't remember the last time I've had my own bike out of the garage, and I miss tearing down the highway after being shut up in here all day. Test-driving my customers' bikes when the repairs are finished doesn't count. That's work and not relaxing."

"I can see that. Come spring, we should plan a long ride somewhere. Maybe over to eastern Washington and stay at Lake Chelan for a couple of days. Moira would enjoy that. Well, as long as you brought someone, too. Got anybody you could ask?"

"Not lately."

Although it would be really nice if he did. Heck, he couldn't remember the last time he went out on a date. It had been even longer since he'd been involved in any kind of relationship. As he finished putting the last few tools back in their places, an image filled his head of him cruising down the highway with someone on the back of his bike. Well, not just someone. Inexplicably, his imagination decided that it was Hailey leaning into his back, her arms wrapped around his waist and holding on tight.

As if reading his mind, Titus said, "Too bad you couldn't bring Hailey. I bet she and Moira would really hit it off."

His friend wasn't wrong. "Yeah, they would, but unfortunately she lives two thousand miles away."

Meanwhile, Titus wiped his hands clean on a paper towel. After wadding it up into a ball, he tossed it into the trash can on the far side of the workshop as if shooting a free throw. "He shoots, he scores, and the crowd goes wild."

Not to be outdone, Finn followed suit with equally spectacular results. Titus immediately took that as a challenge. "Tell you what—first one to hit the basket three times wins. Loser buys the first round the next time we go to Barnaby's for a couple of cold ones."

"It's a deal."

Too bad Lady Luck was clearly on Titus's side. The man had some serious skills and hit the basket with his first three shots. Finn hit two, but the next one bounced off the side of the can. Titus immediately whooped and did a little victory dance that Finn really wished he could have filmed to share with their friends. "Come on, 'Shaq' Kondrat. Let's get out of here."

The two of them walked out through the office, turning off lights as they went. Out in the parking lot, Titus stopped to stare up at the sky. "Thanks again for working on my bike for me. I know you have a lot going on, and I would've understood if you'd needed to give it a pass."

"Like I told you, I make time for my friends. Besides, hanging out with you tonight was fun."

Titus unlocked the door on his truck but didn't immediately open it. "If there's anything I can do to help with…well, anything, don't hesitate to call, even if you just need to blow off steam or something. Regardless, keep me posted."

"Thanks, Titus. I appreciate that. Now, you'd better get going. Even if Moira isn't home yet, Ned will be wondering where you are."

"Sometimes that dog thinks he's the one in

charge." Titus shot Finn one last grin. "Unfortunately, most of the time he's right."

Finn followed Titus's truck until they reached the main road through town where they headed in opposite directions. He wondered if his friend had any idea how much Finn envied him having someone waiting for him at home. Having a woman who loved him would be really great, but even having a dog like Ned would be an improvement.

Maybe he'd check into adopting one after the holidays were over. The right kind of dog would be good company for him not just at home, but at the shop as well. He bet Jim would enjoy having a furry family member come over to hang out with him sometimes. It was definitely something to think about.

For now, he couldn't wait to get home and call it a night.

CHAPTER TEN

HAILEY INSTANTLY FELL in love with the church that was hosting the Christmas carol sing-along. Set deep back in a small clearing, it was surrounded by a scattering of Douglas firs dusted with fresh snow. The white-clapboard building featured a tall steeple topped with a simple cross and a row of stained glass windows above the front entrance. Lit from within, the jewel-toned panels added the perfect finishing touch.

Anxious to get in from the cold, she snapped a couple of quick pictures before following Finn into the church where a lady handed them each a program for the evening's events. Hailey thanked her and trailed behind Finn as he threaded his way through the people clustered at the back of the sanctuary. While he stopped to look around, Hailey admired the decorations inside the church. The arrangement of alternating red and white poinsettias lined up along the front of the stage was especially nice. Two

Christmas trees decked out in flickering white lights flanked the altar. Everything was simple, but lovely.

Finn pointed toward the right side of the room and said, "Titus is waving at us from up near the front. He's signaling that there's room for us to sit next to him."

That was nice of Titus. At least she was acquainted with someone besides Finn, who seemed to know almost everyone they passed. Living in a small town where everybody apparently knew everybody else was far different from anything she'd ever experienced. Judging from the fast-growing crowd, this was obviously a popular holiday event in Dunbar. It wouldn't be long before there would be standing room only.

It didn't take them long to reach Titus, who had staked out territory in a pew near the front. He immediately rose to his feet and stepped out into the aisle. "Hi, Hailey. I'm glad the two of you could make it. My wife will be joining us in a few minutes. She's just finishing up her shift out on patrol."

He then pointed toward the couple at the far end of the pew. "Hailey, I'm not sure if you've met Cade Peters, our chief of police, and his wife, Shelby. She runs the post office and the historical museum here in town."

Hailey smiled at the pair. "It's nice to meet you both."

Finn motioned for her to slide in next to Cade and then sat down next to her. "Titus wants to sit on the end so Moira doesn't have to climb over us to reach him when she gets here."

"Good thinking."

Once she and Finn were settled, Shelby leaned forward to peer around her husband. "Hi, Hailey. Rikki mentioned she had an out-of-town guest staying at her place for the holidays. I'm guessing that would be you."

How much should she share? "It would be. I'm here from Missouri."

Cade joined the conversation. "I heard you drove here. That's quite a drive this time of year. Did you run into any problems along the way?"

"A snowstorm near Denver that shut the highway down overnight. Other than that, it was pretty much clear sailing until right before I started over the mountains here. It snowed a little, but it wasn't sticking to the roads even at the top of the pass."

She suspected Shelby and her husband were likely curious about what would inspire someone to come to a small town like Dunbar for the holidays but were reluctant to pry. At least talking about the weather provided a safe topic of conversation. They'd quickly exhausted the subject but were saved from having to come up with something else to talk about when a woman walked up to the center of the stage at the front of the church. She tapped the microphone in front of her and then said, "Testing, testing."

Satisfied she could be heard and had garnered everyone's attention, the woman smiled. "Welcome, everyone. For those of you who don't know me, I'm Kimberly Dogerty, one of the two pastors here at Dunbar Community Church. If you would all take a seat, we'll be starting momentarily. We'll begin with a few performances and then move on to the sing-along portion of the program. Afterward, we invite you all to join us in the church basement for refreshments, which were provided by Bea O'Malley and Titus Kondrat."

Next, Reverend Dogerty gestured toward a door on the far side of the stage. "Please join me in welcoming the string quartet from our local youth symphony orchestra. They will start off our evening of celebration by playing several pieces for us."

Four young people filed into the room and sat in a row of chairs in front of the altar. The crowd grew silent as the quartet launched into a lovely rendition of Pachelbel's Canon in D.

The quartet continued to play for twenty minutes, their music the perfect introduction to the evening.

When they finished, the room burst into a round of applause. Next, a group of young children were led out onto the stage. The pastor introduced the music director who would direct both the children's choir and the adult one that would follow after the kids finished singing. The kids all looked so cute in their matching reindeer antlers and red noses. Even if a bit off-key at times, their enthusiastic singing was adorable. Hailey loved it.

Finn leaned over to whisper, "Isn't that Carter Volkov in the middle of the back row?"

Hailey was surprised she hadn't already spotted him. "Yes, it is."

She'd have to remember to compliment him and his parents on his performance when she got back to the bed-and-breakfast. "I love the plaid bow tie he's wearing. It's quite the fashion statement."

The church choir followed with some traditional Advent and Christmas hymns. When they finished, the pastor returned to the stage. After thanking the choir, she smiled at the audience. "All right, everyone, it's your time to shine in tonight's festivities."

The music director sat down at the piano.

"Okay, we'll be starting at the top of the list. It's a mix of hymns, Christmas carols and some seasonal secular music. I'm sure you will all find some of your personal favorites among the selections."

Then, with a flourish, she launched into the familiar strains of "White Christmas." Hailey never made any claim of having a great voice, but she had always loved singing. She hadn't been sure if Finn would enjoy himself or even participate, especially since Jim had strong-armed him into going. But when the music started, Finn joined right in, his voice a pleasant baritone. She could also hear Titus, his distinctive voice more deep and gravelly.

Her mother would have loved this event. Hailey really wished she was there, but she knew her mom would be happy that Hailey could forget her grief long enough to enjoy a few moments of the holiday spirit. Even so, her eyes blurred with tears when they sang one of mother's favorite hymns. To her surprise, Finn leaned in closer and asked, "Hey, are you all right?"

She blinked like crazy to clear her vision. "Yeah, I was just thinking about how much Mom would have loved this. Sorry."

To her surprise, Finn slid his arm around her shoulders and pulled her in closer to his side. "No reason to apologize. It means you were lucky enough to have had someone who always made the holidays extra special. You're missing your mom right now, and that's okay. The holidays can be tricky for a lot of people."

That sounded like the voice of experience. "I'm guessing you're thinking about Rhonda."

He sighed and nodded. "Yeah. You already know that I have a lot of special memories of her that are tied to this time of year."

That was true. Even if he hadn't told her that himself, she would've known simply from the look on his face as he'd studied the Victorian village that he and Rhonda had built together over the years. She suspected her mother's snow globe collection would be the same kind of emotional trigger for her for years to come.

It was a relief when the next song was lighthearted and fast-paced. She especially enjoyed Finn holding her close as they joined in the singing and let the music brighten their spirits. Leaning into his strength felt so right, a special connection that she found herself wishing could last beyond this one night.

FINN HESITATED BEFORE heading downstairs to the dessert reception, not sure if Hailey wanted to spend more time in a crowd of mostly strangers. He tugged her out of the way of the people streaming out of the sanctuary. "Do you want to hang around for a while? If not, I'm okay with leaving now."

She gave him a teasing smile. "Seriously? Don't you know me by now? I'd never insult Titus by skipping out an opportunity to enjoy some of those refreshments the pastor mentioned. I can't wait to see what kind of goodies he and Bea have created for tonight."

He slapped his forehead with the palm of his hand. "What was I thinking? Let's go before all the good stuff is gone."

Then he grabbed her hand and all but dragged her across to the other side of the room. "Come on, I know a back way."

Even when they'd reached the large multipurpose room on the lower floor, he found himself reluctant to release his grip on her hand. Telling himself it was only because he didn't want them to get separated in the crowd, he held on as they made their way across the room to where all of the pastries were on display. They picked up paper plates and plastic forks before joining the line of people making their way along the tables. It would be hard to choose from among all of the possibilities, a nice problem to have. He picked up a pair of tongs and asked, "So, what looks good to you?"

Hailey pointed toward the second tray on the

table. "I'm going to start with one of those small chocolate éclairs and go from there."

After picking up one for each of them, Finn moved down the table to stop in front of a variety of Titus's mini pies.

When they'd filled their plates, Hailey asked, "Why don't I get the drinks? Do you want coffee or tea?"

"It's a bit late for caffeine for me, but I could use some water." He took her plate as well as his own. "I'll go stake out a couple of seats over by the wall."

He kept an eye on her as she waited in line to get their drinks to make sure she saw where he'd gone. By the time she reached him, several friends had joined him. Hailey gave Titus a narrow-eyed look as she reclaimed her plate. "I'm going to have to swear off sweets for months after I get back home to Missouri, and I blame it all on you."

"That's not fair." Titus pointed at her plate. "Bea made that éclair. But if it would help, I can refuse to serve you any more desserts while you're here."

Finn and everyone else laughed at Hailey's instant look of horror at that prospect. He nudged her with his shoulder. "I'm guessing you don't have any experience living in a small town, so here's a word of advice. Don't disrespect the man who owns the only café in town. I can pretty much guarantee that will end badly for you."

"Got it." Hailey immediately set her plate and bottled water down on her seat. Then, in a dramatic move, she dropped to one knee at Titus's feet and bowed her head, causing everyone to burst into laughter. "Please forgive me, sir. In the future, I swear to show proper respect to the creator of the pies and all things delicious."

As soon as Finn had realized Hailey was up to something, he'd set down his plate and snapped a quick picture of the interchange with his phone. The horrified look on Titus's face was priceless, and Finn immediately forwarded the picture to their friends as the other man growled, "Fine. You're forgiven as long as you never do anything like that again."

He chuckled a little as he held out a hand to help her up. "Compliments on the proper feudal attitude, though. The rest of you should make note of it should you ever be foolish enough to complain about the effects of my baking. I can't help it that delicious often goes hand in hand with calories."

Moira grinned when she saw the photo and held it up to show her husband. "What's it worth to you for me not to send this off to the mayor? I've heard Ilse has been looking for some lighthearted content for the town's social media accounts."

Titus leaned in close and whispered something into her ear. Moira's face turned a bit red, but she gave her husband a quick kiss. "It's a deal."

When she made a show of removing the picture from her phone. Finn held up his. "That might keep her from sending that to Mayor Klaus, but I still have it. We all do. For the record, I feel safe in saying we'd all prefer baked goods as a bribe."

Everyone else immediately agreed, Hailey included, which had Titus laughing. As they all settled into enjoying their refreshments, Finn couldn't help but notice how easily Hailey fit in with his friends. In no time at all, she was happily chatting away with Shelby Peters, Moira and Rikki Volkov.

He wasn't the only one who noticed. Titus sidled up next to him. "She seems to be enjoying herself, especially considering she's surrounded by a room full of strangers."

Finn pointed out the obvious. "Not everyone is a stranger. She's met you several times, and she's staying with Rikki and Max."

"And she's definitely getting to know you."

Finn wasn't sure how to respond to that.

When he didn't say anything, Titus asked, "Was this outing your idea or Jim's?"

"Jim was the one who told us about it. I used to come with Rhonda, but I've skipped it the past couple of years. It didn't feel right to go without her. I'm not sure I would've come this year on my own, but I'm glad I did."

He wasn't sure where Titus was going with this line of conversation, so he decided to change the subject. "I meant to tell you earlier that your bike is done. I took her for a long ride this afternoon to make sure I hadn't missed any problems. Even with all the dirty slush on the road, everything went great. She's pretty muddy right now, but otherwise she's fine."

Titus's mouth dropped open in shock. "Tell me you didn't."

Finn cracked up. "No, I didn't, but I couldn't resist yanking your chain a little. The paint is done, and I finished putting her all back together. You can pick her up whenever you want."

Moira and Hailey left the other women to stand beside Finn and Titus. Moira asked her husband, "What are you two talking about? You looked kind of upset there for a second."

Titus shoved his hands in his pockets and didn't quite meet his wife's gaze. "Good news.

Finn finished with my bike, and she can come back home tomorrow."

Hailey studied Titus for a second and then frowned at Finn. "What did you really tell him?"

By that point, Moira was looking a bit suspicious, too. "Yeah, what did you do that upset my husband?"

Suddenly Finn was flashing back to his teenage years whenever he had done something that upset Rhonda. Shuffling his feet a bit, he confessed, "I might have let him think that I took his bike for a test drive through the slush and grime on the roads and got her all muddy."

"But you didn't."

"I didn't."

Titus interceded on his behalf. "Hey, it only took me a second to realize it was a joke, ladies. I should've known he wouldn't have abused my girl like that. No need to beat up on the guy, especially when he worked all those extra hours to fix her for me."

Moira smiled as she looped her arm through her husband's. "We both really appreciate what you did for him, Finn. Titus was relieved that he wouldn't have to trust her with a stranger."

By that point, the crowd was starting to thin out, and the cleanup crew was packing things up. It was time to head home. He'd also forgotten something else he'd meant to say to Titus. "By the way, thanks for saving seats for us. If you hadn't, we might have ended up standing in the back. Next year, we'll know to come earlier."

When Hailey shot him an odd look, he realized he'd made that sound as if he expected that she'd be attending the event with him when next Christmas rolled around again. He hadn't actually consciously been thinking that, but it wouldn't surprise him if it happened considering Jim was the only family she had these days. It would only be natural for her to want to spend the holidays in Dunbar again. Not just with Jim, but Finn as well.

Something to think about later. Looking around, he said, "I guess we should be going. I'll be in the shop all day tomorrow, so stop by anytime to pick up the bike."

"Will do."

Hailey wished everyone a good night and then fell into step beside him as they made their way up the steps and out into the parking lot. "Thanks for bringing me tonight. I really enjoyed myself, and I also appreciate how your friends have gone out of their way to make me feel welcome. Maybe it's a small-town thing."

"Actually, only Shelby, Moira and I grew up here. The rest are all recent transplants. Cade moved here to take the job as chief of police after leaving the military, and Titus came when he bought the café. Rikki was hired to manage the bed-and-breakfast and ended up buying out the previous owner. You've already heard Max's story."

"It's nice to know that the town is so accepting of newcomers."

He nudged her shoulder with his. "That's true unless you try to abscond with our chunk of gold. Then it's no holds barred."

"Duly noted. That's two helpful rules I've learned. Don't insult the guy who owns the café, and keep my mitts off the gold. Maybe the mayor should post some guidelines on a sign at the edge of town."

"I'll mention it to Mayor Klaus the next time I see her."

When they reached his truck, he hustled ahead to open Hailey's door for her. She smiled up at him, her eyes luminous in the moonlight. Without thinking, he was hit with an unexpected impulse to kiss her. He caught himself at the last second and took a step back, then waited until she was safely inside before heading around to the driver's door.

As they made the short trip back to the bed-and-breakfast, he didn't know if what he was feeling after the near miss was regret or relief.

The problem was this wasn't really a date even if it had definitely seemed like one at times. After parking in the driveway, he opened Hailey's door for her but made sure to maintain a safer distance than he had back at the church. From the odd look Hailey gave him when they reached the front door, he suspected she was feeling some of the same confusion.

Her smile looked a little hesitant when she finally spoke. "Thanks again for this evening, especially your kindness when I started missing my mom."

He couldn't resist gently brushing a strand of hair back from her face. "I'm glad you enjoyed yourself."

Hailey edged closer to the door. "I should go inside. I know you have to work tomorrow."

She was right. "I guess you'll be spending the day with Jim. I may not have said anything, but I know he really appreciates having some company. Because of his health issues, he's been spending most of his time alone."

"I'm just glad to get so much time with him. I didn't know what to expect when I came, but he's been great."

She reached to open the door, but then spun back and kissed him on the cheek. "You have been, too."

Then she disappeared inside, leaving him

standing there, hand on his cheek where she'd kissed him. It was only when Max and his small family turned into the driveway that he realized he needed to be going.

As he drove home, he caught himself rubbing his cheek two more times. It was one more thing to be confused about. Mostly because Hailey had no doubt meant the kiss as a gesture of friendship, and he foolishly wished it had meant so much more.

CHAPTER ELEVEN

HAILEY CALLED JIM right after she ate breakfast to see if he needed her to pick up anything from the store on her way to his place. As it turned out, he'd forgotten to tell her that he had friends that met on Thursday mornings to play chess. Ordinarily he could have skipped the gathering, but it was his turn to play host. She hastily told him not to worry about it. She needed to do some laundry, so it was no problem to delay coming over until later in the day.

When she asked him if there was a laundromat in town, he offered her the use of his washer and dryer, saying the guys wouldn't mind if she hung around. After a slight hesitation, he then added that there was also a washer and dryer at the shop that she could use. Never let it be said she couldn't take a hint, which was why she chose the second option. Hopefully, Finn wouldn't mind her showing up uninvited.

"I'll see you later then. If you do think of anything you need, just text me."

She hung up and gathered her laundry, which pretty much included everything she'd brought with her. On the way to the shop, she stopped by Bea's bakery to get both her and Finn a tall latte. The only question was whether she could show a little willpower this time and not buy pastries to go along with them. Alas, when confronted by the huge display of fresh doughnuts and other goodies, resistance was futile.

Finn laughed as soon as she walked in. Pointing toward the bag containing the treats, he asked, "Aren't you the same woman who complained to Titus about the adverse effects all of the desserts you've been consuming lately?"

"What can I say? I have no willpower." She gave him his drink. "But in my defense, I picked ones that have fruit filling. That's almost healthy."

Looking amused, Finn fished one of the pastries out of the bag. "You keep telling yourself that."

She sat down on one of the rolling stools and sipped her latte with a happy smile. "Boy, that woman makes a good cup of coffee."

Finn set his drink on a nearby workbench and focused on eating his doughnut. In between bites, he asked, "I thought you were headed over to Jim's this morning."

"Turns out it's his turn to host his chess buddies, and I didn't want to get in their way." She pointed toward the washer in the far corner. "When I mentioned that I'd run out of clean clothes, Jim said you might not mind if I used the washer and dryer here in the shop."

"Have at it. There's detergent and fabric softener in the cabinet over the washer. I do my own laundry here while I'm here working. Saves me from having to do it after I get home."

"Thanks, I really appreciate it."

She went back out to the SUV to carry in the trash bag she'd used to hold her clothes. Back inside, she quickly sorted everything into two loads. After putting the first one into the washer, she picked the right cycle and set it to run. Figuring she'd have at least a couple of hours to kill, she asked, "Is there anything I can do to help you while I'm here? I brought a book to read, but I'd rather be useful if I can."

He glanced around the shop before finally nodding. "Actually, there is something. I've gotten in three large parts orders that I haven't had a chance to unpack. You'd just need to open the boxes and match the part numbers to the packing list to make sure everything is there."

"I can do that. Where would you like me to set up so that I'm not in your way?"

"At the desk in the office would probably be best since the boxes are already stacked along the wall in there. As you finish, you can set the boxes in here and put the packing slips in the red file folder on the desk."

"Got it."

He gave her a box cutter and said to give him a shout if she had questions. She took her latte with her and settled in to work.

FINN POKED HIS head in about forty-five minutes later. "Your load shut off a little while ago."

She looked up from the packing slip she'd been studying. "Thanks. I was about to come check on it, but I wanted to finish going through this last box first."

He came all the way into the office and thumbed through the stack of packing slips. "Any problems?"

"Nope. Everything matched up fine. I was going to start moving the boxes out into the shop after I finished this last one, but I'll go change loads first, if that's okay."

Finn picked up the closest two boxes. "That's fine."

By the time she'd switched loads and set both machines to run, he'd already carried all of the boxes out into the shop and was unloading them onto the counter along the back wall. Rather than simply watch, she offered, "Since I don't know where anything goes, why don't I unload the parts while you put them away?"

"Sounds good."

When they finished, Finn returned to the bike he'd been working on. Not really in the mood to read the book she'd brought, Hailey rolled a stool over to watch what Finn was doing. At the moment, he was methodically stripping bits and pieces off of a motorcycle, setting some on the workbench behind him and the rest into a plastic tub at his feet. After a few minutes, he glanced in her direction.

"Looking for something else to do?"

She felt obligated to point out one small problem with the idea. "I don't know anything about working on engines."

He offered her a small grin. "I didn't think you did, but I'm betting you'll do a bang-up job of cleaning these parts for me. I'll show you how to get started."

As it turned out, she enjoyed the simple job of using a power washer to strip away layers of grease and dirt and then scrubbing away the stubborn bits with a wire brush. It seemed strange to take so much pride in removing the grime to reveal the clean metal beneath, but she found the process quite satisfying. She was finishing up the last piece when she realized that someone else had come into the shop. Glancing back over her shoulder, she wasn't surprised to see Titus standing beside his Harley with a satisfied smile on his face.

When he realized she was watching him, he nodded. "I see he's making you earn your keep."

She set the piece aside and wiped her hands dry on a shop towel. "Actually, I volunteered. Jim had company coming over this morning, and Finn was nice enough to let me hang out here for a while."

Speaking of Finn, where was he? As if sensing the direction her thoughts had taken, Titus answered her unspoken question. "He's on the phone in the office. He should be back in a couple of minutes."

He'd no more said the words than Finn appeared in the doorway. "So does the work I did on the Harley pass muster?"

Titus nodded. "That was never in doubt. She looks great."

Hailey walked closer to admire both the bike and Finn's work. "Did you ever figure out who did the damage?"

Shaking his head, Titus said, "No, and I probably won't at this stage. If they'd been interested in doing the right thing, they would've stepped forward by now."

Finn looked disgusted. "My guess is that it was kids who probably got scared and panicked, especially if they realized it was your bike."

Hailey could understand why they would've reacted that way, but it was too bad. From what she knew of Titus, he was more bark than bite. She suspected he would've worked out a payment plan if they didn't have insurance to cover the damage.

Finn circled the bike, using a cloth to give the front fender one last polish. "Did you tell Cade what happened?"

"Moira may have, but I didn't. What's the point in filing a police report when no one saw anything?"

Titus must have been ready to move on to another subject. He walked away from the Harley to stand by the Vincent Black Lightning. She and Finn trailed along behind him. "When are you going to work on this one?"

"It's next in line. I need to finish the repairs on that one over there, but it should be done later today."

"Do you think the Vincent will run after all this time?"

Finn shrugged. "I'm not going to try that until I have a chance to give it a going-over.

There's no telling what effect sitting that long will have had on the engine and other parts."

He walked over to the counter and picked up a file folder. "I did manage to find something that will help with that, though."

He opened the folder to reveal a rather tattered magazine. Hailey leaned in closer to get a better look and realized it was actually an owner's manual for the bike. "Did this belong to my father?"

"No doubt. If it didn't come with the bike when Nick bought it, either he or Jim would've tracked one down. I knew Jim would've held on to it, but I wasn't sure where he would have stashed it. It took me a while, but I finally found it stuck in the back of the filing cabinet in the office."

Titus held out his hand. "May I? I promise to be careful with it."

When Finn gave it to him, Titus gently leafed through the pages, holding it out so that Hailey could see it, too. It was interesting to see all of the various parts of the bike sketched out in such detail, showing how all of the pieces were designed to go together. When they reached the last page, Titus closed the cover and passed it back to Finn. "When you decide to work on it, give me a call. I'd love to help you. Opportunities to work on a bike like that one don't roll around very often."

"Sure thing. I thought I might get started on it tonight." Finn put the folder back on the counter. "How about you, Hailey? Want to get your hands dirty, too?"

Yeah, she did, but still she asked, "Are you sure you want my help? It's not like I know anything about motorcycles."

"Considering you own one now, this would be an opportunity to learn a few things about them."

The truth was she wasn't convinced the bike should belong to her at all. Her parents had never been married, and there was no evidence that Nick had left a will naming her mother as his heir. Since Hailey hadn't even been born at the time of Nick's death, it was more likely that Jim and his late wife would have been Nick's legal heirs. Regardless, helping to restore the bike would be one more connection with her father. Realizing both Titus and Finn were waiting for her to respond, she nodded. "I would love to help. I might not be of much use with a wrench, but I recently learned how to wash parts."

"Let's meet back here this evening after dinner. Say about seven?"

Titus rubbed his hands together, a big grin on

his face. "I'll be here. Now, let's settle my bill so I can get my lady out of your way."

"Your insurance will pay me directly, so all I need from you is your deductible."

When Finn led Titus back into the office, Hailey checked to see if her first load was dry. She made quick work of folding everything and then started the dryer again with the second load. By that point, Titus was wheeling his motorcycle out into the parking lot. She walked to the front of the garage to watch as he strapped on his helmet and then started his bike and revved the engine. His happy grin had her smiling as he offered her and Finn a cheerful wave and then roared off down the street.

Finn watched until his friend disappeared around the corner and then stepped back into the garage. Hailey waited as he closed the door and shut out the cold. "You probably just gave Titus the best Christmas present he could have hoped for this year. It must feel good to restore a damaged bike like that, especially knowing you just made your friend so happy."

"Yeah, it does. Titus is a good enough mechanic that he could've done most of the work himself. The trouble with that is that it would've taken him a lot longer than it did me since he has his own business to run. I could work on it between other jobs."

He gave her a long look. "Something bothered you about the thought of working on your dad's bike."

There was no use in denying it. "I'm not really comfortable calling it my bike. I can't help but think that my mom should've returned it to Jim and Rhonda as soon as she learned what happened to my father. Under the circumstances, I don't believe she had any legal claim to it."

"That might be true, but you shouldn't feel guilty about it. We both know none of it was your fault. Besides, think how different things would've been if Nick had simply picked up the phone and called his parents to tell them about your mother. If he had, maybe my folks wouldn't have been involved at all."

He met her gaze, his expression bleak. "I'll always be grateful for everything Jim and Rhonda did for me, but I would've rather grown up with my parents alive and well. If I had, who knows where I would be now or what I would be doing."

"I'm sorry, Finn."

He shrugged off her apology. "Again, not your fault."

Then he walked away, leaving her staring at his back and wishing she knew what to say. It wasn't the first time she'd sensed that maybe Finn might have wished he'd been free to choose a different career for himself. She was tempted to ask him, but decided against it. Rather than risk stirring up more painful memories, she rolled one of the stools over by the washer and dryer and settled in to read.

"Sorry to cancel at the last minute, Jim, but tell Hailey she can head this way anytime she wants to. That is, if she still wants to."

Finn mentally crossed his fingers that she'd changed her mind about coming. She'd be better off hanging out with her grandfather while she had the chance. After all, she'd be returning home to Missouri soon. At least he hoped so. Kind of, anyway. The truth was he was all tied up in knots about the thought of her leaving. Sometimes he got the impression that she might have mixed feelings about it, too, even if she hadn't said as much.

"So, what's got your tail in a twist this time?"

The blunt question had Finn regretting that he'd called Jim instead of sending him a text. The man always could read Finn's moods like a book. "Nothing, but you know how it is. Paperwork piles up faster than I can keep up with. I want to see if I can make a dent in the pile before Hailey and Titus arrive."

"Do you want me to have Hailey bring you dinner when she comes?"

"No, that's fine. I can scrounge something when I get home."

Jim abruptly changed the subject. "Hailey said you're going to start working on Nick's bike."

It wasn't a question, but Finn answered it anyway. "Yeah. There's no telling what all is wrong with it after sitting so long. I doubt Hailey's mother knew anything about how to prep a bike for storage. I'm betting it still has the same gas in the tank."

He suspected that he wasn't the only one who shuddered at that thought. After all, Jim was the one who'd taught him what kind of damage time and improper care could do to an engine. "I also need to test the tires. It's a pretty sure bet they'll need replacing."

"No doubt. Order whatever parts you need and don't worry about the cost. Make sure you pay for everything out of my personal account. If you need help sourcing the right ones, make a list and give it to me. I can do that much from home. You've got enough on your shoulders just keeping up with everything else."

Even if Finn didn't actually need the help, he would've accepted the offer knowing Jim would want to be involved in restoring his son's bike. "Good idea, Jim. That would be a big help. By the way, if Hailey didn't tell you, I found the owner's manual you had tucked away. Having the original part numbers will make finding the right stuff a whole lot easier. It looks pretty fragile, and I don't want to damage it. I'm going to photocopy the entire manual and put the pages in a three-ring binder rather than using the original. I'll make you a copy to use."

"I meant to tell you I had that thing. How did you know to even look for it?"

Finn bit back the urge to point out that Jim would have never gotten rid of anything that reminded him of his son. Instead, he went with an easier but equally true answer, laughing a little as he spoke. "Because we still have every manual and parts catalog we've ever had in the shop, starting with the ones as far back as when you and my grandfather first opened the place."

"Don't you laugh at me, boy. Those old things have come in handy over the years, and you know it."

He was right, even though most of the information they contained could be accessed online these days. "Look, I'd better get busy if I hope to get anything done before Titus and Hailey get here. Enjoy your dinner."

"We will. I made my spaghetti and meatballs. Still want to scrounge something at home rather than me sending some over with Hailey? As I recall, it's one of your favorite meals."

He wasn't wrong. "Fine, if you insist."

"I do."

Finn waited for Jim to hang up, but that didn't happen. "Jim, is everything okay?"

"Yeah, I'm good. I'm just sorry that I'm not much help to you these days. I promise to do better after Hailey—" he swallowed hard as if having to force the words out "—after she goes home."

"You know she'll stay in touch, Jim."

"Phone calls aren't the same as having her right here with us."

"I can always teach you how to set up one of those online meeting things that people do where you can see the person you're talking to. It's not perfect but it's still a lot better than a simple phone call."

"I guess. Have fun tonight."

The phone went dead. Finn hated the sadness in the old man's voice at the thought of Hailey leaving town. He had to be dealing with a tangled knot of emotions right now. The excitement of discovering that he had a granddaughter after all this time was understandable. So was the downside of knowing that her life was back in Missouri. Maybe if Jim's health improved, Finn would figure out a way to take him to visit Hailey in the spring.

It would be the right thing to do. Besides, he strongly suspected Jim wouldn't be the only one who would miss Hailey when she was gone.

CHAPTER TWELVE

Hailey got to the garage twenty minutes early to give Finn time to eat his dinner before Titus arrived. She parked her SUV and grabbed the sack that held a salad along with the spaghetti and meatballs. It was no surprise that the lights were off in the office and the door was locked since it was after Finn's normal working hours. She rang the bell and waited for him to let her in.

The door swung open a few seconds later. "I planned to turn the outside lights on before you got here, but you're early."

"I know." She held out the bags. "Seems like I'm always delivering food of some kind to you, but Jim wanted to make sure you had time to eat before we start working on the bike."

"That was nice of him. And you, too, of course."

He led the way back into the shop. "Want something to drink? I have water, coffee, and probably a couple of cold root beers in the fridge."

"Water will be fine."

While Finn made quick work of his meal, Hailey studied her father's motorcycle. Finn had moved it off the trailer and had it set up on the hydraulic lift he used when working on a bike. She was no expert, but she thought the lift was cleverly designed. It allowed him to raise and lower the bike for easier access when he was working. Circling the bike, she studied it from different angles. "I could be wrong, but it looks like this motorcycle is built along leaner lines than Titus's bike."

Finn moved up beside her. "You're not wrong. For starters, it has a smaller engine and a shorter wheelbase. This is my personal opinion—and other people might disagree—but I would find Titus's bike to be more comfortable for long-distance cruising. This bike would be better for zipping around in town."

She trailed her fingertips over the faded leather of the seat. "That makes sense to me."

Finn finally sat down and began eating. "How was Jim today?"

She pulled up another one of the rolling stools and sat down. As she opened her bottle of water, she said, "He seemed fine. He regaled me with a lot of stories about all of the scrapes Nick got into back in the day."

"Did you enjoy that?"

"Yeah, it makes my father seem more real to me. Before this, he was a complete mystery to me."

"That's understandable."

He didn't point out that was her mother's fault, but she knew he was thinking it. So was she, but there was no changing the past. "We also spent a good part of the afternoon going through old family photo albums, so nothing too stressful. I have to say it was a bit weird seeing so many total strangers who looked a little like me. Jim told me who everyone was, but I gave up trying to keep all of the names and relationships straight. I should've taken notes. Maybe next time."

"A better idea would be to put Jim to work labeling the pictures for you." Finn paused to finish the last bite of his salad before continuing. "He doesn't have the energy for a lot of physical labor anymore, but it's not good for him to sit around doing nothing but watching television all day. A project like that would do him some good."

"It would be a lot of work."

Finn shrugged. "It's not like he'd have to do it all in one day or anything. He loves going through those albums. I figure he's never bothered to label the pictures because he thought he was the end of the line for his family."

Finn pointed at her with his fork. "That's changed now since he has you."

She felt obligated to protest his assessment of the situation. "He considers you family, too. He told me that himself."

Shrugging, he said, "Yeah, I know, but it's not the same. I have all of my own family's photos at home. I also have a couple of albums filled with pictures of Jim, Rhonda and me. The people in his albums are your flesh and blood."

It was an intriguing idea. "Is there a store in town that has office supplies? I'm not sure what kind of stickers or pen would be best for a project like this. I could also type the list of names on each page and then print it out or something similar."

A knock at the front door derailed the conversation at that point. "You finish your dinner while I go let Titus in."

She was up and moving before Finn had a chance to respond. Titus was standing outside the door with the same huge dog she'd seen lurking in the kitchen at the café. She was pretty sure animals weren't allowed in restaurants unless they were service animals. Maybe the rules and regulations about such things were different in Washington than they were back in Missouri, but she didn't think so. At the time, she'd considered asking Finn if Titus's customers minded him having his pet roaming around the place. After looking around, though, it seemed obvious that no one cared or they were just used to it by now.

The dog in question charged into the office as soon as she opened the door, dragging his owner behind him. Titus hauled back on the leash to bring the dog back under control. "Ned, behave. You don't want to scare the lady."

Ned plopped down next to his owner, his tail sweeping back and forth on the floor as he awaited further instructions. Hailey held her hand out for Ned to sniff. When the dog gave her fingers a quick lick, she went down on one knee to give the grateful dog a thorough scratching.

"You're a handsome boy, aren't you?"

Titus grumbled a bit as she continued to sweet-talk his dog. "Don't feed his ego too much. He's already spoiled rotten."

Arching an eyebrow, she looked up at Ned's owner and pointed out the obvious. "And whose fault is that?"

Titus didn't bother to dispute the issue. "Mine, but I figure he went through some rough times before he found his way to me. I'm just making up for other people's mistakes."

She patted Ned on the head one last time before standing up. "And I'm sure he appreciates that. It's easy to tell that he's happy with his life these days."

"Seems like it. At least he doesn't complain much." Titus unsnapped Ned's leash. "Are you ready to get your hands greasy?"

She laughed. "I've been looking forward to it all day. Finn should be about ready for us now. He was finishing up his dinner when I came to let you in."

Titus followed her back into the garage proper, rubbing his hands together. "I can't tell you how excited I am to get the chance to help work on your bike. Like I said, chances like this are rare."

"So I've heard. I had no idea what it might be worth until I got here. If I'd known, I probably would've left it in storage instead of bringing it with me." Feeling a bit sheepish, she bit her lower lip and then added, "Seriously, I didn't think anything of leaving it in the motel parking lot every night on the way here. It's a miracle someone didn't hitch the trailer to their own vehicle and drive off with it."

Titus looked a bit sick by her admission, but his expression was nothing compared to the look of horror on Finn's face. He'd clearly overheard the last of their conversation. "Sorry, Finn. I know that was irresponsible of me, but I didn't know the risk I was taking."

He shook his head as if to clear it. "No apology necessary, Hailey. You had no way of knowing. I routinely ship bikes all over the country. It will be no big deal to make similar arrangements to transport it back to Missouri for you."

Actually, she still wasn't comfortable with Finn's assumption that the bike actually belonged to her. Now wasn't the time for that discussion, though. She did a slow lap around the bike. Without commenting on the shipping issue, she asked, "Where do we start?"

Finn took the hint. "Titus and I will start dismantling everything. As we do that, I'll make a list of what parts need to be replaced versus the ones that can be used again once they're cleaned and refurbished."

She grinned and rubbed her hands together. "So I get to clean parts again?"

He laughed at her excitement at the prospect. "Let me know if you get bored, and we can find something else for you to do."

She picked up the bins he'd used earlier to hold the parts that needed her attention and set one within easy reach of both Finn and Titus.

Finn took his usual seat on a rolling stool as Titus did the same on the other side of the bike. Once they got situated, Finn handed his friend a slender three-ring binder. "I made a copy of the owner's manual for each of us."

Titus immediately started paging through his. "This is so cool."

Finn pointed toward the counter next to where Hailey would be working. "I thought you might like one, too. That's yours over there on the counter. I also picked up a box of disposable gloves to protect your hands while washing the parts. They're a size medium, so they should fit you better than the ones I use."

"That was thoughtful of you. I appreciate it."

He grinned at her. "Never let it be said that I don't take good care of my free labor."

With that settled, the three of them set to work.

THE NEXT MORNING, Finn's alarm went off at the usual time. Most of the time, he didn't have any problem crawling out of bed to get ready for work. This was not one of those days. He stared up at the ceiling and debated whether he could get by stealing another hour or two of sleep before getting up. It wasn't as if he was expecting any customers to stop by the shop, and the delivery trucks knew to leave the boxes out of sight around the side of the building behind the dumpster.

The only thing that had him dragging himself up to sit on the side of the bed was the knowledge that Titus was no doubt already hard at work at the café. Titus's workday normally started even earlier than Finn's, and his conscience wouldn't let him slack off. This wasn't the first time he'd gotten caught up in working on a special bike and stayed at the shop beyond his normal working hours. However, it was the first time that midnight had come and gone before he started packing up to go home.

With some effort, he finally stumbled into the bathroom and turned on the shower. It was tempting to set the water on the coldest setting in case the shock would jumpstart his brain. He finally opted for a more moderate temperature, figuring a large dose of caffeine would do a better job of clearing out the cobwebs.

Rather than hanging around his house long enough to make breakfast, he decided to swing by the café to pick up a couple of breakfast sandwiches and a tall cup of black coffee to go. Better yet, two cups.

His grumbly mood didn't improve when he looked outside. It must have snowed again after he got home, because his truck was covered with a dusting of new powder. He bundled up in his warmest gear and headed outside. He started the engine to warm up the cab while he scraped the snow off the windows.

Judging by the lack of tire marks in any of his neighbors' driveways, he was the first one to be out and about this morning. Since the high school kids normally left for class about the same time he went to work, he suspected the schools might be closed for the day. Lucky kids.

Boy, he'd loved snow days when he was in school. Too bad he was now a responsible adult with obligations he couldn't ignore. Now that he thought about it, he couldn't remember the last time he played hooky from work. Rather than dwell on his lack of a social life, he drove slowly through town to the café. He was about to get out of the truck when his phone buzzed. What was Hailey doing up at this hour when she didn't need to be anywhere?

"Hey, what's up?"

"I'm at the garage."

She hadn't mentioned anything last night about spending more time helping him. "Sorry, I'm running late this morning, but I'll be there shortly. I have one more quick stop before I head over. Is there something you needed?"

After a brief hesitation, she said, "I wanted to talk to you about something."

That didn't tell him much, so he made a wild

guess. "And you don't want to discuss it in front of Jim."

"Pretty much."

"Have you had breakfast?"

"A blueberry muffin and a cup of tea."

"Okay, stay in your car and keep warm. I'll be there in twenty minutes or so."

Actually, he made it in less than fifteen. He'd lucked out and hit a brief lull in the usual steady stream of customers at the café. He picked up four grab-and-go breakfast sandwiches along with four cups of coffee on the off chance Hailey was as caffeine-starved as he was.

Titus stepped out of the kitchen just as Rita, one of the servers, was ringing up Finn's bill. He delivered a couple of heaping plates to a pair of brothers who owned a small cattle ranch a short distance outside of town. As soon as he set the plates down, he headed in Finn's direction. If Titus was feeling the effects of their late night, it didn't show. "Working on that bike was fun. Let me know if you want my help again."

"I will. It won't be until the rest of the parts come in, though. Jim is working on tracking them down, but there's no telling how long it will take for everything to get here."

"Will they arrive in time to get the bike done before Hailey leaves town?"

Finn picked up the sack with the sandwiches

and the cardboard tray holding the coffee. "Probably not, but it doesn't matter. I plan to ship the bike back to her anyway."

Titus eyed the four cups of coffee. "You hosting a party this morning?"

"I'm just dragging after our late night and wanted a double dose of coffee. Half of my order is for Hailey. She called right before I came in to say she was already at the shop waiting for me."

"Were you expecting her?"

"No. Evidently she wants to talk about something."

Titus led the way over to the door and opened it for Finn. "Does that sound a little ominous or is it just my suspicious nature jumping at shadows?"

"I'm not sure. All she said was that she wanted to talk without Jim there to listen in."

"Interesting. What do you think—"

Before Titus could finish his question, Rita hollered at him from across the room. "Hey, boss. Gunnar says the sink in the kitchen is backed up again. Thought you'd want to know that he's about to try unplugging the drain himself."

Titus turned pale at that pronouncement. "Sorry, I've gotta go. The last time Gunnar tried to fix the problem, it took an emergency call to the plumber to put everything back together again. You have no idea how much that cost me."

Then he took off running, wending his way between the tables and customers at high speed. Before he even reached the kitchen door, Titus started yelling at Gunnar to stop whatever he was doing. Gunnar hollered right back at him while Ned barked his head off. It was tempting to hang around to enjoy what was bound to be a lively encounter between employer and employee, but it wouldn't be fair to leave Hailey sitting out in the cold for much longer.

Silently wishing his friend the best of luck dealing with the plumbing, Finn left the café, still chuckling. Not that he'd admit it to Titus, but the panicky look on his face had been hilarious. It was also a nice reminder why Finn preferred to worked alone.

It didn't take long for him to reach the shop. He turned into the parking lot in front of the garage and pulled up next to Hailey's SUV. When she got out, he handed her the bag of sandwiches to hold while he locked up his truck and then opened the door to the office. Then he stepped aside to let her go in first.

"Go on back while I turn on the lights. I bought us some breakfast sandwiches, and two of those coffees are for you. I usually make a pot as soon as I get here, but I bought some at the café to drink on the way here. Sadly, I didn't get enough beauty sleep last night, and I'm really dragging this morning."

She winced. "Sorry about that. We should've quit a lot earlier since both you and Titus had to work this morning."

He waved off her concern. "No apologies necessary. We were having fun and didn't want to stop. For now, let's eat."

Hailey didn't say a word as she chose a sandwich at random. After peeling back the wrapper, she took a small bite of the sandwich. It was hard to not notice how she was avoiding making eye contact with him. Something really had her tied up in knots, but he couldn't imagine what it could be. Had he said or done something to upset her without knowing it? Rather than press for answers, he'd give her all the time she needed to marshal her thoughts.

Finally, she set her sandwich down and clenched her hands in her lap. He took a sip of coffee to wash down the big bite he'd just taken. "Hailey, it can't be that bad. Just spit it out. What's wrong?"

"I'm sorry, but I don't want it."

He glanced down at her half-eaten sandwich. "It's okay if you're not hungry."

Her gaze shifted toward the Vincent Black

Lightning and back to him. "Not the sandwich, Finn. The bike. I don't want it."

Okay, he hadn't expected that. "Why not? By the time I get done with the restoration, the bike will be like new. It was your father's. Surely that means something to you."

She was already shaking her head. "Of course it means something to me, but the bike means more to Jim. It disappeared when his son died, and he's been wondering all this time what became of it. Seriously, I can't believe my mother held on to it all these years when it wasn't hers to begin with."

"No, it probably wasn't. That doesn't mean it wasn't yours. Nick was your father. Jim is your grandfather."

He let that much sink in before continuing. "If you tell Jim that you don't want the bike, I'm worried he'll see it as a rejection of both him and Nick."

"That's what I'm afraid of, but I don't know what I'd do with it even if I did take it back home with me. It deserves better than to sit in a storage area, which is what would happen. I don't know the first thing about riding a motorcycle. If something happened to the bike, I'd feel terrible."

"You could always learn to ride. It's not that hard, and I bet you'd love it."

She didn't look convinced, so he tried again. "It's literally in your blood, Hailey. Your father loved riding motorcycles. Jim doesn't ride anymore, but he used to spend a lot of time cruising on his. In the summer, he and Rhonda would take off for parts unknown on his Harley and disappear for a weekend. Here's a shocker for you—she even had her own for a while."

"Seriously? I've only seen pictures of Rhonda, but she sure didn't look the type."

"So you think all motorcycle owners are alike?" Finn couldn't help but laugh. "I swear Rhonda and Jim had a bunch of friends who took long rides together. It's a great way to see the country."

Looking a bit sheepish, she wrinkled her nose. "Sorry, I should know better than to stereotype people like that."

He grinned at her. "Now you've got me trying to picture your grandparents and mine riding the highways decked out in black leather jackets and chaps, heavy boots, and sporting a whole lot of tattoos."

"You have to admit that sounds a lot like Titus."

"True enough, and he'd be the first to admit it. For the record, I wear leathers when I'm out on my bike. Along with a helmet, they provide bikers the best protection from injuries."

"You've never said what kind of bike you own."

"I built it from the ground up myself. It's closer in style to Titus's Fat Boy than to your father's bike. If the weather clears enough while you're here, I'll take you out for a ride. I've got an extra jacket and helmet you can wear."

She didn't look too excited by the prospect, but he bet he could talk her into it. "So let's not tell Jim that you might want to leave the Vincent here with him at this point. It's not ridable right now and won't be for a while yet. You have plenty of time to make up your mind."

"Okay."

With that settled for the moment, he unwrapped his second sandwich. "Eat up, lady. I plan to put you to work as soon as we finish breakfast."

That perked her up a bit. "Doing what? Do you have more shipments to be inventoried or parts to be cleaned?"

Good question.

"Don't worry, I'll figure out something."

CHAPTER THIRTEEN

"And where have you been?"

The tone of Jim's question came across a bit crabby, not merely curious. Rather than respond immediately, Hailey took her time hanging up her coat and removing her snow-covered shoes before answering. Drawing a calming breath, she stepped into the living room. "I was helping Finn at the shop and lost track of time."

Her explanation evidently took some of the wind out of Jim's sails since his next comment was definitely less confrontational. "Sorry, I didn't mean to come across so cranky. I was worried."

"I should've called you earlier. I spent most of the morning working in the storeroom and didn't have my phone in there with me. I didn't see your texts until I was getting into my car to head this way."

He frowned. "What were you doing in the storeroom?"

"Unpacking some shipments that came in. Finn showed me where everything should go, and it freed him up to work on his new project."

"I'd point out that you didn't drive all the way out here from Missouri to spend time in a dusty old storeroom."

She took her usual seat facing him. "To tell the truth, it felt good to do something productive, and I've enjoyed the time I've spent helping Finn. This might sound weird, but I've always liked bringing order out of chaos. Cleaning parts for him and straightening shelves definitely qualifies."

He looked ready to complain more, but then he smiled. "Actually, now that I think about it, that's the perfect way for you to learn about the family business. Back in the day, we started off having both Finn's father and Nick do grunt work around the shop before we ever let them get their hands on the bikes themselves."

Where was he going with this? He seemed to be waiting for her to respond, but she wasn't sure what he wanted her to say. "For sure the experience will make it easier for me understand what you're talking about when I'm back home in Missouri."

Just that quickly his mood switch flipped again. "You know you don't have to be in such a big hurry to leave Dunbar. From what I've gathered, you don't have a good reason to go back to Missouri."

She so didn't want to have this argument right now. Admittedly, there probably wasn't going to be the perfect time for the discussion. "Jim, I have obligations that I can't just walk away from on a whim. I have a job, an apartment, and friends waiting for my return."

"What kind of friends? People you happen to work with or is there some fella waiting for you back there? If so, how come you haven't mentioned him since you got here?"

She didn't appreciate his judgmental attitude about her life back in Missouri. "I have friends besides my coworkers. No boyfriend, though. I had just started dating someone new when Mom got sick. Taking care of her took up most of my free time, and he moved on. To be honest, since we'd only gone out a few times, I hardly noticed when he stopped calling."

Jim nodded as if her answer was exactly what he'd expected. "Those don't sound like obligations. They sound more like excuses."

Then he pointed a shaky finger in her direction. "You know what's missing from that list? Family, and family should trump any of that other stuff."

With that pronouncement, he pushed himself up out of his chair and walked out of the room.

"I'm going to take a nap. Wake me when Finn gets here."

Then he disappeared down the hall, slamming his bedroom door behind him. She sat there in shocked silence for a long time. What should she do next? She'd been up front from the beginning that she'd only come to town for a short visit, one meant to test the waters, so to speak. Maybe she should've kept to her original plan to introduce herself and spend a couple of days getting acquainted before returning home. While she wasn't happy with Jim trying to change the rules now, she was even angrier with herself.

The truth was that the longer she stayed, the harder it was going to be to leave. She already loved her grandfather. Yeah, he could be a bit cranky at times, but he'd also done everything he could to make her feel like she really mattered to him. Like he needed her as much as she needed him, which meant he was right about family trumping everything else. Her mother's death had left a gaping hole in her heart, but Jim and his stories about her grandmother and her father had given the healing process a definite boost.

Then there was Finn. She hadn't been exaggerating about her love of putting things in their place and giving everything a good polish. But what she really liked best about hanging out at the shop was watching Finn while he was working. There was something so fascinating about seeing a true craftsman at work. He was just so…competent. She couldn't help but notice the small scars on his big hands, marks left by years spent wielding tools and shaping metal. Then there was the way his eyebrows rode low over his dark eyes as he dealt with a stubborn bolt or difficult repair.

He'd probably be stunned to learn that she thought of him as an artist, one who created beauty out of the most unlikely materials—chrome, steel and grease.

Her phone jarred her out of her rather whimsical reverie. Checking the screen, she saw it was Finn. Funny that he'd call right when she was thinking about him, not that she'd admit that to him. She swiped the screen. "Hi, what's up?"

"A couple of things. Do you know what the plans are for dinner?"

"Actually, the subject didn't come up while we were talking, and Jim is taking a nap right now. I'll go poke around in the kitchen to see if I can tell what's on the menu. Give me a second."

She quickly checked the fridge and then the pantry. "I don't see anything in the fridge or in the pantry that looks like a meal for three people. I can ask him what the options are when he wakes up, although it's probably already too late to thaw something. Got any ideas? If not, I could put together a quick casserole if I can find all of the ingredients. Seriously, you'd be amazed what I can make with a pound of ground beef, a chunk of cheese and a box of rigatoni pasta. I'll also need a jar of pasta sauce, and to keep things healthy, I should probably throw in a couple of fresh vegetables."

His amusement at her slapdash method of cooking came through clearly. "Sounds delicious. Text me anything you're missing, and I'll pick it up on the way."

"It's a deal."

"How was Jim when you got there?"

She sighed. "A bit testy because I got here later than he expected. I honestly don't know if he was really worried or just lonely. Either way, I probably should've let him know where I was. Once he cooled down, though, he decided that me spending time at the shop doing what he described as 'grunt work' was a good idea. Something about that's how he and your grandfather first introduced their sons to the business. You, too, probably."

"Yeah, they definitely believed everyone should start at the bottom and work their way up. Even when I was in middle school, I spent a lot of Saturday mornings sweeping floors, emptying the trash and stuff like that. I can't say I was always happy about it, but at least I never had to worry about not being able to find a job when I was in high school. That can be a real problem for teenagers in a town the size of Dunbar. It kept me in gas money, anyway."

"That's a big deal at that age. I did a lot of babysitting back then. My friends and I were always having to pool our resources to buy gas. It was that or walk, which was never my first choice, especially in the winter. This close to the mountains, you probably know something about that."

"Yeah, I do."

She knew Finn needed to get back to work, but she wanted to warn him just in case Jim was still upset about her plan to return home. "You should also know that Jim isn't happy that I'll still be leaving after Christmas. Not sure there's much I can do to change that, but I thought you should know."

"Thanks for the warning, but I'm not surprised he's upset. He only just found you, and it's going to be hard for him to see you leave. Having said that, it's not like you didn't warn him. You're already staying longer than you planned in order to spend more time with us. I know it's easier said than done, but you shouldn't feel bad about it."

But she did. "I hope he knows that it won't be easy for me to leave. I'll miss him horribly when I go." After a second, she added, "In case you're wondering, I'll miss you, too."

"Ditto, lady."

"It's funny. I came here to get to know my grandfather. I never expected to meet so many other people that I'll also miss, not to mention Titus's pies. If I thought they'd survive intact, I'd insist on you mailing me one on a regular basis."

Finn laughed again. "I bet Titus would get a kick out of that idea. Maybe he could freeze one of his peach pies for you and ship it on dry ice."

"Don't tempt me. That might work, but it sounds expensive."

"I can't believe you'd worry about a little thing like money if it meant having one of his pies."

"I'm not sure my landlord would be happy if I offered him a piece of pie instead of my rent."

"It could be worth a try."

When another phone rang in the background, Finn said, "Oops, do you mind holding for a second? I need to take this other call."

"Sure thing."

While she waited, she did a more thorough

survey of the pantry and refrigerator. By the time he came back on the line, she'd made a list of what she'd need for dinner.

"Sorry that took so long. It was one of my regular customers, and it takes him a while to get to the point sometimes."

"That's okay. I should let you get back to work, anyway. I'll text the shopping list as soon as we hang up."

"Sounds good. I should get there before five."

"See you then." She hesitated and then added, "And Finn, thanks for listening."

"Anytime."

AFTER HAILEY DISCONNECTED the call, Finn stared at the blank screen on his phone for the longest time. The amount of effort it took for him to finally release his grip on it spoke to his current mood. He took some comfort from knowing he'd managed to carry on a normal conversation with Hailey without her noticing that anything was wrong. That didn't mean he wasn't looking around the shop for something he could pound on for a while.

Hailey had no way of knowing that anything she'd told him would feed into his worst fears. She'd only wanted something useful to do when she'd offered to help around the shop. It never occurred to him that Jim would see that as the first step toward drawing her into the family business. He was pretty sure that Hailey wasn't thinking that way, but there was no telling for sure.

Regardless, it was a problem, at least for Finn, because it gave him a pretty clear glimpse into what Jim was thinking. The old man had promised that someday his half of the business would belong to Finn, making him the sole owner of their business. Despite Jim's recent health scares, Finn sincerely hoped that day was still far in the future. That said, he also looked forward to the day when he'd have full control of the shop. Then he'd finally be free to decide what he really wanted to do with his life.

If someone had ever bothered to ask a six-year-old Finn what he wanted to be when he grew up, he would have said a firefighter. However, no one had ever asked, and he'd never found a way to break the news to the man who had welcomed a lost little boy into his home. Instead, Finn had dutifully gone into the family business and settled for being a part-time volunteer firefighter. He was still young enough to change careers, but eventually it would be too late.

He tried his best not to think of such things. Jim would see it as a betrayal of the worst kind. The mere thought sent a wave of guilt rushing through Finn that had him up and pacing the floor. He owed his godparents everything. It would crush Jim if he even suspected that Finn might want to choose a different path than the one he'd been on since he was born.

After all, everyone in town knew that the members of the Cooper and Morris families all worked on motorcycles. It was as if it had been magically ordained that Finn would be a third-generation bike mechanic.

Back when Finn's grandfather and Jim started the business, they had intended to pass it down through the generations, maybe even expanding to other locations as the families grew in size. For a short time, their plan seemed to be working. Finn's father had dutifully followed in his father's footsteps, and Nick hadn't completely rejected their expectations. Everyone knew he'd return to the fold as soon as his time in the army ended. But now, in only three generations, the clans had reduced in number to just two people—Jim and Finn.

But now that had changed. There was new blood in town. Finn didn't know what Hailey's long-term plans were, but he knew without a doubt Jim was already envisioning her producing a whole new generation of kids to carry on the family tradition. It was becoming increasingly obvious that Hailey stood to inherit

Jim's half even if she had no desire to work in the shop herself. Finn couldn't blame Jim for wanting his granddaughter to reap the benefits of his creation.

The problem was that Finn couldn't afford to buy her out. The reverse was probably equally true—it was highly doubtful that she had the financial wherewithal to buy his half of the shop. Even if she did, why would she want to when she knew next to nothing about motorcycles? The bottom line was that he'd be stuck with a new partner, one who couldn't pull her own weight when it came to running the business. That made it a recipe for disaster as far as he was concerned. He'd have to continue to take on enough work to keep the business afloat. That made it nearly impossible to take any time off. He was already working six days a week most of the time, sometimes even seven. Heck, it had been over three years since he'd managed to take a real vacation.

The whole mess made him tired just thinking about it.

His phone pinged, jarring him out of his pity party. It was the shopping list Hailey had promised to send him. He quickly scanned it and was relieved the few things she needed would all be available at the store in town. Checking the time, he decided to put in another hour working on the design for the new project before knocking off for the day. And if time allowed, he might reward all of his hard work with a quick stop at the café to buy one of Titus's pies.

JIM MUST HAVE really been tired because he was still asleep when Finn finally arrived at the house. Finn peeked in on him and then helped Hailey with dinner. After putting together a tossed salad to go with the casserole, he got the garlic bread ready to pop into the oven right before it was time to eat.

Hailey had the radio set on a station that played nothing but Christmas music while the two of them worked at the kitchen counter. He'd never seen anyone dance in place to a Christmas song before, but it was cute. Giving in to temptation, he caught her hand and swung her around, twirling her out and then back in closer. The surprise move had her stumbling a bit, but she quickly caught her balance and got with the program. There wasn't much room to maneuver in the kitchen, but they made the most of the space, laughing at the missteps when one or the other bumped into something. The song finally ended, leaving them a bit breathless and grinning at each other.

The applause coming from the kitchen door startled them both. Finn took two steps back from Hailey and turned to face his godfather. "Jim, I was about to come wake you up. Dinner is almost ready."

"You two were sure enough cooking up something, but it wasn't dinner." He leaned against the end of the counter and sighed, his faded eyes staring into the distance. "Hailey, you wouldn't know this, but Rhonda and I loved to dance together. We preferred the living room because there was more room to maneuver, but we were known to dance in here, too. Tell her, Finn."

"He's right. The two of them had some serious moves."

In fact, those were some of his favorite memories, even though he'd been embarrassed by their behavior back when he was a teenager. "In fact, Rhonda was the one who taught me the basics of ballroom dancing. She said any guy worth his salt should know how to dance. Something about the ladies liking that in a man."

Hailey gave him a shy smile. "She wasn't wrong."

Turning back to Jim, she continued. "My mom and I took line dancing lessons together back when I was around thirteen. We also loved Jazzercise and Zumba."

The timer on the stove chimed, and Hailey

grabbed a pair of oven mitts. After taking the casserole out of the oven, she put the bread in to heat up. "Dinner will be ready in five minutes."

As Finn added dressing to the salad, a thought occurred to him. "I have an idea. Shay Barnaby has a tavern over on the far edge of town. We should go there for dinner sometime. It's not fancy, but the food is good, and there's an old-fashioned jukebox that blasts dance music. I'd bet you'd like it."

"Sounds like fun." She carried the casserole over to the table and set it on a trivet. "I'd love to go if there's time before I leave."

Just that quickly, Jim's smile faded. "You two go ahead and eat. Seems I've lost my appetite."

Then he walked out, leaving the two of them staring at the empty doorway.

CHAPTER FOURTEEN

JIM WASN'T THE only one who was no longer hungry. At a loss for what to do next, Hailey took the bread out of the oven. After tossing the oven mitts on the counter, she dropped down into one of the chairs and rested her head in her hands for several seconds. Finally, she looked up to meet Finn's gaze. "I'm the one he's upset with. Maybe he'll eat if I leave."

Finn didn't look much happier than Jim as he ran his fingers through his hair in obvious frustration. "Don't go anywhere just yet. I'll talk to him. He might not realize it right now, but he's going to regret if his behavior makes you reluctant to stay here."

"It won't help if you force him to spend time with me if that isn't what he wants to do." She blinked hard to clear the tears that were blurring her vision. At the same time, Finn edged closer to her as if unsure of his welcome. But when he held out his arms, she stood and stepped into his embrace. Being surrounded by the comfort of his warmth and strength went a long way toward helping her regain control of her emotions.

"When I came here, I swear I didn't mean to knock anyone's life sideways."

Finn stroked her back. "I know that, and so does he. I'll go talk to him."

She stayed right where she was, holding on to Finn for another few seconds before finally stepping back. "Tell him I'm sorry."

"You're not the one who needs to apologize."

Without waiting for her to respond, he stalked out. She briefly considered making a quick exit while Finn dealt with her grandfather, but immediately rejected the idea and sat back down at the table. If she and Jim were going to maintain a healthy relationship, they had to be honest with each other. She'd made it clear that she was there to meet him in person, and that afterward she would return home to pick up the pieces of her life. Regardless of what Jim thought, she had legitimate obligations, ones she couldn't shirk for much longer without it causing her long-term problems.

That didn't mean she wouldn't stay in frequent contact with him. She made a mental list of all the ways that could happen. They could make phone calls, exchange texts and e-mails, and set up regular video visits. Heck, they even could write letters if he'd rather go old-school. The bottom line was that she'd do whatever it took to fill in the gaps in between actual visits to Dunbar.

She could hear the distant rumble of the two men having a heated discussion down the hall. Finn had closed Jim's bedroom door, making it impossible to make out specific words. Even so, tempers were definitely running hot. Being so upset couldn't be good for Jim and might even put a strain on his heart. Before she could decide what to do to calm things down, the bedroom door opened and not one, but two sets of footsteps headed her way.

She started to stand up but decided against it. A few seconds later, Finn walked back into the kitchen with Jim following close on his heels. Someone needed to say something to get the conversation started, but any useful words refused to come to her. Surprisingly, it was Jim who took charge of the conversation.

"I owe you an apology, Hailey. I'm sorry that I acted like a jerk and walked out. I really hate the idea of you leaving town, but I promise that I'm grateful that you chose to come visit in the first place. Your being here means everything to me, and I hope you know that."

Deciding actions would speak louder than words at the moment, she rose and headed straight for her grandfather. Wrapping her arms around him, she hugged him close and said, "I'm sorry, too, Grandpa. I can't help that I'll need to leave soon, but I do promise I'll come back as often as I can."

He jerked back far enough to look her in the eye, his eyes glistening with a sheen of tears. "That's the first time you've called me that. I thought all chance of me every having a grandchild died with my son. Even if I get a bit cantankerous at times, never doubt that you are a gift in my life."

"As you are in mine." She hugged him again and then stepped back. "Now, we should eat while the casserole is still warm."

He sniffed the air. "It smells great. Let's dig in."

Jim breezed past her to take his usual seat at the table. After he passed by her, she caught Finn's eye long enough to mouth, "Thank you."

He nodded and motioned for her to sit down. "I'll get the salad. Sorry, there's no dessert tonight. I ran out of time to stop at the café."

Jim brightened up. "Not a problem. We have some of those sugar cookies left, and I have ice cream in the freezer. For now, pass the bread."

The rest of dinner passed peacefully. Hailey listened with interest to the men discussing the progress on restoring her father's motorcycle.

Jim glanced in her direction. His smile was a bit sad as he seemed to get lost in the past for a minute. "Boy, that thing was a proper mess when he bought it, but Nick did a fine job of restoring it. He had a real talent for that kind of work."

Hailey could just see the two of them huddled around the bike for hours at a time as they brought it back to its original glory. No wonder those were such special memories for Jim. "Did he always enjoy working on bikes?"

"Yeah, he did. From the time he was old enough to hold a wrench, he liked to help me and Finn's grandpa work on the mechanical repairs. I gave him his own set of tools when he was just ten. He wasn't much for the design end of things, but there wasn't an engine he couldn't make purr."

Hailey could hear the parental pride in his voice. "I bet that was a fun father-son project for the two of you."

Jim nodded. "Those days have always been some of my favorite memories of my son. When we first started working on the bike, your father was just a teenager, which meant we didn't always see eye-to-eye on things. Doing right by the Vincent was one thing we could both agree on."

While she digested that newest nugget of information about her father, Jim turned his attention back to Finn. "Be sure to let me know when the parts come in. I'd like to get my hands greasy, too."

"I will."

Jim went silent again. Finally, he sighed. "I admit knowing how good a mechanic he was is why I wasn't real happy when Nick joined the army instead of taking his rightful place in the business. That wasn't the only reason, though. I understood a young man's need to explore the world, but I knew it would worry Rhonda. I never liked seeing her unhappy. To be fair, neither did Nick."

She noticed that Finn didn't comment. Maybe he'd also felt pressured into joining the business. If so, that was between him and Jim. Before she could think of a safe topic of conversation to pursue, Finn's phone rang. While he took the call, she started clearing the table.

"HEY, RYDER. WHAT'S UP?"

"Tomorrow is Saturday, and I'm calling to make sure you can still drive the fire truck in the parade."

"Yeah, I can, but it's a good thing you called." Because with everything that was going on, it had totally slipped his mind. "I'd almost forgotten about it. Sorry about that."

Finn gave Hailey a quick look and switched

the call over to speaker mode. "Do you know if anyone else is scheduled to ride in the truck with me? Jim's granddaughter is here for the holidays, and she might like to come with me."

"There should be room, but the kids usually ride in the back and toss candy to the spectators."

Finn winked at her. "Yeah, but this kid is about our age."

There was a short pause, and then Ryder asked, "Is she single?"

Boy, now he wished he hadn't put the call on speakerphone. Regardless, why on earth would Ryder care about that? "I'm pretty sure your fiancée wouldn't like to learn that you've been asking about other women."

Ryder's laughter rang out across the kitchen. "Don't worry, I wasn't asking for myself. I just thought a couple of the other guys might be interested in showing her some of the sights here in town."

Finn didn't want to know who Ryder was talking about. "Tell them Hailey will be my guest tomorrow. Besides, she's only here for a short visit."

Still chuckling, Ryder said, "Message received and understood. Don't worry, I'll warn them off. Got any questions for me?"

"Nope. I'll see you bright and early at the station."

Finn disconnected the call and set his phone aside. "So, Hailey, about tomorrow. Like I told Ryder, I'd almost forgotten that I had promised to drive in the annual Christmas parade here in town. Would you like to ride in a fire truck with me?"

At least Hailey didn't hesitate to accept. "Sounds like fun. I've never been in a parade before, or a fire truck, for that matter."

Jim chimed in. "Don't get your expectations too high. It's a small-town event, not the Rose Parade. The kids love it, though. A member of the city council has an old Cadillac convertible that he's restored to like new. It's huge and bright red. He puts the top down so Santa can ride in the back seat and wave at everybody as they drive through town."

"It still sounds like fun." She gave Finn a hopeful look. "Back to the fire truck, though. Any chance I can play with the siren?"

This was getting better and better. He loved how she always took such pleasure in simple things. "It can probably be arranged."

Hailey's eyes glittered with excitement. "Then count me in. What time would I need to be ready?"

"I'll pick you up around eight. You might

want to stop by the drugstore in town on your way back to Rikki's tonight and pick up a Santa hat or some such thing to wear."

"Good idea. I might also check to see if they have some kind of holiday sweatshirt or sweater I can wear. Should I get something Christmassy for you, too? Maybe reindeer antlers and a red nose? You'd look cute wearing them."

He felt mildly insulted. "Not really. Besides, I'll be wearing my firefighter gear. It's part of the tradition."

She muttered "Stick in the mud" under her breath, which set off a round of laughter from Jim. Even Finn grinned a little.

"One more question. Should I buy candy to throw?"

"Nope. All of that is donated by businesses in town. All you need to do is dress warm and be ready to go by eight."

Hailey gave him a mock salute. "Yes, sir. Will do, sir."

Cute. He shook his finger at her. "Keep it up, lady, and maybe there won't be room for you in the cab after all."

"If so, I bet if I play my cards right Ryder will let me ride in the back with the kids."

Jim picked up his empty plate and headed for the sink. "She's right about that, and don't forget about those other guys Ryder mentioned. Treat her right or the sharks will be circling."

Finn shot his godfather a dark look. "Don't worry. There won't be any circling."

Hailey looked understandably puzzled by his reaction. It wasn't as if the two of them were going on a date. If anything, she was more of a tagalong getting a chance to experience one more small-town event. In an effort to steer the conversation in a different direction, he asked, "So should we have ice cream now or let dinner settle a bit?"

At least Hailey was willing to follow his lead. "Let's clean up the kitchen first, and then I'll dish up the ice cream."

Jim looked back over his shoulder at them. "If you two will take care of the leftovers, I'll handled the dishes. Hailey, if you don't mind, pack up some of the casserole for Finn to take home. There's plenty for all three of us to have for lunch tomorrow."

"Will do."

Crisis avoided, they all got to work.

SATURDAY MORNING DAWNED clear and cold. Finn pulled into the driveway at the bed-and-breakfast. Hailey must have been watching for him, because she was out of the house and down the steps before the truck stopped moving. She greeted him with a huge smile as she climbed up into the passenger seat. "It's a beautiful day for a parade."

"Yeah, it is. Last year it rained, which wasn't nearly as much fun." He waited for her to get buckled in before backing out onto the street. He eyed her attire and tried not to laugh. She had her hair pulled back in a ponytail and wore a headband that had reindeer antlers attached at the top. Glittery snowmen dangled from her ears.

He had to wonder where she'd gotten that oversize sweater on such short notice. It came halfway down her thighs, and she'd had to roll up the sleeves to make them short enough. Fire engine red, it had a green Christmas tree on the front that was decorated with real bells that jingled with every move she made. It also looked as if she'd stuffed it with pillows.

"I just want to make sure you'll be warm enough. The heat will be on in the cab of the fire truck, but it will still be chilly. Most of the time the windows will be down so we can wave at the crowd. What all are you wearing under that, uh, shall we say interesting sweater?"

"Hey, I love this thing. Good thing I don't have to sneak up on anyone, though." She tugged on the front of the sweater, setting off all of the bells to demonstrate the problem. "But to answer your question, I'm wearing a thermal undershirt, a wool sweater and my winter jacket. I bought a men's extra-large so it would fit over all my layers."

"Good thinking."

He drove to the fire station where Ryder and some other volunteers were getting the fire truck ready for the parade. Two guys were busy attaching a giant wreath to the grille in front while a couple of others were tying an inflatable snowman on top of the cab. Hailey immediately asked Finn, "What happens if you get called out to fight a fire or something while the parade is going on?"

"I guess we'll see how good you are at handling a fire hose or using an ax to break through a roof."

"You think you're funny."

"I am funny, but the county fire department will cover for us and take our calls for a couple of hours. They do the same thing whenever we have a parade."

"Does that happen a lot?"

"I don't know how it is in other small towns, but the fine citizens of Dunbar really love their parades. Most years we have five or six."

"Do you always drive the truck?"

"No, we trade off, but I usually drive in this particular parade."

After parking his pickup, Finn hustled around

to join her on the passenger side. "Let's head inside so I can introduce you to everybody."

He took her hand and led her into the building. They came to a stop at the front end of the fire truck where Finn released his hold on her and waited until he had everyone's attention before speaking. "Hey, everybody. This is Jim Morris's granddaughter, Hailey Alston. She's in town for the holidays, visiting from Missouri."

Then he moved on to introducing his friends starting with a burly guy standing next to a boy who looked to be about seven years old. "Hailey, this is Shay Barnaby and his son Luca. Shay owns the tavern I mentioned to you. If you have any questions about the fire truck, then Luca's your guy. There's not much he doesn't know about it."

That had Luca grinning big-time. "I can get you a coloring book about it if you want. That's how I learned about them."

What a cutie! "I would love that, Luca."

"I'll go get it now."

When he took off running, Finn continued with the introductions. "The two guys bagging up the candy are Trace and Logan Calland. They run a small cattle ranch and trucking company on the outskirts of town. And finally, the guy headed this way is Ryder."

"Nice to meet you." She stepped forward,

her hand held out. "Thank you for saying it was okay for me to ride in the truck today."

"The more the merrier."

Finn touched her arm to get her attention. "I'm going to run upstairs and get a cup of coffee to take with me in the truck. Would you like one?"

"That would be nice. No sugar, heavy on the cream."

"Got it. I'll be right back."

Shay Barnaby waited until Finn disappeared up the steps before approaching her. "Are you enjoying your visit here in Dunbar?"

"I am. I've never been to the Pacific Northwest before, but it's every bit as beautiful as I'd heard it was. The mountains are spectacular, and I love all of the huge trees."

"Yeah, I get that. I'm a transplant myself, but I really love it here."

She smiled at him. "I'm guessing you didn't pick up that hint of a Southern accent in this part of the country."

"Nope, that's pure Georgia. I moved here when I was a teenager."

Before he could say anything else, his son came pounding down the steps with what had to be the coloring book he'd promised her clutched in his hand. He skidded to a halt next to his father. "Here's your book."

She immediately paged through it. "Thank you, Luca. I'm sure I'll learn a lot from this. I promise I will read it cover-to-cover after the parade is over."

He frowned a little. "Just so you know, Ryder and Shay both say it only has the basics. But don't worry, there are lots of better ones you can read if you want."

She thought it was interesting that he'd call his father by his first name, but that was their business. "Good to know."

"Mr. Ryder said you're going to ride inside the truck. I get to ride in the back to toss out candy to people." His chest puffed out a bit in pride. "This is my second time."

"That sounds like fun."

"It is."

Finn was back with her coffee. "Thanks."

"You're welcome." He ruffled Luca's hair. "Giving her that coloring book was a smart idea, Luca. I wish I'd thought of it."

The boy shuffled his feet a little, but it was clear Finn's praise pleased him. At that point, Ryder joined them. "Luca, I meant to ask you how Beau and Bruno are doing."

"They're great. I wanted them to ride on the fire truck with me today, but Shay said we needed the room on the truck for other kids."

"I'm sure they understood. You can always slip them an extra treat or two to make it up to them."

Luca looked up at his father as if reluctant to respond to Ryder's suggestion. "I know treats shouldn't be used as bribes, but they looked so sad I just had to give them some."

Hailey bit back the urge to laugh at the soft-hearted boy's dilemma. It had taken her a second to realize that Bcau and Bruno were Luca's dogs, not his siblings. His father gave the boy's shoulder a squeeze. "That's okay, kiddo. Sad, puppy-dog eyes are hard to resist. I promised them we'd take them to the park for a walk when we get home."

Okay, that was even funnier, especially when Ryder caught Shay's eye and mouthed "sucker." Then he checked the time. "Okay, folks. Time to get loaded up if you're riding on the truck. We have to be at the parade staging area in twenty minutes. The rest of the kids will be waiting for us there."

Finn handed her his coffee. "Can you take this for me? I've got to gear up."

"Sure thing."

Ryder approached her. "Why don't I hold your things while you get situated in the truck? You can ride in the front passenger seat since Finn is driving."

Luca's obvious excitement when he and his

father climbed onto the back of the fire truck had nothing on hers. She'd never expected to have the chance to ride in a parade, much less doing it in a fire truck. It took some effort to haul herself up into the front passenger seat. Once she was buckled in, Ryder passed her the coffees and the small pack she was using to hold her phone and wallet.

Then he joined her inside the cab, but in the back seat. Was she sitting where he'd planned to ride in the parade? "I can sit in back if you're supposed to be up front."

"No, you're good where you are. I'm only going as far as the staging area. I volunteer at a local no-kill animal shelter, and I'm working at our information booth today."

"Oh, so that's why you know Beau and Bruno."

He looked around and then lowered his voice. "Yeah, Shay and Luca adopted them right after the kid came to live with Shay. He lost his parents in a car accident a while back, and Shay became his guardian."

That explained why Luca referred to Shay by his first name. "Poor kid, but it's obvious he's doing okay."

"Yeah, they had a few rough patches along the way, but that's to be expected when both of them have gone through so many changes in such a short time. Not only did Shay become a father with no warning, he fell head over heels in love at the same time. Now he and Carli are married, and the three of them are doing great. This is their first Christmas as a family, and I'm glad they found each other. This is a hard time of year to be alone."

Yeah, she knew something about that herself. No doubt Finn did as well, although he'd been even younger than Luca when he lost his parents. She counted herself lucky to have found a new family so soon after the loss of her mother. The driver's door opened and Finn climbed in, effectively derailing the downward emotional spiral she'd been on just thinking about her mom. As he started the engine, he asked, "You ready to wave and smile at everybody?"

"I can't wait. One question, though." She waved her hand at all the buttons and switches on the dashboard. "Which one is the siren?"

"Just so you know, the guys in back will be playing Christmas music. They won't appreciate it if we constantly drown them out with the siren." Despite that, he pointed toward a dial. "I'll give you a crash course in operating it, but we can't blast it the whole length of the parade."

Ryder piped up from the back seat. "Where's the fun in that?"

They were all laughing as Finn drove out of the garage.

CHAPTER FIFTEEN

EVEN AS A KID, Finn had always enjoyed being part of the parades in Dunbar. This one, though, was turning out to be extra special. The reason for that was sitting next to him and having the time of her life. Recent holiday seasons had been hard for both him and Jim, but not this year. By rights, they should've been the ones cheering up Hailey. Instead, she'd somehow managed to put the bright colors and sparkle back into Christmas for both of them. Every time she turned in his direction, her eyes alight with excitement, his pulse kicked it up another notch. He'd snapped a few pictures to share with Jim and to remind himself of the warmth of her smile even after she left town.

Despite the chilly temperature, Hailey kept the window down the whole time as she waved at absolutely everybody they passed, most of whom were complete strangers. Her excitement doubled whenever she spotted a familiar face in the crowd.

So far, she'd made judicious use of the siren, only giving a short blast at each stopping point along the parade route. As soon as he slowed the truck to a complete halt, people would surge closer to catch the candy that Luca and the other kids were tossing into the crowd. When it was time to move on, Hailey gave the siren three short blasts to warn everyone to move back out of the way again, laughing every time she did it.

"This is our last stop before we return to the staging area."

Hailey looked disappointed at that news. "So soon? We can't do another lap through town? Maybe roar down a street or two with the siren going full blast?"

"Sorry, but no." He hated to ruin her fun, but he had no choice in the matter. "We have to get back and get ready to take any calls that come in. The county can cover for us for only so long."

She sagged back in the seat. "Well, rats. I forgot about that. Still, it's been fun."

"I'm glad you enjoyed yourself."

"Me, too."

"Just so you know, I'm on duty this afternoon. I'll give you a lift back to the bed-and-breakfast beforehand, but I'll be bunking down at the station for the night. I told Jim that's where I'd be, but you might need to remind him."

"I will." After a second, she gave him a concerned look. "I don't want to give you the impression that all I think about is food, but when will you eat lunch? Do you have food at the station for dinner?"

"Unless a call comes in, I can pick something up at Titus's. We also stock a few frozen dinners at the station, so I won't starve. They're not my favorite, but they're not totally awful."

Hailey wrinkled her nose, making her feelings on that subject all too clear. "I'm not a fan. But after Mom got sick, there were nights I didn't have the energy to do more than push a few buttons on the microwave."

She started to say something else, but stopped. "Sorry, I didn't mean for the conversation to take a downward turn. I want to enjoy every minute of this experience. Who knows if I'll ever have another chance to ride in a fire truck with a handsome firefighter?"

If she said anything else, Finn didn't hear it. His brain got stuck on the idea that she thought he was handsome. He appreciated the thought even if he wasn't sure that was actually true. Based on what he saw in the mirror every day, he'd always thought his nose was a little too strong, and his other features were ordinary at best. In his experience, most women commented on his muscular build. He worked hard to keep in shape, because an out-of-shape firefighter wasn't just a danger to himself. All of that aside, it was nice to know Hailey found him attractive.

The feeling was mutual, because he'd always been a sucker for blond hair and big blue eyes. In this case, however, the attraction went beyond Hailey's physical appearance. At the beginning, he might not have been comfortable with her unexpected arrival in their lives, but he'd come to like so much about her. Just having her around was good for Jim. It had been a long time since he'd shown much enthusiasm about anything at all, and it was good to see him enjoying life more.

She took such pleasure in everything they'd done together, from cutting down her first Christmas tree to riding in the fire truck. He also liked how she fit in with his friends. He could easily get used to having her at his side long-term.

Too bad she'd be gone soon. He didn't like to think about how lonely it would be when she left.

"You've gone pretty quiet over there."

He blinked and realized he'd been staring at

her. She smiled and pointed out the front window. "The parade is about to leave us behind."

"Sorry about that. Hit the siren so we can get moving."

She hit three short blasts, once again grinning big-time. "That would never get old."

As they waited for the crowd to move back, she pointed to another button on the console. "You never said what that one does."

"It's my favorite." He waggled his eyebrows. "When we approach an intersection where our light is red, it sends a signal that turns the lights facing the cross street and oncoming traffic red and ours back to green."

"Seriously? It can do that?"

"Yep."

Hailey stared at the small button in wonder. "I never even thought about fire trucks having something like that. Of course, it only makes sense. You firefighters get all the cool toys."

She wasn't wrong. "It's why I volunteered in the first place. That and the fact that I totally rock the gear we wear."

Hailey gave him a long, considering look and then shook her head. "You can tell yourself that, but we both know there was more to it than that. I admire you and the others for stepping up to protect the people in town."

He felt his cheeks flushing hot. "Don't paint

me as some kind of hero, Hailey. The fire department was short on volunteers and needed more people to volunteer. It only made sense that I should help out. I know Jim hates the choice I made, and I really don't like to worry him. However, the work is satisfying and important."

She stopped to wave at a few people before speaking again. "Did you ever think about becoming a full-time firefighter? You know, instead of joining the family business?"

This conversation was treading on treacherous ground. He tried to come up with an answer that wouldn't reveal too much about a sore subject. Unfortunately, the truth slipped out before he knew it. "Yeah, I did. When I was in high school, I went so far as to talk to the people at the county fire department about what kind of schooling I would need and all of that."

"How come you didn't follow through on it?"

He paused to think about how to explain. "Because I owed Jim and Rhonda. I couldn't walk away from the business and live with myself."

"Did you even discuss it with them?"

"No. It would've only hurt both of them, especially Jim."

To lighten the moment, he forced a smile. "Being a volunteer firefighter is the next best thing. I still get to drive the truck, blare the siren, and mess with the stoplights."

He tapped on the side of his helmet. "And don't forget how good I look when I'm all decked out in my gear."

She took the hint and let him veer off any more serious discussion. Instead, Hailey snapped a quick picture of him. "You're right about that. Like I said, I'll be the envy of all my friends back home when I show them the gorgeous firefighter I got to hang out with."

He laughed as she put the phone in her pocket. She smiled back at him, and then added one more comment. "I'm glad you found a way to follow your dream while also honoring the business your grandfather and Jim built together."

The admiration in her voice made him uncomfortable. "Again, the fire department really needed help, and unlike some of the others, I'm single with a job where I can set my own hours. If my situation changes at some point, I might have to walk away and let someone else step up to take my place. That's what Shay had to do when he adopted Luca. He still covers an occasional shift for us in a pinch, but he has other priorities now."

When the line of floats and vehicles suddenly picked up speed, he focused on his driving, grateful for an excuse to stop talking for a while. Hailey hadn't meant to tread on painful subjects, but some dreams died hard. By the time they arrived back at the staging area, he'd managed to tamp down his emotions again. Slowing to a stop, he parked the truck so Shay and the other volunteers could help all the kids to climb down. Then they kept the munchkins corralled until they were claimed by their parents. When the last one was gone, the firefighters and Luca returned to their seats on the truck. Once they got settled, Finn started the engine again and carefully steered the truck out of the parking lot and back to the station. There, he and Hailey helped make quick work of removing all of the Christmas decorations and putting them away.

Ryder came back just as Finn finished putting his gear back in his locker. "Hey, Ryder, I'm going to give Hailey a ride to Rikki's place. On the way back, I'm going to pick up lunch and dinner at the café. If you'd like, I can grab something for you, too."

"I'd appreciate that. I'll have whatever you're having."

When he reached for his wallet, Finn waved him off. "I've got it. You can buy next time."

"It's a deal." Then Ryder nodded his head in Hailey's direction. "Take your time. I can hold the fort until you're back."

"Thanks. I won't be gone long."

He grabbed his regular coat and caught up with Hailey, who was busy listening intently to whatever Luca thought she really needed to know about the fire truck. The little guy had definitely come out of his shell since he'd first arrived in Dunbar. Having lost his own parents at a young age, Finn knew better than most what that felt like. He really admired how Shay had stepped up to bat for the kid.

Speaking of whom, Shay waved to catch his attention. "Hey, Finn, gotta second?"

"Sure."

Shay led him over to the far corner of the garage. "You know my tavern is closed to the public on Sundays. Well, Titus and I got to talking about how it might be fun if a bunch of us got together there this Sunday evening for a private party. We're asking for a small donation to cover food and drinks. To keep costs down, I'll handle the grill to make burgers and stuff for everyone and pay one of my bartenders to cover the bar for the event. We'll crank up the jukebox so people can dance. Carli and Moira suggested we do a ten-dollar gift exchange. Evidently, there will be a prize for the cleverest gift and another for the most creative wrapping job. They also insisted on having an ugly

Christmas sweater contest, but participation in that will be optional."

Then he looked past Finn to where Luca was still talking to Hailey. "I don't know what the situation is between you and Hailey, but I thought you two might like to come. It's short notice, so don't feel bad if you already have plans."

"Sounds like fun. What time would we need to be there?"

"Considering almost everybody has to work on Monday, we thought we'd start at five o'clock and end by ten. You also wouldn't have to stay for the whole time. Bring Jim, too, if you want."

"He doesn't much like going out at night these days, but I'll give you a call after I have chance to talk to him and Hailey."

Shay clapped Finn on the shoulder. "I hope we see you there. Now I need to grab my kid and head home."

When he stopped to collect Luca, Hailey said something to the boy that had him laughing and then headed in Finn's direction. "I'm ready to go if you are."

"It looked like Luca was giving you quite the lecture on how we operate around here."

"All I can say is that is one very bright little boy. I'd love to have him in my class."

They started toward his truck. "I don't think you ever said what grade you teach."

"I teach at an elementary school, but the grade level varies from year to year. It all depends on where they need me. I was assigned to a third-grade class this term, which is a fun age. They're old enough to work independently, but they still get excited when I put stickers on their graded homework."

"I bet you're looking forward to getting back to them."

He was surprised when she sighed. "Yeah, sort of. After being gone this long, it will be like starting a brand-new school year. Even if the long-term substitute tried her best to duplicate how I do things, there are bound to be differences. That means the kids will have to learn a whole new routine when I take over again."

"They'll be glad to see you, though."

"I hope so. I only had them for a short time before I started my leave of absence."

He waited until they were on their way to Rikki's place to bring up Shay's invitation. "I know I mentioned that we should go to Shay's tavern one night while you're here. Well, it looks like we're going to get the chance. Barnaby's is normally closed on Sunday, but Shay is hosting a private holiday party for his friends. He invited us to come."

To his surprise, she hesitated instead of immediately accepting the invitation. "Look, it's okay if you don't want to go or have other plans. He'll understand, especially on such short notice."

"That's not it. I don't have other plans, but I thought you might. If there's someone else you'd prefer to go with, I'd certainly understand. I've already commandeered a lot of your time since I've been here, and I can always hang out with Jim."

"Actually, Shay said Jim would be welcome to come. I said I would ask him, but I'm pretty sure he'll say no. He doesn't much like going out at night anymore."

Finn glanced in her direction before continuing. "As for me, I'm not seeing anyone special right now if that's what got you worried. If you'd like to go to the party, I think you would enjoy it."

"If you're sure, it does sound like fun. I can't remember the last time I went dancing."

"Same here." Feeling better about the situation, he decided to tease her a bit. "A word of warning—if you have some steel-toed boots, you might want to wear them to protect your toes until I knock the rust off my dancing skills."

Hailey gave him a long look. "Don't forget—

I've seen your dancing skills, and they're not all that rusty."

"If you say so, but don't say you weren't warned."

"Duly noted."

They'd reached the bed-and-breakfast. When he pulled into the driveway, Hailey started to get out of the truck, but then hesitated. "Do we need to bring anything to the party?"

"Nope. Shay is organizing all of the food and drink in exchange for a small donation. We're encouraged to wear an ugly Christmas sweater—which you've got covered." He made a point of eyeing her outfit and they both laughed. "There's also going to be a ten-dollar gift exchange, so we'll need to make a quick trip to one of the shops in Leavenworth tomorrow morning to pick something up. There would be a lot more choices there than here in town. He also mentioned there will be a prize for cleverest gift and one for the most creative wrapping. Not sure what that last one would look like."

"I'll give it some thought tonight. What time do you get off in the morning?"

"Unless I'm out on a call, I should be done around nine, but I'll need to go home first to change clothes. I'll text to let you know when I'm on my way to pick you up to go shopping."

"Okay." She got out of the truck and looked back at him. "Stay safe out there tonight. Jim isn't the only one who'll be worrying."

Then she gently closed the door and walked away.

He sat and watched until she disappeared into the bed-and-breakfast. Okay, then. Now he had two people worrying about him. Perhaps he should feel guilty about that, and he did—at least a little. But the truth was guilt was only a small part of the tangle of emotions he was feeling. For some inexplicable reason, he rather liked knowing that Hailey cared enough to be concerned.

With that confusing thought, he headed for the café to pick up the food he'd promised to get for himself and Ryder. Maybe taking Hailey to the party was a mistake. For one thing, he suspected Shay assumed that the two of them were something more than friends, and it was likely his other friends were also thinking along those same lines. All things considered, that shouldn't have surprised him. After all, they'd been spending a lot of time together since she'd come to town.

More time, in fact, than he'd spent with any other woman in ages. It had been even longer since he'd had anything that approached being a serious relationship. He'd had a long-term relationship with a girl that started back in high school. From the beginning, he'd thought she was the one he would spend the rest of his life with. After all, they both had deep roots in Dunbar and so much in common. He was a small-town boy, and Brooke was a small-town girl—what could go wrong?

As it turned out, everything. He'd started working with Jim while Brooke left to attend college on the other side of the state. It wasn't until she was about to graduate that she finally told him that she had outgrown both him and life in a small town. He might have tried to convince her to change her mind, but there was no point. She was already wearing someone else's ring. The last he'd heard, Brooke and her husband were living in Chicago and had a couple of kids.

He'd eventually started dating again, but so far none of the relationships had lasted more than a few months. Next time around, he'd sworn he wouldn't settle for anything less than the kind of relationship that Jim and Rhonda had.

That brought him back to thinking about Hailey. Circumstances may have thrown them together, but it wasn't as if he'd done anything to avoid the multiple outings they'd been on. In fact, now that he thought about it, he'd actually been looking for ways to spend more time in her company. The question was why, especially when his life would be that much simpler when she was gone.

Then a small voice in the back of his mind whispered that *simpler* wasn't the right word. That *emptier* or even *lonelier* would be a better description.

Deciding that was something better left to ponder while he was alone in the night, he parked by the café and hustled inside to pick up meals for him and Ryder. At least feeding a friend was uncomplicated, and he needed that right now.

CHAPTER SIXTEEN

Hailey frowned as she studied her image in the mirror over the dresser. Finn had assured her that Shay's party was supposed to be casual, especially since most people would be competing in the ugliest sweater contest. She and Finn had considered giving that a hard pass, but they'd finally decided to go all in on their choice of attire. The oversize red sweater covered in jingle bells that she'd worn in the parade was big enough to fit Finn, and she'd picked up a smaller one in green for herself. She'd also bought plastic holiday earrings in the shape of green and red striped mittens.

She turned her head side to side to check her makeup and hair. The blue-gray shadow she'd chosen set off the color of her eyes, so that was a plus. She'd also put in extra effort on her hair, pulling it back in a French braid.

"Well, that will have to do."

Especially since it was time to head downstairs to wait for Finn. She put on her coat and grabbed her purse before stepping out into the hallway where she paused to listen. The house was so quiet that it felt as if she were alone in the old Victorian. Rikki and Max had left two hours earlier to do some shopping before heading over to the party. Carter was upstairs in their private quarters watching movies with the teenage girl who was babysitting him for the evening.

Hailey reached the lobby and finished buttoning her coat just as Finn stepped onto the front porch. She didn't wait for him to knock before joining him outside. She held up the decorative bags that held their gifts for the exchange. "The wrapping isn't exactly fancy, so I wouldn't expect to win any prizes."

He studied the gift bags and the strands of curly ribbon that trailed down from their handles. "They definitely look better than anything I would've managed to do."

She wasn't sure that was the compliment he thought it was. "Thanks... I think."

Earlier Rikki had asked Hailey to make sure the front door was locked when she left. After taking care of that, she held on to Finn's arm as they walked down the snow-covered sidewalk toward the driveway. "I still can't believe how early it gets dark here."

"I'd say you'd get used to it eventually, but I'm not sure that's true. We go to work before the sun comes up and return home in the dark. It can get pretty gloomy this time of year."

"Well, I'm betting this evening won't be gloomy. I'm actually pretty psyched about this party, even though I still feel a little bad about leaving Jim home alone. I know it was his choice, and he assured me he didn't mind. Something about us only being young once, and we shouldn't spend all of our time babysitting an old man."

Finn shrugged his shoulders. "I'd take him at his word. Jim rarely pulls his punches. If he was unhappy, we'd both know it."

He was probably right about that. She waited until they were in the truck and underway to ask, "How many people do you expect to be there tonight?"

"I'm not sure. Shay never said who all he'd invited. I'm guessing you've probably met a lot of them already."

That was a relief. She didn't want Finn to feel as if he needed to stick right by her side all evening if he had friends he wanted to hang out with. On the other hand, she really hoped he'd been serious about wanting to dance with her.

A short time later, they pulled into a parking lot outside of a rustic building with an unlit neon sign over the door that simply read Barnaby's. Finn parked next to a row of other vehicles and then came around to help her down out of the cab. They joined a small group of people heading for the entrance of the bar. She recognized the two brothers from the fire department and the chief of police and his wife. There was a note taped to the door that announced that the evening's event was a private party and to knock to gain entry.

Finn rapped his knuckles on the door. Seconds later, it opened just a crack. Shay peeked out and then swung it open all the way. "Come on in out of the cold, everybody. When you're ready, you can place your drink orders at the bar. I don't have any servers here tonight since we're actually closed for business, but the bartender will get you set up with whatever you need. We have soft drinks, alcohol, coffee and hot chocolate."

Boy, that last one sounded good. Hailey wasn't much of a drinker, and hot chocolate would hit the spot on a chilly night like this one. Finn pointed toward the back corner. "Let's grab a table over near the dance floor."

He took her hand as they made their way across the room. She was relieved to see Rikki and Max at a nearby table and that Titus and Moira had just walked in the front door. Once they reached an empty table, Finn stripped off his coat and hung it on the back of his chair. "I'll go put our gifts under the tree and then see about getting us something to drink. What would you like?"

"Hot chocolate would be great, preferably with either marshmallows or whipped cream on top."

"I'll be right back."

A minute later Moira appeared by the table. "Mind if Titus and I join you?"

Hailey smiled and nudged the chair next to her out from the table. "Please do."

Moira sat down. "I'm glad you and Finn could make it despite the short notice."

"It was nice to be invited. I really appreciate how welcoming everyone has been since I arrived. I'm also glad Finn doesn't seem to mind me tagging along with him."

"On the contrary. Titus said Finn has enjoyed showing you around."

"That's nice to hear, especially since I appeared in his life with no warning at all."

"That wasn't your fault. From what I understand, Jim had every chance to tell him and didn't."

"He also didn't tell me about Finn. I understood him not saying anything to anyone before we got the DNA tests back, but he's never explained why he kept my existence a secret after that."

"Maybe he was afraid you wouldn't actually show up or something." Moira shrugged. "It's all worked out, though, so that's good. On a different subject, I was out on patrol during the parade yesterday, but I heard you got to ride in the fire truck and blast the siren. I bet you enjoyed that."

"Yeah, it was a lot of fun! I guess you've had plenty of experience yourself with sirens in your line of work."

Moira offered her a wry smile. "True enough, but rarely for fun."

Hailey laughed. "Yeah, I can see how that would be true."

Titus dropped down in the seat next to his wife's. "Hi, Hailey. Is Finn still keeping you busy washing bike parts for him?"

"Not the past couple of days, but I thought I would stop by the shop again tomorrow afternoon for a little while. I'm not used to having so much free time on my hands, and I like to feel useful. Jim called to let me know he has an appointment of some kind and won't be home until close to dinnertime."

She glanced around to see what was keeping Finn. He was talking to a young woman working behind the bar. The pretty brunette batted her eyes and laughed at something Finn said as she prepared the drinks he'd ordered. Hailey forced herself to look away when watching the interchange sent a surge of what felt suspiciously like jealousy zipping through her. She shoved it down deep inside, knowing she had no claim on Finn. Yes, she found him attractive and liked him a whole lot more than she should. He'd definitely carved a place for himself in her heart. However, it wasn't as if she could stick around Dunbar long enough to explore the possibility of any kind of romantic relationship with the guy. If Finn wanted to flirt with someone who looked way too young for him, that was his business.

Something of what she was thinking must have shown on her face, because Titus glanced back over her shoulder to see what had caught her attention. His eyebrows shot up, but then he quickly did a far better job of schooling his expression than she had. No doubt he'd mention the interaction to his wife at some point, but at least he wasn't going to embarrass Hailey by bringing it up now.

Desperate for a safe topic of conversation, she pointed toward Titus's sweatshirt, which had a caricature of a tough-looking chef that looked suspiciously like its wearer. Underneath the picture were the words "You'll eat what I fix and like it. Merry Christmas."

"Nice sweatshirt, Titus. It looks just like you and the big cleavers are a nice touch."

He gave his wife a dark look. "Moira sprung it on me when she told me we had to participate in the ugly sweater contest. I have no idea where she got it, but it makes me think this shindig wasn't as spur-of-the-moment as I was led to believe."

His wife looked pretty proud of herself. "Actually, I bought it a month ago. I was going to make you wear it to dinner at my mom's on Christmas Eve, but this was an even better occasion."

Moira's own sweater was only slightly more subdued. The colors were a garish mix of red, green and white with words written in bright orange, which simply said, "I even make this ugly Christmas sweater look good!"

Hailey glanced down at her own. "On the upside, Titus, at least you don't jingle with every step you take."

Titus watched as Finn finally started back toward their table. "So was it your idea or Finn's to wear matching outfits?"

"Actually that's just how it turned out. I bought the one he has on to wear over my winter coat when I rode in the fire truck yesterday.

It fits him better than it did me, so I went back to the store to see what else they might have. Seems there was an unexpected rush on buying Christmas sweaters, and this was the last one they had in my size."

Moira snickered. "I can't wait to hear all those bells jangling when the two of you hit the dance floor. You'll be your very own rhythm section."

Hailey hit her forehead with her palm. "I didn't even think about that."

Finn set her hot chocolate down in front of her and then took his seat. "Okay, what did I miss?"

She tugged on the front of her sweater, setting off the bells. "Moira kindly pointed out the racket you and I will make when we're out on the dance floor. How loud do you think we'll be?"

He pointed toward her cup. "Drink that while it's hot and then we'll find out."

She dutifully took a sip. "Oh, that's really good. She must have put a shot of espresso in it or something. I love mocha hot chocolate."

"If you decide you'd like a refill, I'll let Cassie know you want more of the same."

Meanwhile, he and Titus reached into the front pocket of their jeans and brought out small plastic bags filled with quarters. Moira picked up her husband's and studied it. "I take it you're in the mood to do a whole lot of dancing."

His mouth quirked up in a small smile. "Yep, and there's no time like the present."

He stood and offered Moira his hand, and they headed over to the jukebox. The two of them studied the selections for a minute or two before Titus began feeding quarters into the slot. When he was done, Moira pushed a series of buttons. Seconds later, the music started playing.

Hailey was relieved that the volume was loud enough to mute the sound of their jingle bells. She downed the last of her drink and set her cup aside. "You ready to show off your best dance moves?"

"Let's do it."

Moira had picked a country song, one that was perfect for them to dance like they had the other night in Jim's kitchen. This time there was no awkwardness, no struggle to find the right rhythm together. Finn spun her out and then back into his arms as they moved around the dance floor together until the song ended. The next one was a salsa, and Finn proved to be equally adept with the Latin dance style. Hailey managed to keep up with him, but the fast-paced rhythm left her a little breathless. Thank goodness the one after that was a slow ballad.

A few seconds in, however, she realized the slower pace presented her with a few problems of its own. For one thing, she could no longer blame the way her pulse was racing on the music. No, that stemmed directly from how nice it was to be cradled against Finn's broad chest as the two of them swayed to lyrics about old heartaches and lost loves. How long had it been since she'd enjoyed a night like this? The answer was simple—too long.

As if sensing the direction her thoughts had taken, Finn murmured, "I'm glad Shay decided to throw a party. This is nice."

"It is."

She looked up to meet his gaze. His dark eyes glinted in the dim light over the dance floor, his gaze dropping to focus briefly on her mouth. His eyes flared wide, as his head tipped down, narrowing the gap between them. She was afraid he was going to kiss her—and even more afraid that he wouldn't.

He was close enough now that his breath mingled with hers. She found herself rising up on her toes, trying to narrow the small distance that still separated them. Her eyes drifted closed as she waited for him to make the final move. She was almost sure he was about to do that when a loud, clanging noise rang out across the bar. The obnoxious racket brought everything to a screeching halt. Even the jukebox went silent.

Finn looked every bit as confused as she felt. He had several inches over her in height, which give him an advantage when it came to tracking down the disturbance. "What the heck?"

He gently turned her to face the other direction. What was Shay doing standing on top of the bar? When the murmuring in the room hadn't completely died off, he held up a pot in one hand and once again whacked it several times with a large metal spoon.

"Sorry, but I had to get your attention somehow." He held up a piece of paper. "I need all of you to step up to the bar in an orderly fashion to fill out one of these for your dinner orders. Write your name at the top and then mark how you want your burger cooked and what you want on it. The available sides are coleslaw, baked beans, French fries, onion rings and Tater Tots. Also, Titus donated a bunch of his mini pies for dessert, so you can pick the flavor you'd prefer, too. No guarantees on that, but we'll try. When your order is ready, Moira or Carli will call out your names. Raise your hand if you have questions."

When no hands appeared, he called out, "Okay, let's get to it."

"Do you want to try to shove our way to the

front of the line or let others go first to avoid the crush?"

"Ordinarily I would suggest the latter, but I don't want to risk them running out of Titus's pies."

"Good thinking."

Finn started working his way through the crowd as Shay jumped down off the counter. When they got there, she realized he'd set stacks of the forms at intervals along the length of the bar. Cade and Shelby had gotten there first and had already finished filling out their orders. They stepped aside to give her and Finn room to work on theirs. The bartender walked up and down on her side of the bar collecting the completed slips.

Once she picked up theirs, Finn led the way back to the table. Hailey wasn't sure if she was relieved or disappointed that Shay's announcement intervened before she and Finn could step over a line out on the dance floor that she wasn't sure they should cross. The music came back on before they reached their seats. Rather than head back onto the dance floor, Finn pulled out her chair for her. Leaning in closer so she could hear him over the music, he said, "I'll go see about getting us another drink. Do you want more hot chocolate or something else?"

"I'd like a soft drink. Whatever cola they have is fine."

"Got it. I'll be right back."

Hailey watched him approach the bartender. Maybe it was her imagination, but it was obvious the bartender he'd called Cassie was only too happy to wait on Finn again. Didn't it occur to the woman that if he was ordering two drinks it meant he was with someone? Maybe she didn't care. Regardless, it seemed inappropriate for the pretty brunette to be flirting while she was on the clock, but that may be the same streak of jealousy Hailey had felt earlier talking again.

To Hailey's surprise, Finn nodded and the woman immediately popped out from the end of the counter to follow him out onto the dance floor. Hailey gritted her teeth as the pair started dancing together, but Finn made no attempt to hold the other woman's hand. In fact, when the brunette moved closer to him, he immediately backed up, restoring the distance between them.

Okay, then. Hailey still wasn't happy, but she wouldn't throw a hissy fit when Finn finally returned to the table. Probably, anyway.

Deciding there was no use in torturing herself by watching their every move, she deliberately turned away to watch the hustle and bustle as Moira started calling out people's names when their orders were ready. She couldn't help but notice she wasn't the only one who had taken notice of Finn and his dance partner. A guy sitting at the end of the bar had his attention laser-focused on the pair. He was one of the two brothers she'd met briefly at the fire station. As if sensing her attention, he glanced in her direction. After finishing off his drink, he set the glass down on the bar and headed straight for her.

When he reached the table, he offered her a smile that didn't quite reach his eyes. "Hi, I'm Logan Calland. Finn introduced us at the fire station. Since he's otherwise occupied with Cassie, would you care to dance?"

It was tempting, but she didn't want to get drawn into whatever drama was going on between Logan and the pretty bartender. "I'm pretty sure I'm not the one you want to be dancing with."

This time his smile was a little more genuine. "I wish I could say you were wrong about that."

Before she could say anything in response, Moira called out, "Finn and Hailey, your order is up."

"Sorry, Logan, but I'd better go pick our meals."

He nodded in the direction of the dance floor.

"No need. Finn is already on his way to get them."

By that point, Cassie had noticed Logan watching her. When she gave him a hopeful smile, he deliberately turned his back and disappeared into the crowd. Hailey might have imagined the look of hurt on the other woman's face when Logan walked away, but she didn't think so. The couple clearly had a problematic past history, which was too bad. Logan seemed like a nice guy, and Finn obviously liked Cassie. Regardless, it wasn't Hailey's problem to solve. Instead, she smiled at Finn when he returned with their burgers and decided to focus on enjoying her dinner.

CHAPTER SEVENTEEN

Finn set a basket containing an enormous cheeseburger and a heap of sweet potato fries in front of Hailey. He then plunked down his own before returning to the bar for their drinks. After reclaiming his seat at the table, he offered Hailey an apologetic smile. "Sorry I abandoned you for so long. Cassie was going on her break and wanted to dance while she had a chance."

Hailey trailed a fry through the puddle of ketchup she'd just squirted onto her plate. "I take it she's an old…friend?"

He'd been about to take a bite out of his hamburger, but the way Hailey phrased that question had him setting it back down. Something about her tone left him confused. "Yeah. I went all the way through school with Cassie's older brother. She was a couple of years behind us, but sometimes he had to bring her with him when we were doing something because their parents both worked. That sort of made her an unofficial little sister to the rest of us."

He glanced toward the bar where Cassie was talking to Shay's wife. "She's home between semesters from college and asked Shay if he needed any extra help over the holidays. He hired her as a temp to cover shifts for some of his employees who wanted extra time off."

"That was nice of him."

Somehow Finn didn't think she really meant that, but he didn't push her for clarification. Instead, he asked, "How is your burger?"

"It's delicious."

"He also makes really great chicken wings, but you should be careful if you ever decide to try them. The heat level runs the full gamut from mild to scorching hot." He shuddered at the memory from the time he'd tried the hottest version. "Trust me, the hot ones will make a grown man cry."

Hailey gave him a considering look. "Are you speaking from experience?"

Even the memory of that night had him reaching for a cold drink. "Sadly, yes. Not one of my finer moments, that's for sure."

Titus had just returned to the table. "What he isn't telling you is that people usually only order the hottest level of Shay's wings to settle a bet."

Hailey turned her attention in Titus's direction. "So, have you lost any bets?"

"I'm proud to say I haven't, mainly because I don't get drawn into betting on something I can't control." He nodded in Finn's direction, his mouth quirked up in a small smile. "That, and I was here the night your boy there lost that bet. It happened right after I moved to Dunbar. I have no desire to bite into something that sets off a five-alarm fire in your mouth. Basically, I learned from Finn's mistake."

Finn growled, "Glad to have been of service."

Hailey didn't even try to hide her amusement from him. "That just leaves one question. Did you also learn from your mistake?"

"I did." He took another swig of his ice water. "It took me a long time to work up the courage to try even the mildest ones again. Next time we come, we'll order a basket of them so you can see how good they are."

"It's a deal."

Moira finally joined them. "Whew! I thought we'd never get everyone served. At least Shay has shut down the grill, so he and Carli can enjoy the rest of the evening. Once everyone finishes their meal, we'll start the sweater contest and then do the gift exchange."

All of that sounded like fun even though Finn kind of hoped they could get through all of that quickly. He wanted a lot more time out there on the dance floor with Hailey and had a bag full of quarters burning a hole in his pocket. He'd even let her pick out most of the songs, but he'd hold back a few quarters to ensure there would be a couple of slow dances toward the end of the evening.

Not that he didn't enjoy the faster-paced numbers, too. He hadn't been kidding when he'd warned Hailey that his dancing skills might be kind of rusty, and he was surprised how easy it was to get back up to speed. Considering how rarely he dated, it had been ages since he'd spent an evening out on the dance floor. Moreover, he couldn't remember a time when a woman had felt so right in his arms. He very much wanted to know if that had been a fluke.

With that in mind, he concentrated on finishing his meal. The sooner they were all done eating, the sooner they could get on with the rest of the night's festivities. He was just reaching for his dessert when he happened to see Hailey taking the first bite of her coconut cream pie. Her eyes drifted shut as she slowly savored the creamy goodness. His gaze remained riveted on her as she repeated the process with her second bite.

She finally realized that not only was Finn watching her every move, but so were Titus and

Moira. Her face turned rosy pink in embarrassment. "What?"

Moira answered before Finn could even figure out what to say. "We shouldn't have been staring. Everybody loves Titus's pies, but you seem to take that enjoyment to a whole new level. Sorry if we made you uncomfortable."

Thankfully, Hailey waved off Moira's concern. "Don't worry about it."

Then she grinned at Titus. "Of course, if you want to make it up to me, some more of this coconut cream pie would be a good way to go about it."

Titus's rusty laugh rang out. "It's a deal. Just call the café when you want to collect, and I'll make sure to set one aside for you."

Finn tugged on Hailey's sleeve. He waited until she turned to look at him to stage-whisper, "Please tell me you're going to share it with me. Well, and I guess Jim. It would be rude for us to eat it in front of him."

She rolled her eyes, but then laughed. "Fair enough."

Hailey started to say something else, but then she pointed toward the bar. "Everybody, cover your ears. Shay is up on the bar and about to start banging on his pot again."

Sure enough, he walloped it half a dozen times before the crowd grew quiet. "Okay, folks. First, we're about to start the sweater contest. We have a panel of volunteers who will be judging the entries. Prizes will be awarded to the top three entries."

He reached down and picked up three envelopes and a bottle of wine. "If you've chosen to participate, please line up along the wall over there. The judges will view the entries and either send you back to the end of the line for the second round of voting or dismiss you to return to your seat. Once they winnow the possibilities down to the final three, we'll announce the winners."

Carli tugged on Shay's arm and said something. He nodded and held up his hand to regain everyone's attention. Pointing in the direction of the Christmas tree in the corner. "I'm being told that Santa has arrived and will pass out the gifts from under the tree. Be sure to stop by to get one. I also want to congratulate Max Volkov for winning the wrapping contest. We don't know what's inside the package he brought, but whatever it is must be shaped a lot like the Trillium Nugget."

He paused as he gave Max a suspicious look. "Well, unless he decided to make off with the nugget again, which means what's in the package might be the real deal."

Max laughed and called out, "Guess you'll

have to wait until someone opens the package to find out!"

As Shay climbed back down off the bar, Finn looked at Hailey. "Are we in or are we out?"

"I say we're in."

With that, they stood up and headed for the line forming up across the room. Titus clearly didn't want to participate, but Moira wasn't having it. "You promised. Besides, I happen to know that's a bottle of Malbec."

She arched an eyebrow as she trailed her fingertips down the side of his face. "We both know how much you enjoy a good bottle of Malbec."

A slow smile spread over Titus's rugged face. "I do indeed."

The look Titus and Moira exchanged was the kind married couples sometimes gave each other that Finn could only envy. One where they shared a memory, a special connection between them that no one else knew about. It reflected a depth of knowledge that came from their love for each other. Jim and Rhonda had always shared that kind of connection, too.

Finn hoped someday to find a little of that for himself. An unexpected image of him and Hailey dancing in Jim's kitchen popped into his head, followed by so many others—the two of them picking out the Christmas tree, working side by side at the shop, and cooking dinner together. It wasn't hard to imagine a future filled with so many more of those moments.

Too bad she wouldn't be sticking around long enough to explore that possibility.

Meanwhile, the line of contestants moved forward at a pretty fair clip with more people heading back to their tables than returning to the end of the line. Finn wasn't at all disappointed when the judges thanked them for joining in the fun and let them go. Titus was less pleased when he and Moira were sent back to go through the process again.

Finn offered him a cocky wave and followed Hailey toward the Christmas tree where Santa was posing for pictures as he handed out the gifts everyone had brought to the party. They stood on each side of Santa, held up the packages he'd given them, and dutifully smiled for the camera. From there, they headed back to the table where they sat down to unwrap their gifts.

Finn's package contained a T-shirt with Santa riding a motorcycle emblazoned on the front, wishing everyone a Merry Christmas. Considering what he did for a living, it was the perfect gift. It was even his size—an extra-large. That left him wondering how it happened that he ended up with that particular gift. Maybe somehow Santa's choices weren't so random after all, not that he was complaining. He was pretty sure Jim would get a kick out of seeing him wear it.

At the same time, Hailey was checking out what Santa had given her. The gift bag contained a large container of hot chocolate mix and an envelope. Her face lit up and she whooped and did a little jig when she peeked inside the envelope. "It's a gift certificate for a free pie at Titus's café! That's two of his wondrous creations he owes me now."

He understood her enthusiasm. "Better put that somewhere safe. You wouldn't want someone else to put it in his pocket. Totally by accident, of course."

She gave him a narrow-eyed look. "You wouldn't dare."

Holding up his hands, he tried to look shocked by her accusation. "Hey, I wasn't talking about me. I figure I stand a good chance of getting a piece of that pie honestly."

Still looking suspicious, she folded the coupon and stuffed it into her purse. "What do we do next?"

Reaching into his own pocket, he pulled out a few quarters. "Let's get the dancing started again."

He liked that Hailey didn't hesitate and headed straight for the jukebox. She fed the coins into the slot and then made quick work of picking songs. The first one started to play as the two of them joined the growing crowd out on the floor. They started off dancing without touching as they got lost in the rhythm of the music. Halfway through the second song, the jukebox suddenly shut off as Shay once again climbed the bar to announce the winners of the ugly sweater contest.

Finn was standing next to Hailey when someone accidentally jostled her hard enough to knock her off-balance. To prevent it from happening again, Finn stepped behind her, wrapped his arms around her waist and held her close to his chest. He liked the way she immediately leaned back against him and relaxed as the three winners filed up to where Shay was waiting. Once they were in position, he started speaking. "Here are the winners of the first, but hopefully not the last, Ugly Christmas Sweater Contest."

He held up the first envelope. "Third place goes to Jody Livick."

After a brief round of applause, Shay moved on. "Second place goes to Trace Calland."

When Trace collected his prize, Shay held up the third envelope and the bottle of wine. "And finally, first prize goes to Titus Kondrat!"

The crowd went wild, applauding like crazy probably for no other reason than that being at the center of all of that attention clearly made Titus so uncomfortable. When Finn put two fingers in between his lips and let loose with a shrill whistle, Titus gave him a look that made it clear that there would be retribution headed Finn's way when he least expected it.

Moira finally took pity on her husband. She took him by the arm and gently led him away. Hailey might have worried that they'd managed to offend Titus. Then she noticed he was grinning as he and Moira headed back toward the dance floor.

When the jukebox resumed playing again, the song was a ballad that spoke of two people dancing together and wondering where the night would lead them. Finn wasn't sure if it was one of the songs that Hailey had chosen or if someone else picked it, not that it mattered. Right then, holding her close in his arms felt as if the lyrics had been written with the two of them in mind.

He loved the way Hailey tucked her head under his chin as the song played. Their last slow dance had almost ended with them kissing. Unfortunately, that moment had been shattered when Shay had started banging away on a pot to get everyone's attention.

But now, Finn was pretty sure that he wouldn't let another chance pass them by. No sooner had the thought crossed his mind than Shay's voice rang out across the room once again. "In case some of you haven't noticed, some unnamed person or persons hung bunches of mistletoe on the ceiling in various places in the bar. Feel free to look up and see if you happen to be lucky enough to be under one. Just know that it's strictly up to you if you want to take advantage of the situation, but time is of the essence. The cleanup crew will be leaping into action soon, so they can get home at a decent hour. If anyone wants to stick around and help, it would be much appreciated. The more the merrier."

As soon as he quit speaking, the lights overhead dimmed except for a few centered over the bar itself. The shadows offered everyone a small bit of privacy as the music continued to play. Finn leaned down to whisper near Hailey's ear, "How about it? Shall we see if we're under the mistletoe?"

He loved that she didn't hesitate to look up. Sure enough, there was a bundle of mistletoe directly above them, but he wasn't sure luck had anything to do with it. How had he not noticed earlier that there were similar bundles scattered about every five feet across the entire ceiling. Someone had been busy.

Still, it would be a real shame not to honor the tradition. "So, what do you say?"

Hailey's hands had been resting on his shoulders, but now she slid them up higher to encircle his neck as she rose up on her toes and offered him a siren's smile. "I say yes."

Finn brushed his lips across hers, not sure how far to go with this. When she made a small sound of disappointment, he tried again, this time lingering longer. She murmured her approval as he deepened the kiss even as they continued to gently sway together until the song came to an end. A few seconds later, the lights flickered on and off briefly before returning to full brightness.

Finn had no idea how he looked, but Hailey's pretty face was flushed as she stared up at him before taking a step back. That left him feeling confused about what to do next. Should he apologize? If so, for what exactly? Because he was sure she'd been right there with him, enjoying the kiss as much as he had. Then she smiled at him as she took his hand in hers, and the world righted itself again.

CHAPTER EIGHTEEN

WITH SO MANY people pitching in, it didn't take long to restore order in the bar while Titus and Shay cleaned up the kitchen. When the pair finally reappeared, Shay looked pleased as he scanned the room. "Wow, you people did a great job. Thank you."

Finn shook his head. "No, we should be the ones thanking you instead. You and everyone who helped you pull all of this off on such short notice. It was a genius idea, and we had a blast."

Shay pegged him with a sly look. "For that, I'm putting you at the top of my list to help organize the next one."

Finn didn't even hesitate. "It's a deal."

Shay turned his attention in Hailey's direction. "And how about you? Should I put your name on the list, too?"

How was she supposed to answer that? Yes, she wanted to be on that list, but right now she had no idea where she'd be spending Christmas next year. Even if she did return to spend the holidays with her grandfather again, there was always the possibility that Finn would be dating someone else. She was already amazed that a great guy like him was currently unattached. The idea of seeing him with another woman didn't exactly set well with her, especially after the kiss they'd just shared.

In fact, it was a shock how much she hated the whole idea. It hit her then that her feelings for him had somehow crossed the line from liking him...to maybe even loving him. That realization hit her hard, leaving her badly shaken. Doing her best to maintain her composure, she hedged her bets when she finally answered Shay. "If I'm in town, I'd be glad to help."

"Good. I'll pencil you in."

While Shay seemed content with her answer, Finn was a different matter. He didn't say anything, but the strong hint of tension around his eyes made it seem as if her answer had struck a nerve. Maybe she wasn't the only one fighting some strong feelings. This wasn't the time or place for questions, but maybe he'd explain his reaction on their way home. By that point, everyone had collected their personal belongings and headed for the door. She and Finn walked out with Rikki and Max. When the couple offered her a lift back to the bed-and-breakfast, she accepted to save Finn a trip.

Even so, he walked with her to their car. "What are your plans for tomorrow?"

She'd been thinking about that herself. Avoiding him would only raise questions she didn't want to answer, and she needed to know if she would feel the same about him tomorrow. "Would it be okay if I hang out with you at the shop in the afternoon? I'm supposed to see Jim in the morning, but then he has to leave for an appointment. I offered to take him, but he said he could drive himself since it was here in town."

Finn finally managed a small smile. "Come by anytime. I'm expecting another parts delivery that you can unpack, and there's a bin full of dirty parts with your name on it. If you're not in the mood to work, you can always sit at the desk and read."

"Sounds like fun. I'll see you after lunch."

He took a small step toward her. For a second, she thought maybe he was going to kiss her again, but the sound of Max and Rikki getting into the car had him backing away. "Tonight was fun."

"Yeah, it was." In fact, it was the best time she'd had in recent memory. Funny, she'd come to Dunbar to meet her grandfather, and she was so very glad she now had Jim as part of her life.

But the special connection she felt for Finn had allowed her to set her grief aside long enough to enjoy the beauty of the season and to make new friends.

"Thank you for tonight, Finn. It meant a lot to me."

"To me, too." He reached out to touch her face ever so gently. "See you tomorrow."

Then he surprised her with a hit-and-run kiss and then opened the back passenger door for her. Once she was safely inside, he disappeared into the night. On the way back to the bed-and-breakfast, she found herself smiling. His parting kiss wasn't anything like the one they'd shared on the dance floor, but it wasn't any less special.

HAILEY GOT A later start on Monday morning than she'd meant to and hoped it wouldn't upset Jim this time. When she arrived at his house, he wasn't in his usual spot in the living room. She finally located him upstairs in the small bedroom that did double duty as his home office. He was busy shuffling through a stack of papers, shoving some into a worn leather briefcase and others back into the two-drawer filing cabinet next to the desk.

Jim muttered something under his breath as he picked up another legal-sized file folder and started thumbing through it. When he still hadn't noticed her standing in the doorway after several seconds, she cleared her throat to catch his attention. He had been so focused that he nearly jumped out of his skin and scattered the papers all over the desk. Shooting her a distinctly crabby look, he quickly gathered up all the files and stuck them into his briefcase. "You shouldn't sneak up on people like that."

"Sorry I startled you, Grandpa. Maybe I should go back downstairs since you're busy. Would you like me to bring you a cup of coffee or anything?"

"No, that's all right, although a fresh cup of coffee does sound good about now. I'll be down shortly."

"I'll see you then."

She returned to the kitchen and started the coffee. With that done, she checked the time. Jim usually ate lunch pretty early and probably needed to leave for his appointment soon. After fixing some sandwiches, she opened some canned soup to heat up when he came downstairs.

It was another twenty minutes before Jim finally appeared in the doorway, briefcase in hand. "Sorry that I snapped at you upstairs. I had a lot on my mind and didn't hear you come in."

"No problem. I should've called your name as soon as I came up the steps."

He made his way to the table. "Thanks for making lunch. I appreciate it."

"I thought you might want to eat before you had to leave."

She glanced at the briefcase and wondered exactly what kind of appointment he had. Considering Finn's concern about Jim's overall health, she'd assumed it was a doctor's visit, but that didn't appear to be the case. It was tempting to ask him what was going on, but she decided against it. If he wanted her to know what he was up to, he would've told her by now. Maybe Finn knew who Jim was meeting with, but she didn't think so.

"Have a seat." She picked up the coffeepot and poured each of them a cup of coffee. "The soup is almost ready."

As she set his coffee on the table, she noticed he'd put on a tie before coming downstairs. "You're looking pretty snazzy. That shirt-and-tie combo brings out the color of your eyes."

He glanced down at the dark blue shirt. "Thanks. Rhonda said the same thing when she bought them for me."

Now that she thought about it, this was the

first time she'd seen Jim wear anything other than jeans and a flannel shirt. It made her even more curious about what kind of appointment warranted dressing up for the occasion.

"Looks like the soup is boiling."

She hustled back to the stove where the soup had been just seconds from boiling over. "Oops, sorry. I got lost in thought there for a second."

"No problem."

After setting the sandwiches on the table, she ladled the soup into bowls and set one in front of Jim and the other at her spot. Jim dug right in to his meal, leaving her no choice but to do the same. She couldn't help but suspect that there was a reason he was being so mysterious about what he was up to today. When he finished the last of his lunch, he put his dishes in the sink. After checking the time, he sat back down at the table.

"I've still got a few minutes before I have to go. How was the party at Barnaby's last night? Did you have fun?"

She smiled at the memory. "Yes, I did."

Jim enjoyed her description of the ugly sweater contest, especially when she told him about some of the more memorable entries. He laughed out loud when she told him about the one that garnered Titus the first prize. "There was a lot of dancing, too. Everyone seemed to really enjoy themselves."

Then she shared one of her favorite parts—the fact that Titus now owed her two whole pies. "Of course Finn says I have to share them with him and you as well. Something about it being rude if he and I were to eat them in front of you."

Jim's eyes twinkled with amusement. "That's generous of him. But keep in mind there's nothing written in stone about how big—or small—his slices have to be."

Hailey cracked up. "I love the way you think. I can't wait to point that out to Finn when I get to the shop this afternoon."

Jim reached for his briefcase. "I should head out. Tell Finn to come by for dinner, and we'll eat at six o'clock sharp. To keep things simple, I'll order pizza, which should make him happy."

"I'll let him know."

"Okay, then." Jim checked the time again. "I'll see you later."

He headed for the foyer to get bundled up. "You're welcome to stay here for the afternoon if you're tired of hanging out at the garage with Finn."

"I promised I'd give him a hand this afternoon. I might also go back to Rikki's to rest for a while before dinner."

"You could do that here if you want."

"That's true. But if you're not back yet, I won't be able to get in."

"I swear that I don't know where my head is lately." Jim had had his hand on the doorknob, but he stopped and turned back. "I've been meaning to give you a key to the house for days now. I always keep an extra one in the junk drawer in the kitchen. Let me see if I can find it for you real quick."

She waited where she was while he stalked back into the kitchen. She could hear him rummaging around in a drawer for several seconds before he called out, "Found it."

Jim dropped it in her hand on his way back to the door. "You can keep that."

"Thanks, Grandpa. Guess I'll see you later."

She watched from the front window as he backed his car out of the driveway and drove off. Once he was out of sight, she turned off all of the lights except one in the living room and the overhead light in the foyer. After a second's hesitation, she also turned on the porch light since it got dark so early.

With all of that done, it was time to head off to see Finn. Just the thought had her pulse picking up speed, not because she'd be spending the time unpacking boxes and washing greasy parts. No, it was knowing she'd be spending more time with Finn. Before leaving the house, she called the café to see if she could use her gift certificate to pick up a pie for dessert. Luck was with her. Not only was a pie available, they had coconut cream, her new favorite.

Today was a good day.

IT WAS PAST time to lock up the shop and head for Jim's place for dinner. The only reason Finn was still working was that he'd come to the unexpected realization that he was in serious trouble, and it was all Hailey's fault. Normally, when he first started working on a new design, he preferred to have the shop to himself and absolute quiet so he could concentrate. That meant no music blaring and no dancing together when a favorite song came on. Also, no interruptions to answer a bunch of random questions, and definitely nobody humming along to classic rock while she worked.

But none of that was true as long as it was Hailey sharing his space. He'd actually accomplished a lot more than he'd expected to today. At the same time, Hailey had quickly finished the entire list of chores he'd written out for her. The parts shipments were unpacked and put away. With that job done, she'd cleaned the parts in no time and handled a few phone calls like a pro. When she left to head back to Jim's house, the shop went back to normal—quiet and lonely. Just that quickly, his ability to focus disappeared. Instead, he kept finding himself staring at the door and wishing she would come walking back in. That was when the truth had hit him hard—he really, really liked having Hailey share his space. And that was a problem.

A big one, in fact.

Mainly because she wasn't going to stick around for much longer, although she hadn't yet set a specific departure date. Allowing for the amount of time it took to drive back to Missouri, she'd probably have to leave no later than a day or two past Christmas. Finn had known from the first that it was going to be awfully hard on Jim when she left. That was to be expected. After all, the man had only just found out he had a granddaughter, so having her living halfway across the country was far from ideal.

He also knew he'd be the one who had to help Jim through the rough days after Hailey finally drove out of town. What he hadn't figured on was that Jim wouldn't be the only one with a huge, empty hole in his heart when she left. He tried telling himself that if he hadn't given in to the temptation to kiss her, he would've been able to maintain some emotional distance. That argument didn't hold water, though. Even before they'd crossed that line, he'd known that she'd somehow managed to slip seamlessly into his life. Heck, even his friends had immediately welcomed her into their circle as if she belonged there.

There'd been something in the way she'd looked at him last night when they danced that made him think maybe she felt something for him, too. Even if that were true, he had no idea what to do about it. Heck, they'd only known each other for a short time. Who even thought about things like love and commitment that quickly? Did he even have the right to ask her to give up the life she'd known on the chance they might eventually figure out what was going on between them?

Would it be better to keep silent and let her leave as planned? Maybe not better, but definitely safer.

This was getting him nowhere, and it was time to get a move on.

Fifteen minutes later, he parked his truck out front of Jim's place. When Finn got out, he stopped for a few seconds to admire the Christmas lights that cast a warm glow up and down the street. It brought back other favorite memories from when he was a kid, like when Rhonda and Jim would drive him around on Christmas Eve to admire the decorations in town. They'd also pick a night to make hot chocolate and popcorn before watching a favorite holiday movie together. Such good times.

Feeling calmer, he started up the driveway just as a car pulled up in front. A teenager got out carrying two pizza boxes. Reaching for his wallet, Finn asked, "I can take those. How much do I owe you?"

"The bill is already paid. Mr. Morris took care of it when he called in the order."

Finn pulled out a twenty and handed to the kid. "Merry Christmas."

The kid gave the bill a wide-eyed glance. "Same to you, sir, and thank you for this."

He jumped back in his car and drove off. Having spread a little holiday joy, Finn headed toward the house. The door swung open right before he reached the porch. Jim didn't notice him at first. He was too busy watching the delivery boy drive off down the street. "Where is he going with our pizzas? It's bad enough that Finn is late."

Finn stepped into the light cast by the porch light. "Two things, Jim. The kid gave me the pizzas, and I'm not late."

"Fine."

Jim took the boxes from him and marched back into the house, leaving Finn to follow on his own. Inside, Hailey had been sitting on the sofa, but she got up after Jim walked by. She waited until he was out of sight before whispering, "I don't know what's going on, but he's been really restless—pacing the floor and staring out the window."

"Did he ever say who he went to see?"

"No, he didn't. All I know is that he dressed up for the meeting. He also took a bunch of papers with him."

Before Finn could process that much, Jim came back. "If you two want to hear about where I went today, you'll have to wait until after we eat. Afterward, I'll explain everything and then we can celebrate with that pie Hailey brought."

He turned and headed back into the kitchen. Knowing Jim, he'd only dig in his heels and refuse to tell them anything if they pressed him for information before he was ready to share. "We'd better do as he says."

If Jim figured they'd be in the mood to celebrate, he must think whatever he was going to tell them was good news. Crossing his fingers that was true, Finn followed his godfather into the kitchen.

CHAPTER NINETEEN

THE PIZZA WAS Finn's favorite, but he limited his intake to two slices to save room for dessert. He watched as Jim made serious inroads into the veggie-style he preferred while Hailey took a middle-of-the-road approach by eating a slice of each. As soon as she finished the last bite, Jim jumped up to clear the table and shove the leftover pizza into the fridge.

Something sure had the old man wound up. Finn had enjoyed seeing him take more interest in things since Hailey came to town, but this was definitely over the top. Instead of looking forward to the big reveal of Jim's news, Finn found himself fighting an unexpected sense of dread. Maybe that was unfair to his godfather, but all the secrecy bothered him. Rather than ask what was going on, he sat back in his chair and tried to look more calm than he actually felt at the moment.

Finn suspected he wasn't the only one with

questions. Whenever she didn't think Jim would notice, Hailey studied him with a slightly puzzled look on her pretty face. As soon as the last few things were loaded into the dishwasher, Jim returned to his seat. On the way, he grabbed his old briefcase off the counter and tossed it down on the table.

He looked at each of them in turn. "I've actually been surprised that neither of you even asked what kind of appointment I had scheduled today."

Hailey shrugged. "I figured when you wanted me to know, you would tell me. I didn't want to pry into your personal business."

Jim stared at Finn until he responded as well. "Same here."

He then pointed a knobby forefinger in Finn's general direction. "You probably assumed I had a doctor's appointment."

"No, actually I didn't. You've been having me drive you to those, and there weren't any on the calendar."

"True enough." Looking pretty pleased with himself, Jim rubbed his hands together and then unlatched the briefcase. "The fact is that I met with my lawyer today."

Okay, that had Finn sitting up straighter. Why would Jim need to talk to his lawyer? Was there something going on with his health that had him worried?

The announcement had Hailey looking as confused and concerned as Finn felt. He watched in silence as Jim pulled three legal-sized folders out of his briefcase. After checking the labels, he set one in front of Hailey, another in front of Finn, and kept the last one for himself. "We'll get to those in a minute. Before that, I have a few things I want to say to the two of you."

Finn leaned in closer to rest his elbows on the table. "We're listening."

"Okay, then. I guess I'll start with you, Finn. I know I haven't said this enough, but I appreciate how hard you've worked to keep C&M Custom Bikes a going concern. After all these years, the company remains widely respected for the quality of work and design that we turn out. I'm so proud of the way you've maintained the high standards that your grandfather and I set for the company. Thank you for that."

He paused again as if waiting for Finn to say something. "You're welcome, Jim. I learned from the best."

That was true. Jim had always been the creative member of the team while Finn's father and grandfather were the ones who had executed his designs. Early on in Finn's career, Jim had been a tough critic with exacting standards. There had been times Finn thought Jim had asked too much of him, but he'd also basked in the glow of his godfather's praise when he finally got something right.

Next, Jim turned to his granddaughter. "Hailey, having you appear from out of nowhere has been nothing short of a miracle. My only regret is that we didn't find each other years ago. I know your mother had her own reasons for the secrecy, but Rhonda and I would've loved watching you grow up just like we did Finn. That said, better late than never."

Hailey blinked several times as if fighting tears. "I'm glad I found the courage to reach out to you, Grandpa. I will admit that I almost didn't. My biggest fear was that even if the DNA tests proved we were related, you might not be happy about that. Instead, you and Finn have both made me feel welcome in your lives. That means so much to me."

By that point Jim looked a bit teary-eyed himself, not that Finn blamed him. To be honest, he also had some pretty strong feelings about Hailey's sudden appearance in their lives himself, but now wasn't the right time for that discussion. In fact, considering she'd be leaving in a few days, he wasn't sure there would ever be a right time. He wasn't into long-distance relationships, and she hadn't shown any inclination to change her mind about returning to Missouri.

It came as no surprise that Jim had similar thoughts on the situation. "I've never been a fan of family being scattered all over the place. That was one reason I hated it when our son decided to enlist rather than join the family business right out of high school. Maybe that was selfish thinking on my part, but your grandmother and I barely saw Nick after he reported for duty. Yeah, he got to see a good part of the world just like he wanted, but the two of us missed him every day he was gone."

He put his hand on Hailey's. "I don't want to miss you like that, too. I want you close at hand where we can share pizza and pie and whatever time I have left in this world."

Just that quickly, Hailey looked downright panicky. "I want time with you, too, but I have to go back home or I'll lose my job. I promise I'll come back to visit as often as I can."

Jim reached over and tapped the folder in front of her. "See, that's why I went to the lawyer. You might not need that job anymore when you could have one right here in Dunbar."

What on earth could he be talking about? Hailey sat there looking stunned and floundering to come up with a response. Finn knew exactly how she felt. To buy her some time, he pointed out the most obvious problem with Jim's thinking. "She's a teacher, Jim. You can't just snap your fingers and get her a job in our school district."

He aimed his next question directly at Hailey. "Even if there was an opening in a local district, would your teaching credentials be accepted in here in Washington?"

Hailey blinked several times as if clearing her mind. "I haven't actually checked, but I'm pretty sure that they would. A lot of states have mutual acceptance agreements if certain requirements have been met. For example, you have to have graduated from an accredited program with a degree at the right grade level. With my certificate, I can teach any grade in elementary school but not at the secondary level."

Turning back to Jim, she frowned. "Regardless, I promised my principal that I would be back in early January. I love the school where I work, and it's past time for me to get back to my students."

Finn figured he and Hailey might as well have been speaking pure gibberish for all the attention Jim was paying to what they were saying. Instead, he opened his folder. "I never said it was a teaching job. We have a family business, and you're family. If you'll open your folders, I've got big news for both of you."

Okay, from the way Jim avoided looking at Finn directly, Finn figured this news was bad. In fact, really bad. Feeling a bit sick, Finn stared at the folder and shook his head. There was no way he wanted to see what was inside, and he wasn't the only one. Hailey was looking at her own as if it were a rattlesnake poised to strike.

Jim nudged each of their folders a little closer to them. "Go ahead and open them. I want to share the good news, and then we can move on to celebrating with the pie."

Finn ignored the folder. "Jim, just tell us what you did. Now, please."

"Fine. I've decided that it's time to pass the baton to a new generation." He picked up the first in a stack of forms from his own file and tossed it into the middle of the table. "I had papers drawn up to sign my half of the business over to Hailey. As soon as we finalize everything, she can start receiving a salary from the company. I haven't worked out the exact amount yet, but obviously it will have to be close to what she makes as a teacher."

Finn's temper usually did a slow burn, but not this time. It went from mild concern to flaming fury between one heartbeat and the next. Lurching to his feet, he clenched his fists hard enough to hurt. "Hailey, I'm sorry, but could you please excuse the two of us for a few minutes? Jim and I need to talk, and it would be better if we did that alone."

He didn't know how he looked at the moment, but it must have been pretty bad from the way Hailey bolted to the dubious safety of the living room. All things considered, he wouldn't be surprised if she packed up and left instead of waiting around to see how their discussion turned out. If so, he'd track her down later and apologize for upsetting her. As mad as he was, he still knew that none of this was her fault.

As soon as she was out of sight, he focused all of his attention on his godfather. "Jim, have you lost your ever-loving mind?"

The old man glared right back at him. "Not at all, and I don't appreciate you ordering Hailey to leave the room like that. It was rude."

"I asked her to leave so she wouldn't get caught in the crossfire, and I said please."

Rather than give Jim time to respond, Finn sat back down and glared at him. Doing his best to keep his voice down to a dull roar, he asked, "Did it even occur to you to ask my opinion before you pulled a stunt like this? The last time I checked, the business was half mine. I should have some say in what happens to it."

Jim slammed his hands down on the table. "I

don't need your opinion when it comes to my half. I'm entitled to sign it over to my granddaughter if I want to. Period. No discussion needed. You can pay her the same salary you've been paying me, so it won't affect the bottom line at all."

"And what are you supposed to live on?"

The old man wasn't about to back down. "My finances are none of your business."

Finn prayed for patience. "Funny, I seem to remember that I'm the one who recently had to set up most of your bills on autopay to help you keep up on top of things."

That clearly scored a direct hit, because Jim's face flushed red. "Between my social security and savings, I'll be fine."

After a brief silence, Jim slowly drew a deep breath and then let it go. "Okay, you're right that I should've talked to you first. That said, I knew exactly how you would react to the idea, and not just because I promised you that my half of the business would come to you someday. Lord knows you've earned it."

He glanced toward the door to the living room. By the time he finally spoke again, all the defensiveness and anger had disappeared from his voice, and only sadness remained. "The problem is that I can hardly stand the thought of her leaving. I'm afraid I'll never see her again."

He pointed toward his folder of papers. "This was the only thing I could think of that might convince her to stay."

Finn paused to listen. So far, he hadn't heard the sound of the front door opening and closing, which meant Hailey was still in the other room. Keeping his voice barely above a whisper, he made a confession of his own. "I don't want her to leave, either, but blindsiding her like this wasn't the right way to do it."

Jim looked relieved that at least they were on the same page when it came to Hailey remaining in Dunbar. "Probably not."

Hailey stepped into the doorway. "Hey, guys, can I come back in now?"

Finn glanced back over his shoulder at the woman standing behind him. He did his best to muster up a welcoming smile as he pulled her chair out from the table in invitation. "Sure. I think we're all done yelling at each other."

Jim mumbled, "For now, anyway."

Hailey's smile looked a bit strained when she asked, "Would either of you want coffee? I'm going to get myself a cup."

Finn nodded, but Jim waved her off. "No, thanks."

While she poured their drinks, Finn tried to

judge how she was holding up. It was far from the first time that he and Jim had had a vocal disagreement on things, but it was the first time she was the topic of the discussion. On the surface, Hailey looked calm, but he couldn't help but notice how her hand shook as she set his mug down in front of him. He reached out to capture her hand in his and gave it a quick squeeze. "Sorry if I upset you."

"It's all right. Jim's announcement knocked both of us sideways." She settled herself at the table and sipped her coffee before finally addressing her grandfather. "Grandpa, I know you have good intentions, and it means a lot to me that you want me to stay that badly. I'll even admit that I am not looking forward to leaving."

"Then don't."

"I'm sorry, but it's not that simple." She was clearly struggling to find the right words to explain what she was thinking. "I have to go back. There are obligations that I can't ignore, and people who are depending on me to return."

She heaved a sigh. "For starters, I haven't finished settling Mom's estate, and some of that can't be done long-distance. I've packed up her personal stuff, but it's all still sitting in her condo. I was paralyzed by the thought of getting rid of anything, like it made her passing all too real for me. It still needs to be done."

Her eyes glittered with a sheen of tears. "Right before I left to come out here, the attorney notified me that the paperwork transferring the condo to my name had gone through. Now it's up to me whether I want to move into it myself. My other choices are to rent it or sell it outright. It's a really nice place, but I'm afraid living there would be a constant reminder that Mom is gone. If I do choose to keep the condo, then I'll need to pack up my apartment and move."

Finn scooted close enough to take her hand in his. "How does your contract with the school district work?"

"It runs until the end of the school year, around the last week of May."

Stubborn man that he was, Jim clearly wasn't about to give up. "If you sold the condo, you'd have the money to buy a place here."

Finn released his hold on Hailey and dropped his chin down to his chest in frustration. "Jim, stop pushing. She needs more time to think all of it through."

"I'm just saying…"

Hailey bit her lower lip for a few seconds before speaking again. "Like I said, I have a lot of decisions to make, and I need to go back to Missouri to do that."

Then she shot Finn a worried look as if she

had something she wanted to say but wasn't sure she should. Finally, she picked up the file folder with her name on it. "Grandpa, I'm honored that you would want to do this, but I can't accept it. I've enjoyed hanging out at the shop with Finn, but I'm not really of any use there. I'm not a designer or a mechanic. All I would be doing is taking money I didn't earn. I'm a teacher, and I love my job. It's all I ever wanted to do."

Jim didn't look happy, but he didn't argue. "I bet you're good at it."

"I'd like to think so."

Then she set her folder on top of Finn's. "I do have a suggestion I think you should consider. Instead of signing the business over to me, give it to Finn instead. He's earned it. And like me, there's something he's always wanted to do. If he owned the business, that would free him up to choose his own path forward."

Then Hailey gave Finn a pointed look, maybe questioning if he wanted to share his dreams with Jim himself or if he'd prefer she do it for him. When he didn't immediately jump into the conversation, she nodded and drew a breath to start speaking again. Suddenly, Finn knew what she was about to say; what he didn't know was how to stop her. Diving across the table to plant his hand over her mouth would work, but his body refused to cooperate. He couldn't even choke out a simple order like "No!" or "Don't!"

Meanwhile, Jim's attention bounced between the two of them, his eyebrows riding low over his eyes. Finn wasn't sure if the man looked confused or suspicious. Right now, it didn't matter as Hailey braced herself and started talking again.

"I wanted to be a teacher." She pointed toward her grandfather. "You and Finn's grandfather wanted to build motorcycles. My dad wanted to serve his country. We've all had dreams and made the choice to follow them. Do you have any idea what Finn would've done with his life if he'd ever been given a choice?"

She paused, letting the import of the question hover in the air between the three of them. Finn finally managed to string some words together. "Please drop it, Hailey. It won't change anything, and it's too late to matter."

The woman had definitely inherited her fair share of stubborn from her grandfather, because she didn't back down. "No, it's not, Finn."

Jim crossed his arms over his chest and stared at Finn. "Okay, I'll bite. What do you want to be when you grow up?"

Ignoring the question, Finn focused all of his attention on Hailey. "If I had wanted to have this discussion with him, I would have brought it up myself. You don't have the right to stir up even more trouble like this. Especially when you're still determined to go back to your life in Missouri, and I'll be stuck here dealing with the fallout."

Her grandfather jumped to her defense. "Show some respect, Finn. Don't talk to her like that!"

Hailey must have finally realized that she'd seriously overstepped her bounds. "No, Grandpa, he's right. I shouldn't have said anything."

Looking stricken, she turned back to face Finn. "I'm sorry... I didn't mean to..."

"You know what, I'm out of here."

Her sound of distress as he walked out of the kitchen cut through the fog of anger that clouded his thinking. He was the one overreacting now and knew it, but he couldn't seem to help himself. It was impossible to decide who he was mad at right now. Jim, for sure, for not talking to him first. Hailey for leaving when Finn very much wanted her to stay. And finally, himself for being too much of a coward to tell her that he loved her. He might not appreciate Jim's heavy-handed actions, but at least the old man had the courage to lay it all on the line.

Grabbing his coat, Finn walked out into the chill of the winter night, alone and with no idea of where to go next.

CHAPTER TWENTY

Hailey cringed as Finn walked away. What had she been thinking?

She folded her arms on the kitchen table and dropped her head down, wishing she was anywhere else than sitting there with her grandfather. It had never been her intention to cause trouble between him and Finn, but she should've guessed that was a possible outcome of the conversation.

After all, Finn was a grown man, and he had every right to be angry with her right now. If he'd really wanted to change careers, he'd obviously had ample opportunity to speak up long before now.

Jim finally cleared his throat. "Are you all right?"

Hailey closed her eyes as she lifted her head, not wanting to face the disappointment she fully expected to see reflected in his faded blue eyes. "No, I'm not. I didn't mean to upset Finn and hurt you like that. I foolishly thought I was helping."

"Your intentions were good, Hailey. I know that. For that matter, so does he." He scooted close enough to wrap his arm around her shoulders. "Besides, you weren't wrong."

She risked a quick peek at him to gauge if he was serious about that. "Really?"

He patted her on the shoulder and then sat back, maybe to give each of them some room to breathe. "Yeah, I admit I never asked Finn if he'd rather do something else with his life. I was afraid if I did, it might have ended up with him leaving this small town to pursue his own dreams like Nick did. When you've lost as many people you care about as Rhonda and I have, you like to keep the few who are left close at hand. I've had other friends, but none like Finn's grandfather. Bill was the brother I never had. The shop actually started off as his dream, and I kept it going to honor his memory."

The pain in Jim's voice finally gave Hailey the courage to really look at him. From the way he was staring off into the distance, it was clear his focus was on the past and people she'd never known. "When we lost Nick and Finn's parents in one fell swoop, I'm not sure I would've been able to carry on if it weren't for Finn. I couldn't close down the business when it was also his family's legacy, not just mine."

He swiped at his eyes to clear away a few tears. "To be honest, I always suspected Finn wanted to be a full-time firefighter. It's why I hated it when he joined the volunteers here in town. I was afraid it was his way of taking that first step away from our business. I had good reason to think that way, too. Back when it was time for him to decide what he wanted to do after high school, Rhonda warned me that he'd checked out several programs that offered the training to become an EMT and firefighter. If he'd insisted that's what he wanted, I'd like to think I would've found the strength to encourage him. The truth is, he never mentioned it to me, and I never asked."

Jim left the table and got the pie out of the refrigerator. After cutting three slices, he packed two up in plastic containers and set them aside. He brought the third back to the table and sat back down. "Again, I couldn't stand the thought of losing the last real connection to all of the people we'd both lost. If C&M Custom Bikes no longer existed, then neither did they. In the end, Finn took specialized classes in design and mechanics. He's been working at the shop ever since."

Jim ate a bite of his pie. It seemed odd that

he hadn't offered her any, but right now she wouldn't actually enjoy the wonder that was Titus's coconut cream pie. He pointed his fork in her direction. "I could be wrong, but I suspect you and Finn might be developing some strong feelings for each other."

She swallowed hard and struggled to give Jim an honest answer. She settled for trying to sidestep the issue. "We haven't known each other long enough to be thinking along those lines. Sorry, Grandpa, but people don't fall in love that fast."

That startled a laugh from her grandfather. "Listen to yourself, girl. Your own parents did exactly that. My son cared for your mother enough to put his whole life on hold while she finished college even though he knew we probably wouldn't approve. People only make huge sacrifices like that for people they love. Your mother would've had an easier time of it if she'd given you up for adoption, but that wasn't the choice she made. I'm betting she didn't look at raising you as a hardship, but as an amazing gift that kept Nick alive in her heart."

"If that was so, why did she never tell me who he was?"

Jim shook his head and sighed. "We'll never know for sure, but there's no doubt she loved you. If things had turned out differently, my son would've loved you, too. The thing to remember is that even though she couldn't bring herself to tell you about Nick directly, she did the right thing in the end. She left you a trail to follow if that's what you wanted to do. I'll always be grateful for that, and I hope that you feel that way, too."

For the first time since finding the letter, the pictures and the motorcycle, the small knot of anger in her heart started to unravel. "You're right, and I am grateful."

While they were dealing with hard truths, there was one last thing she needed to get off her chest. "My father's Vincent Black Lightning doesn't belong to me, Grandpa. It's really yours."

He cupped the side of her face with his hand. "No, Hailey, it's not. It's yours to do with what you will. Finn can teach you how to ride the bike if you're interested. If not, it's worth a lot of money these days. Sell it if that's what you want to do. There's a lot that can be done with that amount of cash. Either way, there's no rush in deciding. Right now, you need to track down Finn and see if you can't mend some fences."

He was right. She had to at least try. "Where do you think he would have gone?"

"I doubt he headed home. Whenever he's got things on his mind, he usually either loses himself in work or hangs out with his friends. I'd try the shop first. If he's not there, maybe Barnaby's or the café."

She kissed Jim on the cheek. "Wish me luck."

He held up both hands with his fingers crossed. "Don't let fear get in the way of things. Tell him that I'm sorry, too. One more thing—don't feel bad that you have to go back to Missouri. It should be your choice whether you want to stay there for good or only long enough tie up all those loose ends you mentioned. I promise I'll do my best to support your decision either way."

That had her on her feet and hugging him. "I love you, Grandpa."

"I know, sweetheart. I know."

Then he pointed toward the counter. "Take those slices of pie with you. They might not solve all your problems, but they certainly won't hurt."

Feeling far better than she had only minutes before, Hailey laughed and bagged them up to go. Jim walked with her into the living room. He stopped briefly to study the Victorian village and then moved onto the Christmas tree, a small smile teasing at the corner of his mouth. "Don't forget about the meaning behind all of these decorations."

He pointed to the few presents under the

tree. "Christmas is the season of giving, Hailey. Those packages are meaningless unless there's love and friendship involved. I've already gotten a better gift than I could have ever imagined, and that's you. I think you and Finn have the chance to gift each other with something pretty special, too."

Then he hugged her. "I'll be here if you need me."

FINN HADN'T BOTHERED to turn on any of the lights in the front of the building. Considering his current mood, he preferred to lurk in the shadows in the back of the shop. He pulled a stool next to the Vincent and sat down to work. For a brief second he considered texting Titus to see if he wanted to come join in the fun but decided against it. No use in inflicting his bad mood on anyone else.

He tried to tell himself that he wasn't even angry anymore, but that wasn't true. He was really mad at himself for storming out of Jim's house, leaving Hailey thinking that she was the one who was in the wrong. Granted, he would've preferred that she not bring up his old dream of becoming a firefighter. He'd actually managed to make that come true the day he qualified to become a volunteer for his hometown fire department. It was important work, and he took great satisfaction in serving his friends and neighbors in that capacity.

Like Jim, he was all tied up inside knowing that the days were flying by, and Hailey would be gone by the end of the week. He loved her, but that didn't give him the right to ask her to stay unless by some miracle she loved him, too.

He studied the pile of new parts neatly arrayed on the nearby counter and tried to decide where to start. When he couldn't come up with a plan of action, he briefly considered simply giving up on doing anything useful and heading home. The problem was that he'd only rattle around alone in an empty house. His time would be better spent doing something useful, even if it was grunt work like sweeping the floors or wiping down the countertops. Something mindless that would keep his hands busy while he figured how he was going to get through the next few days without begging Hailey to uproot her whole life to stay in Dunbar.

A knock at the front door derailed that train of thought. With luck, it would be one of his friends showing up to share a six-pack and some conversation. If it happened to be Titus, maybe the two of them could spend a couple of hours on Hailey's motorcycle after all. His mood momentarily improved, he hustled to unlock the front door only to realize that his unexpected guest was the last person he would have expected.

"Hailey, did you forget something?"

She held up a plastic shopping bag. "No, you did. You left without getting a slice of pie. I thought you might need it."

He hesitated for two seconds and then held out his hand to take the bag. Rather than surrendering it, Hailey whipped it back out of his reach. She arched an eyebrow and gave him an admonishing look. "Slow down there, mister. There are two containers in that bag. I will trade you one of them for a fork, but the other one is mine. Do we have a deal?"

Funny how even that little bit of teasing from Hailey was enough to temper his bad mood. "Yeah, we do. Come on in."

He flipped on more lights as they walked through the office to the shop. "Pull up a seat while I get the forks and some bottled water for us."

She cleared the bike parts off one of the carts and rolled it over next to the stool he'd been using. After pulling another one over for herself, she sat down and waited for Finn to join her. When he did, she removed two containers from the bag and set them on top of the cart. "Jim was the one who cut the pie, so blame him if the slices aren't the same size. Being the nice person I am, you can have whichever one is the biggest."

He eyed her with suspicion. "How come you're being so generous?"

"Like I said, I'm a nice person. Besides, Titus still owes me another pie. There's nothing saying I have to share that one with anybody."

Cute. He popped the tops off the containers and then picked them up as if weighing the contents. "Looks like Jim did a good job keeping them equal."

He started to set one in front of Hailey and then stole it back at the last second and gave her the other one. Scooping up a huge bite on his fork, he smirked, "But this one has a little more toasted coconut on the top."

She laughed and settled in to enjoy her own piece. It didn't take long for them to finish off the delicious treat. That was a shame and not only because he could have easily eaten a second slice. Once they were finished, they'd have to talk, and he wasn't sure how that was going to go. There was more than one topic of conversation he should discuss with her, starting with her outing him to Jim about his dream of being a firefighter. To buy himself a little more time, he unscrewed the cap on his water and took a big drink. It did little to wash away the dry-as-dust taste of dread. He had no idea how this conversation would go or where he should even start.

A minute later, Hailey saved him from having to come up with an opening salvo. She'd already set her fork and empty container aside. Instead of looking at him, she got busy picking the label off her water bottle. "I'm sorry I told Jim about the whole firefighter thing. It wasn't my story to share."

Leaning forward with his elbows on his knees, he stared at the concrete floor beneath his feet. "I'm sorry, too. Not about you telling him, but about how I overreacted. Maybe I would have been happier as a full-time firefighter, but we'll never know. The truth is Jim couldn't keep the family business going all by himself, and I'm proud of what he and I have accomplished over the years. That said, I also enjoy my time volunteering with the fire department here in town. In a lot of ways, I've had the best of both worlds. I'll make sure to tell Jim that when I see him."

"I suspect he already knows, but he'll like hearing it from you."

She finally set the bottle aside and sat up straighter. "He and I also talked about my father's motorcycle. He insists it's mine to do with as I want."

She shot a worried look in the direction of the

Vincent. "I've never even considered learning to ride a motorcycle, but I should probably give it a try before I make a decision."

He nodded in approval. "I can teach you the basics, and there are also courses available that specialize in teaching beginners of all kinds how to ride."

"Good to know."

They'd managed to cover two topics pretty peacefully, but that left the biggie—the two of them. Avoiding the issue wasn't going to make it any easier, so he just went for it. "Have you decided when you're going to leave for Missouri?"

Hailey scooped up all the bits and pieces of the label she'd destroyed and carried them over to the trash can. "Probably on the twenty-seventh, the twenty-eighth at the latest."

Even though he'd been expecting that would be the case, it still hit him hard. They both knew that she had to go, so there was no use in trying to convince her otherwise. He settled for offering up one bit of advice. "Make sure to keep an eye on the weather reports. This time of year, crossing the Cascades can be pretty iffy. That said, one pass might be better than the other, so plan accordingly when it comes time to leave."

"I will. I'll also have to check on the weather predictions between here and home. If it looks bad enough, I might fly home and leave my

SUV here. Selling Mom's car is another one of those things I haven't gotten around to doing. I can drive it until I get back here to pick up my car."

"That sounds like a good idea."

He knew she had said she'd come back to visit Jim again at some point, but knowing she might have to return to pick up her car gave more weight to that promise. "I'll drive you to the airport if you do decide to fly."

"I would appreciate that."

It was time to change topics. "What time do you want to go shopping tomorrow?"

Hailey frowned. "Shopping?"

He forced a smile and tried again. "Tomorrow is Tuesday. The day after that is Christmas Eve. We still need to pick up all the groceries to make that big Christmas dinner you promised Jim and me."

"Oh, that." Then she wagged her finger in his direction. "And the deal was that the dinner would be a group project. You and Jim aren't going to park yourselves in the living room watching football while I toil away in the kitchen. It isn't all up to me."

"Can't blame a guy for trying." He grinned and held his hands up in surrender. "But for the record, I've already ordered a fresh turkey at the store up in Leavenworth to make sure one the right size will be waiting for us. It's all of the other stuff we need to get."

"I don't have any plans for tomorrow, so whatever time works best for you is fine with me. Early would be better, because I need to bake more Christmas cookies." She paused to give him a suspicious look. "Seems those first batches I made have all mysteriously disappeared. You wouldn't know anything about that, would you?"

"I think I'd better take the Fifth on that. How about I buy you breakfast at the café in the morning before we head for the store? I'll pick you up at eight."

"I'll be ready." She got up. "I should get going."

He escorted her out to the parking lot. As Hailey got into her car, he found himself wanting to stop her from going. Anything to be able to spend even a little more time in her company. Ignoring the urge, he stepped back and watched as she drove away, his pulse running hot. Those extra few minutes wouldn't matter in the grand scale of things. At least he knew he'd be seeing her again in only a matter of hours.

Besides, waving goodbye while masking his pain with a smile was good practice for when it came time to watch her leave Dunbar behind with no idea when or even if he'd see her again.

CHAPTER TWENTY-ONE

Rikki's bed-and-breakfast had almost become a second home for Hailey over the short time she'd been in Dunbar, to the point that people who lived on the same street now waved and smiled whenever they saw her driving by. To thank her hosts for making her feel so welcome, she'd slipped small gifts for them and their son under the tree in the living room last night when she'd gotten back from Jim's house. To her surprise, there had been one with her name on it sitting on the dresser in her room. She'd felt like a kid again as she'd torn off the bow and paper to find a lovely scarf and gloves that matched the color of her coat. Such a thoughtful gesture on their part.

As she got ready to head over to Jim's house for the day, she reflected on everything she'd experienced since arriving in Dunbar. Just two months ago, she'd stared up at her bedroom ceiling and wondered how to survive the upcoming holiday season. She'd never been really into Halloween, but there was no way to avoid it completely when the kids at school were all so excited about their costumes and candy. Luckily she'd already been on her leave of absence, and the day had slid by almost unnoticed. Thanksgiving had been much the same.

But she'd known Christmas would be different, mainly because it had always ranked high on her list of favorite days of the year. Her mom's, too. They'd loved the season's promise of good things to come—from gifts that magically appeared under the tree to the chance to spend special time with loved ones. Then there were all those seasonal holiday treats. Not knowing how she could bear to face it all alone had been the driving force behind her decision to make the trek all the way from her home in Missouri to Dunbar.

The plan had been to introduce herself to her grandfather, spend a day or two getting to know him, and then head right back home. Her hope was that if she spent the actual holiday on the road, she could simply pretend it was just another day, nothing special at all. Boy, had she been wrong about how things would play out.

Not only was she spending Christmas with family, she was actually enjoying herself. It helped that Jim and Finn were introducing her to how their side of her family had always celebrated the holiday. There were a few similarities to how she and her mother had done things, but not everything was the same. Somehow the differences made it easier for her to relax and explore new ways of doing things.

Jim and Finn hadn't done much to celebrate the holidays after Rhonda passed away. Now they were doing their best to resurrect family traditions to make the occasion extra special for her. To help that along, she'd used her late grandmother's cookie recipes rather than only making the kind she and her mom had always baked.

The two of them had always had their big dinner on the twenty-fourth and ate the leftovers on Christmas Day. In contrast, Jim had served up another pot of his chili for dinner last night. Afterward, the three of them had taken a long drive to admire the Christmas decorations in town. They'd ended the evening by attending the Christmas Eve service at the community church in town before returning home. She'd loved sitting between the two new men in her life as they'd celebrated the season with friends and neighbors.

It had been nearly midnight when Finn took Jim home and then drove Hailey back to the bed-and-breakfast. Gentleman that he was, he'd walked her to the front porch and waited as she unlocked the door. Finn had lingered only long enough to give her a quick hug. The gesture had been friendly and warm, but she'd found herself wishing for something more—maybe like the night at Barnaby's where Finn had kissed her under the mistletoe. Too bad Rikki hadn't included some in the decorations on her front porch ceiling. That might have given Hailey the courage to ask for what she wanted.

She regretted her cowardice as soon as he walked away. By the time his taillights disappeared into the night, she missed Finn so much that her heart hurt. It was also a stark reminder that all too soon, she would be the one leaving.

And that it was the last thing she wanted to do.

So now she was on her way to spend Christmas Day with Jim and Finn, determined to enjoy every minute of time she had with them. There would be plenty of time for regrets in two days when she saw them waving goodbye in her rearview mirror on her way out of town.

IN YEARS PAST, it was Jim who got up extra early on Christmas morning to make a huge breakfast for himself, Finn and Rhonda. His explanation for why he did all the cooking on Christmas Eve and Christmas morning was that it was only fair since Rhonda always did the heavy lifting when it came to preparing their huge turkey dinner. Since Jim had cooked last evening, this time Finn volunteered to make breakfast for everybody. He'd already prepped everything but waited to start the last-minute cooking until Hailey texted that she was on her way.

While Finn puttered in the kitchen, Jim was slipping a few last packages under the tree. Finn had added his own gifts right after he'd arrived. From the size of that huge pile of presents, they'd both gone a little over the top in their efforts to make the day extra special for Hailey. The moments when her mother's death hit her hard had grown farther apart. But knowing today might still be hard for her, they'd do their best to keep her distracted and busy.

He finally heard the front door open and put the skillet on the burner to heat up. A few minutes later, Hailey poked her head into the kitchen. "Merry Christmas! What can I do to help?"

"Merry Christmas to you, too. I like your outfit."

They were both wearing the matching sweaters they'd worn to Shay's party. He jingled his bells with a grin and then pointed her toward the mugs and glasses sitting on the counter. "You can pour the coffee and the orange juice. The rest of breakfast will be ready in a couple of minutes."

Jim followed her into the room and took his usual place at the table. "So, Hailey, Finn will be more than happy to help with dinner, but you'll have to tell him what to do and when."

"Good to know. I wrote out a timeline yesterday showing when everything needs to be done. Rikki let me use her printer to make copies for me and both of you."

Meanwhile, Finn shot his godfather a suspicious look. "Just a reminder, Jim. I volunteered to help, but so did you."

Jim grinned at him, his arms crossed over his chest. "Someone has to supervise, and that's me. I can't keep an eye on you and work at the same time."

Hailey joined in the discussion. "Well, I'm pretty sure that people who don't do their fair share won't get a slice of the pie I picked up at Titus's café yesterday afternoon. I'm sure Finn and I can manage the cooking on our own. I'm also just as sure that neither of us will feel the least bit guilty eating pie in front of you."

"So that's how it's going to be, is it?" As he spoke, Jim tried hard to look as if he were upset by the prospect, but there was no missing the way his mouth quirked up in a small grin. Conceding the inevitable, he patted his granddaughter on the shoulder. "I'm right handy with a potato peeler and know how to set the table for a holiday dinner."

She kissed him on the cheek. "That's a good start."

The give-and-take of teasing had Finn smiling. It was a definite improvement over the past few holidays. Hailey's unexpected arrival in Dunbar might have knocked him a bit sideways at first, but now he couldn't imagine his life without her in it. He needed her there in Dunbar permanently and living under the same roof with him. It was past time for him to man up and tell her how he felt.

He had just retrieved the bacon from the oven when that last thought crossed his mind. The sudden realization startled him into dropping the platter on the table, causing both Hailey and Jim to jump. Looking concerned, Hailey asked, "Is everything okay?"

Scrambling for a reasonable explanation that skirted the truth, he blew on his fingers. "Yeah, I didn't realize how hot the platter was and burned my fingers a little."

To lend credence to the lie, he ran some cold water over his hand before returning to the table to sit down. "Let's eat, folks. Those presents won't open themselves."

Jim pointed at Finn with his fork as he spoke to Hailey. "When that guy was little, he'd roust

Rhonda and me out of bed at four in the morning to open presents. When he turned thirteen, we told him he was old enough to wait until a more decent hour. Even then we were lucky if we got to sleep past six."

She snickered. "That makes him a man after my own heart. Mom knew better than to insist we eat breakfast before opening presents. I've never outgrown the little-kid excitement of getting up early on Christmas morning to see all those gorgeous presents under the tree."

So that was another thing they had in common. Good to know. "Like I said, eat up. I've been known to open a few presents that belong to other people because I'm not done having fun tearing up wrapping paper."

"He's not kidding, Hailey. I learned that the hard way when he unwrapped some lingerie I bought for Rhonda one year. Luckily, it was classy stuff—a silk robe with a matching gown that she'd been wanting—but still."

Hailey grinned at each of them in turn. "I have one question. Can we wait until after presents to clean up the kitchen?"

Finn rolled his eyes. "Did you even have to ask?"

FIFTEEN MINUTES LATER, they topped off their coffee and headed for the living room where

Hailey joined Finn on the couch while Jim sat in his usual chair. "I have one question, guys. People have different techniques when it comes to opening gifts. Since we've been sticking to your traditions, do we rip open our gifts as fast as possible or do we stop in between to admire everything? That's how Mom and I always did things."

Finn pretended to give the matter some hard thought. "Since this is your first Christmas with us, I suppose we should follow your lead. How about I play elf and dole out the presents?"

Hailey was already shaking her head. "No way. I'll do it. Someone has to make sure you don't 'accidentally' sneak a few of our gifts into your pile."

That had Jim laughing. "She's got your number, boy."

After sorting through the presents, she delivered the first stack to Jim. She brought the next pile to Finn, winking as she set them on the coffee table in front of him. It took her another two trips to finish handing out the presents. As soon as she sat down, Jim picked up one of his gifts. "Let's get started."

After admiring each other's gifts, they moved onto the next one. Finn held his breath when Hailey picked up the one gift he was a little nervous about. As it turned out, he hadn't needed to worry. She held the snow globe close as if it was the most precious thing she'd ever seen. That didn't mean she wasn't blinking back a few tears. "You remembered."

Looking puzzled, Jim asked, "Remembered what?"

"The night we went to the tree farm, we wandered through the gift shop in the barn. I mentioned that my mother would have loved this particular globe because she adored cardinals. Thank you, Finn."

"You're welcome."

She carefully set the snow globe on the table before picking up the final package in her stack. "Interesting. This one says to open it last."

Finn glanced over at Jim, who was now perched on the edge of his seat, his eyes riveted on this granddaughter as she removed the ribbon and set it aside. Then she gently peeled off the wrapping paper to reveal a box. After removing the lid, she lifted out what looked like a photo album. He leaned over closer to get a better look. The label on the front cover read "Our Family" in gold script.

Hailey slowly started flipping through the pages, pausing to study the pictures. Finally, she unfolded a paper that was tucked into a pocket in the cover. After looking at it, she got up and headed straight for Jim to hug him. "Thank you so much, Grandpa. You must have spent hours and hours organizing all those photographs and putting together that family tree for me. I especially love all the pictures of my father, from when he was a baby right up through his time in the army."

He hugged her back. "I wanted to let you know who you came from."

Finn found it hard not to feel a little left out, but then Hailey turned to smile at him. "You were a really cute baby, Finn. I love all the pictures of you dressed up for sports from T-ball all the way through high school football. You were quite the athlete, I see."

When he shot a confused look in Jim's direction, the old man smirked just a little. "Did you think you weren't part of the family? You're my godson, and I couldn't be prouder of you than if you were my own flesh and blood."

Okay, Hailey wasn't the only one blinking back the burn of tears. "Thanks, Jim. I hope you know how much you mean to me, too."

Hailey cleared her throat and pulled two more packages from the tote she'd left by the front door. She handed the first one to Jim. "It looks like we were on the same wavelength when it came to gifts."

He made quick work of unwrapping it to find another photo album. His hands were shaking as he opened it to the first page, to reveal a picture of a newborn baby sporting a stocking cap tied with a pink bow. Finn moved to stand beside Jim to be able to see Hailey's life start unfolding in front of them. The last page held the pictures she'd taken the night they'd decorated the tree.

"I put the album together before I came here to meet you. I know we missed a lot of time together, but I thought that might help fill in the gaps for you." She paused to look at Finn. "I was so glad I could add those last ones after I got here."

Then she held out the second gift to Finn. Rather than an album, it was one of those picture frames that held multiple photos. It had the same one of them in front of the Christmas tree, but there were also several of him working on her father's bike, and one from when they'd ridden in the parade. He loved it.

"It's perfect, Hailey. Thank you."

He set it down and gave in to the urge to hug her, holding her close and breathing in the warmth of the woman who had somehow become an essential part of his life. It was tempting to linger a little longer but he had to step back when a timer went off on someone's phone. Hailey hustled over to pick up her cell to shut off the alarm.

"Okay, guys, that means it's time to start dinner. Once I get things organized, I'll let you know what you can do to help. For now, relax while you can."

Then she disappeared into the kitchen leaving both men staring after her. After a few seconds, Jim pushed himself up out of his chair. "While she's busy, I have something I need to give you. Come with me."

Finn followed him upstairs to the bedroom that also served as Jim's office. Jim motioned for him to sit in the chair in front of the desk while he unlocked the small safe he'd installed in the closet. What was he up to now? Surely he wasn't going to ask Finn to sign off on giving Hailey half of the business again.

But when Jim sat down, he set a small drawstring bag on the desk and sat down. "This is something Rhonda wanted you to have, but she told me to wait until the time seemed right. I could be wrong, but I think that time might have come."

He patted the bag and then pushed it across the desk. "Go ahead and open it."

Finn tugged the top of the bag open and found a small velvet-covered box inside, the kind of thing jewelry came in. He removed the box and set it on the desk, not quite ready to open it. There were times in a man's life when he knew everything was about to change, and he wasn't sure he was ready for that.

"It won't bite you, boy. Open it. If I've misread the situation and now isn't the right time, just say so. I won't pressure you into anything this important. It has to be your decision. I can always put it back in the safe for now."

After drawing a deep breath, Finn gently lifted the lid. Somehow he wasn't surprised to see Rhonda's engagement ring tucked inside. He picked it up and held it up to the light. "She wanted me to have this?"

"Yeah, she did. She said you could have the diamonds put into a new setting if you'd like. The style of the ring is pretty old-fashioned, and your lady might want something more modern."

Finn stared at the ring and thought of the woman who had worn it for so many decades. Finally, he blurted out the first thing that crossed his mind. "How did you ever find the courage to ask Rhonda to marry you? Weren't you terrified?"

Jim chuckled. "Of course I was. It's a huge decision, and there was always the possibility Rhonda might have said no. I barely had a dime to my name when I proposed to Rhonda, but she was brave enough to take a chance on me. The bottom line is that if you love the woman, you have to take the chance. You do love her, don't you?"

"She should be the first one to hear how I feel about her." He stared at the ring for a long time. "Thank you for this, Jim. I can only hope it brings me the same kind of luck and happiness that it brought you."

Then he put the ring back in the box and stuck it into his pants pocket. "I'll be keeping the ring with me."

"Let me know if I need to make myself scarce." Jim came around the desk to give Finn a quick hug. "We'd better get back downstairs before Hailey thinks we've deserted her."

Finn followed his godfather back downstairs, feeling as if the weight of the small box increased tenfold with each step he took back toward the woman who had already turned his world upside down.

CHAPTER TWENTY-TWO

SOMETHING WAS BOTHERING FINN, or at least it seemed that way to Hailey. Although he'd done his fair share of work in preparing their dinner, he'd been quieter than usual. She had no idea what might have happened, but she'd noticed the change in his mood right after they'd finished opening their gifts. It could simply be that he was tired. None of them had gotten much sleep the previous night.

At least their combined efforts in the kitchen had produced a meal worthy of the holiday. Jim had offered up a toast to celebrate Hailey's first Christmas with them and to express his hope for many more to come. They'd all clinked glasses and then gotten busy passing the various dishes around the table.

Afterward, she'd shooed Jim out of the kitchen while she and Finn dealt with the dishes and the leftovers. When that was done, she served the pie. It was no surprise that Jim had dozed off during the football game he had been watching while Finn and Hailey had been finishing up in the kitchen.

"Should we let him sleep?"

Finn gave it some thought before shaking his head. "No, he'll want to spend every minute of time with you that he can."

Jim blinked sleepily when Hailey shook his shoulder. "Here's your pie, Grandpa."

"Thanks, sweetheart."

He only ate half of it before setting it aside. "I enjoyed today more than you'll ever know. It's brought back so many good memories. Normally, I only get sad when I think about Nick and Rhonda. But thanks to the two of you, this year is different. I'm able to get past the loss to be grateful for having had them in my life at all. Thanks to them, I have you, Hailey."

Turning to Finn, he added, "And I don't know where I'd be if you hadn't been there for me all this time. I might forget to tell you often enough, but I am grateful."

Hailey struggled to get any words past the big lump in her throat. She settled for keeping it simple. "I'm grateful to both of you for everything you've done to make this Christmas so special for me."

Jim stood up and stretched. "I'm sorry, but I need to call it a night. Let's all meet at Titus's cafe in the morning so Hailey can have one more of his breakfasts before she has to leave. I'll see you there at eight."

Then he swiped at his eyes with his hands and took off down the hall without saying another word. It was tempting to go after him, but Finn shook his head. "Let him go. He wouldn't want you to see him crying."

Hailey hated how fast the remaining time on her visit was running out. They'd have tomorrow together, but come Saturday morning she'd be gone. Driving away from Dunbar would be one of the hardest things she'd ever done, especially because she'd be leaving the two men she loved behind. Maybe her feelings would fade with time, but she didn't see that happening. It was time to listen to her heart, and it was telling her that she was her mother's daughter after all, destined to love only one man in her life.

She stood by the Victorian village, watching as the skaters continued their endless dance across the icy pond. "I'm sorry that it will hurt him when I go."

Finn moved up behind her, settling his hands on her waist. "Don't focus on that, Hailey. It only hurts because you've made him so happy. Me, too."

She gave a shuddering sigh. It was time to admit the truth to the man who had claimed her heart. "Finn, I meant what I said. I don't want to go back, but I have to for all the reasons I told you."

"I know, and so does Jim." He gently turned her to face him. "The thing to remember is that those reasons don't mean you have to stay there."

Then he pulled something out of his pocket and held out his fist. "I need to tell you something."

Then he opened his hand, revealing a diamond ring. She stared at it in confusion. "I don't understand."

"This was your grandmother's engagement ring, the one Jim gave her all those years ago. I just found out this afternoon that she left it to me for when I found the woman I was meant to spend my life with."

Then he waited for her to look up at him before continuing. "I know that you have to go, Hailey, but I hope the fact that I love you might be reason enough for you to come back."

Something more powerful than hope bloomed inside her heart. "Really?"

His smile was tentative, but so sweet. "Really. I know it's too soon, but I couldn't let you leave without telling you how I feel."

She traced the shape of the ring with her fingertip. "Jim told me that he thought that you and I were on the brink of something special. When

I said it was too quick, that people didn't fall in love this fast, he pointed out that my parents had done exactly that. It must run in the family, because I love you, Finn. So very, very much."

Finn let out a huge breath. "I was so afraid it was just me."

She blinked back tears as she smiled at him, her heart full. "No, we're in this together. I promise I'll get things tied up back home as fast as I can and let you know when I'll be headed this way for good."

He captured her hand and slipped the ring on her finger. "Consider this a placeholder until you come back. Then we can decide if you want to have the diamonds reset in a different ring."

"When should we tell Jim?"

"Let's surprise him over breakfast tomorrow, and then the three of us can start making plans."

She studied the ring on her finger and smiled. "The last gift I expected to get for Christmas was a whole new life with you and Jim."

"Me, too."

Then he kissed her, and it was everything she could hope for—an acknowledgement of what they meant to each other, and a promise of the life they'd build together.

* * * * *

Get up to 4 Free Books!

We'll send you 2 free books from each series you try PLUS a free Mystery Gift.

FREE Value Over $25

Both the **Harlequin® Special Edition** and **Harlequin® Heartwarming™** series feature compelling novels filled with stories of love and strength where the bonds of friendship, family and community unite.

YES! Please send me 2 FREE novels from the Harlequin Special Edition or Harlequin Heartwarming series and my FREE Gift (gift is worth about $10 retail). After receiving them, if I don't wish to receive any more books, I can return the shipping statement marked "cancel." If I don't cancel, I will receive 6 brand-new Harlequin Special Edition books every month and be billed just $6.39 each in the U.S. or $7.19 each in Canada, or 4 brand-new Harlequin Heartwarming Larger-Print books every month and be billed just $7.19 each in the U.S. or $7.99 each in Canada, a savings of 20% off the cover price. It's quite a bargain! Shipping and handling is just 50¢ per book in the U.S. and $1.25 per book in Canada.* I understand that accepting the 2 free books and gift places me under no obligation to buy anything. I can always return a shipment and cancel at any time by calling the number below. The free books and gift are mine to keep no matter what I decide.

Choose one: ☐ Harlequin Special Edition (235/335 BPA G36Y)   ☐ Harlequin Heartwarming Larger-Print (161/361 BPA G36Y)   ☐ Or Try Both! (235/335 & 161/361 BPA G36Z)

Name (please print)

Address   Apt. #

City   State/Province   Zip/Postal Code

Email: Please check this box ☐ if you would like to receive newsletters and promotional emails from Harlequin Enterprises ULC and its affiliates. You can unsubscribe anytime.

Mail to the Harlequin Reader Service:
IN U.S.A.: P.O. Box 1341, Buffalo, NY 14240-8531
IN CANADA: P.O. Box 603, Fort Erie, Ontario L2A 5X3

Want to explore our other series or interested in ebooks? Visit www.ReaderService.com or call 1-800-873-8635.

---

*Terms and prices subject to change without notice. Prices do not include sales taxes, which will be charged (if applicable) based on your state or country of residence. Canadian residents will be charged applicable taxes. Offer not valid in Quebec. This offer is limited to one order per household. Books received may not be as shown. Not valid for current subscribers to the Harlequin Special Edition or Harlequin Heartwarming series. All orders subject to approval. Credit or debit balances in a customer's account(s) may be offset by any other outstanding balance owed by or to the customer. Please allow 4 to 6 weeks for delivery. Offer available while quantities last.

Your Privacy—Your information is being collected by Harlequin Enterprises ULC, operating as Harlequin Reader Service. For a complete summary of the information we collect, how we use this information and to whom it is disclosed, please visit our privacy notice located at https://corporate.harlequin.com/privacy-notice. Notice to California Residents – Under California law, you have specific rights to control and access your data. For more information on these rights and how to exercise them, visit https://corporate.harlequin.com/california-privacy. For additional information for residents of other U.S. states that provide their residents with certain rights with respect to personal data, visit https://corporate.harlequin.com/other-state-residents-privacy-rights/.

HSEHW25